DATE DUE

MAY 2 4 2011			

FRANKLIN EVANS, OR THE INEBRIATE

FRANKLIN EVANS,

OR

THE INEBRIATE

A TALE OF THE TIMES

WALT WHITMAN

Edited by Christopher Castiglia
and Glenn Hendler

DUKE UNIVERSITY PRESS
DURHAM AND LONDON 2007

Introduction, Selection of Texts, Notes, and Bibliography
© 2007 Duke University Press

All rights reserved
Printed in the United States of America on acid-free paper ∞
Designed by Jennifer Hill
Typeset in Bulmer by Tseng Information Systems, Inc.
Library of Congress Cataloging-in-Publication Data appear
on the last printed page of this book.

CONTENTS

vii Acknowledgments

ix Introduction
*Christopher Castiglia and
Glenn Hendler*

I. FRANKLIN EVANS, OR THE INEBRIATE
1 *A Tale of the Times*

II. SUPPLEMENTARY TEXTS
117 *The Madman*

123 *The Child and the Profligate*

135 *An Address Delivered by Abraham Lincoln
Before the Springfield Washingtonian Temperance Society,
at the Second Presbyterian Church,
Springfield, Illinois, On the 22d Day of February, 1842*

145 Bibliography

ACKNOWLEDGMENTS

CHRIS CASTIGLIA would like to thank Nick Hurley and Kristen Egan for their research assistance. GLENN HENDLER thanks Cheryl Reed for transcription of the text, Brooke Cameron for help with proofreading and research, and the American Antiquarian Society for supporting work on this volume through an AAS/Northeastern Modern Language Association Fellowship. The editors would like to thank Leo Blake of the Walt Whitman House, Camden, New Jersey, John Powell of the Newberry Library, Chicago, and Paul Rascoe of the Tanner Library, University of Texas, Austin, for their assistance with images. And to the ever-patient Ken Wissoker, our deepest thanks.

INTRODUCTION

Christopher Castiglia and Glenn Hendler

THE mere existence of *Franklin Evans, or The Inebriate* will surprise many readers, even students and scholars well versed in nineteenth-century American literature and culture. Of course, Whitman specialists have always been aware of the book's place in what Ralph Waldo Emerson called the "long foreground" preceding Whitman's poetic career, and social historians have placed it on their lists of writings devoted to the cause of temperance. Beyond such scholars, few know that more than a decade before making his mark as a poet with the publication of *Leaves of Grass*, Whitman was heralded as "one of the best Novelists of this country." *Franklin Evans* forces those who thought they knew about Whitman, and about nineteenth-century American literature and culture in general, to look closely at both the text itself and the rich and complex context its existence reveals. What biographical, social, and cultural factors would lead Whitman to write a full-length temperance novel in 1842? Why did he and his publishers believe that *Franklin Evans* would "create a sensation" and get "the widest circulation," as the book's publicity promised? How might such a publication have been received in 1842? And why should we read this novel today?

WHITMAN'S EARLY LIFE

Walter Whitman, Jr., was born on May 31, 1819, to Walter and Louisa Van Velsor Whitman; he was the second of eight children who survived infancy. Whitman's father was descended from farmers who emigrated from England in the mid-seventeenth century, and his mother's family was of Dutch and Welsh descent. At the time of Whitman's birth, the family lived in West Hills, in Suffolk County, Long Island. In 1823, Walter Whitman, Sr., failing to find employment on Long Island, moved his family to the thriving city of Brooklyn, where he found work as a carpenter and contractor. Louisa's father, Major Cornelius Van Velsor, traveled to Brooklyn once a week to sell produce and traded horses in Manhattan, so Louisa was no stranger to urban life.[1] Throughout Whitman's childhood his family moved within Brooklyn, often changing residences annually. Always partial to his mother and his sisters Hannah and Mary, young Whitman had more troubled relationships with most of the men in his family, particularly his father, his older brother, Jesse, and his younger brothers, George and Andrew, all of whom Whitman avoided — along with his chores — by writing stories, one of which, the tale of an intemperate farmer, seems a precursor to *Franklin Evans*.[2]

In Brooklyn, Whitman attended the strict Lancaster School, as well as Sunday school classes at St. Ann's Episcopal Church, although the single strongest influence in the Whitman family's eclectic mixture of religious influences was probably Quakerism.[3] At eleven Whitman abandoned his formal education and began work as an office boy in the law firm of James B. Clarke and his son Edward. The latter assisted young Whitman with his writing skills and introduced him to the library, where he read romances and novels, particularly works by Walter Scott and James Fenimore Cooper. Equally important for his subsequent literary career, Whitman became intimately acquainted with the city by running errands.

Like many American authors from Benjamin Franklin to Mark Twain, Whitman learned about the physical and material side of publishing early in his life. In 1831 he began operating the hand press for the Long Island *Patriot*, a weekly publication edited by Samuel E. Clement, and known as the "organ of the Democratic Party in Kings County."[4] A year later, Whitman left the *Patriot* to work for the *Star*, a Whig publication that competed with the *Patriot*. Whitman continued to work as a printer during his teens, and he spent his free time attending the theater and reading novels, romances, and poetry. When his family returned to rural Long Island in 1833 (the cause of the move — Louisa's illness during the birth of her eighth child, Walter's financial dis-

1. Allen, 3. 2. Kaplan, 62. 3. Kaplan, 70; Reynolds, 35–40. 4. Kaplan, 75.

appointments, or the cholera epidemic in New York—is unclear), Whitman remained in Brooklyn and began his journalistic career during an apprenticeship for the *New York Mirror*.[5] When his apprenticeship ended in the spring of 1835, Whitman became a typesetter in Manhattan, until fires in the summer and winter destroyed much of the printing district, leaving Whitman—and many others—out of work.

In May 1836, Whitman returned once again to Long Island, where at the age of seventeen he became a teacher, a post he held, off and on, until 1841. Schools during that period were required by law to be open a minimum of three months out of the year, and many did not exceed this requirement.[6] Teachers earned scant pay, often only thirty-five dollars per term, and had to move among families who supplied free room and board.[7] Whitman was usually responsible for between twenty and fifty pupils, although more than once he found himself with eighty. Students were of various ages, usually ranging from five to fifteen, and Whitman was not much older. He changed schools frequently; many of his teaching appointments were not renewed, suggesting that some communities were unhappy with his permissive pedagogy.[8] Whitman was asked to leave one school after a disapproving father alleged that Whitman spent too much time with his young son, an incident reflected in Whitman's stories "Bervance" and "The Child's Champion" (a version of which is reproduced in this volume).[9] Between teaching jobs, Whitman resided with his family, where his refusal to help with farm work increased the antagonism between the young writer and his father.

In 1838, Whitman started his own weekly paper in Huntington, the *Long Islander*, but he proved a poor manager, incapable of keeping accurate accounts, and his financial backers sold the paper.[10] In 1839, Whitman went to work for the *Democrat* and lived with its editor, James Brenton. When Whitman left teaching for good in 1841, he moved back to Manhattan, where he became a fixture at Tammany Hall, a hotel that served as Democratic Party headquarters. A speech Whitman delivered to fifteen thousand people at a Democratic rally in City Hall Park was later printed in the *New Era*.[11] In 1841, Whitman also began writing, a career change that brought him into contact with many of New York's most influential editors, including Park

---

5. Allen, 22; Kaplan, 73. 6. Allen, 28. 7. Allen, 28. 8. Kaplan, 83. 9. Kaplan, 87.
10. Kaplan, 93. 11. Kaplan, 97.

Daguerreotype of Walt Whitman,
1848, unknown artist. *Courtesy of
the Walt Whitman House, Camden,
New Jersey.*

Benjamin, whose *New World* published two Whitman poems — "Each Has
His Grief" and "The Punishment of Pride" — as well as an early tale, "The
Child's Champion." The following year, Benjamin would solicit Whitman's
first novel, *Franklin Evans*, for the paper. John L. O'Sullivan's *Democratic
Review* published three Whitman tales in 1841: "Death in the Schoolroom" in
August, "Wild Frank's Return" in November, and "Bervance" in December.[12]
Whitman revised "Fame's Vanity," gave it the new title "Ambition," and pub-
lished it on January 29, 1842, in *Brother Jonathan*, another Benjamin paper.
Early in 1842, Whitman left his job as compositor at the *New World* to write
for the *Aurora*, an independent paper without ties to any political party. The
Aurora published "The Death and Burial of McDonald Clarke," a parody
of Reverend Charles Wolfe's "The Burial of Sir John Moore," on March 18,
1842.[13]

Journalism was a business with fierce competition and often unpredictable
alliances in 1840s New York, and Whitman quickly became a player, publishing an attack in the *Aurora* on Benjamin, his former employer, titled "Bam-

12. Allen, 44. 13. Allen, 46.

boozle and Benjamin," perhaps prompted by a quarrel with the often tem-
peramental Benjamin.[14] Two days after Whitman's article appeared, *Brother
Jonathan*, which Benjamin had previously edited, ran a similar attack. Perhaps this attack was provoked by Benjamin's early publication in one large
"extra" of Edward George Bulwer-Lytton's *Zanoni*, which *Brother Jonathan*
intended to publish serially. Whitman biographer Gay Wilson Allen has con-
jectured that, while Benjamin was scooping *Brother Jonathan*, Whitman was
doing the same, publishing his attack in the *Aurora* on the Thursday before
Brother Jonathan's weekend editorial.[15]

Whitman prospered at the *Aurora*, becoming editor on March 28, 1842, a
position he held until April, when he quit after owner Nelson Herrick meddled
with his editorials.[16] Whitman then began editing the *Evening Tattler* and continued to publish stories with the *Democratic Review*. On November 5, 1842,
the *New World* announced the upcoming publication of *Franklin Evans*, "by
a popular American Author." On November 23, 1842, *Franklin Evans, or the
Inebriate* appeared as a stand-alone "extra" edition of the *New World*. Though
by some estimates the paper sold as many as twenty thousand copies of the
story, Whitman had sold it for only $75.[17] Although Whitman would continue
to publish as a journalist and, most famously, a poet, this was his first and last
extended work of fiction.

WHITMAN'S NEW YORK

In a review of *Franklin Evans* published in the *New York Sun* on December 1,
1842, the reviewer, most likely Whitman himself, writes:

> The author of the lately published novel of "Franklin Evans" takes, for his plot,
> the coming of a young countryman to New York, to seek his fortune. It would
> not be amiss for every youth, whether he be of city or of country, to read this
> book, and receive a warning from some of its incidents. Franklin Evans was
> led onward to the very verge of ruin by his weak and womanly desire to ape
> the habits and manners of the town. And how often do we see this propensity
> illustrated in real life! Worthy and very intelligent men and women, who have
> been bred up in the country, and, compared to whom nine out of ten of those

14. Allen, 46. 15. Allen, 47. 16. Allen, 53. 17. Kaplan, 104–5.

who promenade Broadway would prove far inferior in point of real worth, good manners, or education, evince that they feel themselves *lesser*, in comparison with "genteel" New Yorkers, because the latter have better fitting clothes and are possessed of more brazen self-conceit!

Young men who come to the city are surrounded by a thousand dangers; and that parent makes a very foolish mistake, if he would but know it, who prefers having his son a pert clerk or second-rate lawyer to bringing him up an independent and sturdy farmer — than whom no avocation is more respectable, and no class in the republic contains more examples of happiness and honor.

We have in New York places that draw their principal support from the extravagance of the thoughtless young men — a great portion of them new comers to the city. In some, the attractions are music and intoxicating drinks. In some, is gambling in all its detestable varieties. Every kind of wickedness that can be festered into life by the crowding together of a huge mass of people is here to be found. Youth, inexperienced and unwary, too often falls an easy and an irretrievable prey to these whirlpools of sin.[18]

The review offers a somewhat inaccurate account of the lessons taught by *Franklin Evans*, which depicts the "countryside" from which the young protagonist departs as a location, not of "real worth, good manners, [and] education," but of illness (often occasioned by alcoholism), lost opportunity, and cold-hearted neglect. In the city, moreover, Franklin encounters, not simply "whirlpools of sin," but the opportunities for wealth made possible by the city's chance meetings and anonymity (no one knows about Franklin's shameful lapses into drunkenness).

Nostalgic, highly romanticized depictions of America's fading rural past are typical of reform literature of the 1840s, however, and Whitman nods to that convention in his fanciful summary of *Franklin Evans*. The review takes up other features of reform rhetoric as well, especially the characterization of the city and the desires it generates as feminine. *Franklin Evans* also echoes reform literature of its time in representing class differences as matters of "habits and manner," in which working-class culture generates a series of character flaws easily correctable through increased self-management rather than through structural changes to the production and distribution of capital.

18. *The Sun* (December 1, 1842). Reproduced in Whitman, *Journalism, Vol. 1* (hereafter *WWJ*), 164–65.

Above all, the review — like *Franklin Evans* itself — echoes reform's suspicion of the new urban landscape: the threadbare attractions of the music halls, the licentious illusions of the theaters, the besotting inebriation of the saloons, and the vicious criminality of the streets.

Except for short episodes such as Franklin's initial departure from the countryside and his disastrous residence on a southern plantation, *Franklin Evans* take place in New York City, and readers of Whitman's poetry, with its enthusiastic celebrations of urban democracy, will be surprised by the tale's virulent anti-urbanism. There are several possible explanations for such anti-urban sentiments, which suffused temperance literature throughout the 1840s. For one thing, alcohol consumption was more visible, more concentrated, and more public in cities, due in part to the large numbers of Irish and German immigrants who lived in dense and clearly demarcated neighborhoods in the city and brought with them forms of sociality centered on pubs and beer halls.[19] Particularly as wards populated by immigrants gained political clout, the drinking places where ward leaders and their constituents gathered became sites of power that threatened the traditional leaders of city government.[20] Finally, the dramatic population growth from the 1820s to the 1860s resulted in the reorganization and segregation of residential neighborhoods, and thereby, as Richard Stott notes, "broke down the paternalistic private relief system."[21] In the face of that breakdown, anxieties about the regulation of proper "character" among the citizenry grew sharply, resulting in vigorous efforts to reform perceived sources of civic unruliness such as alcohol consumption.

No city experienced greater changes during the 1840s than New York, which, according to Sean Wilentz, transformed "from a major seaport where the vast majority of citizens were native born to a metropolis where more than half of the population had been born abroad and where more than four-fifths of the immigrants had come from either Ireland or Germany."[22] The population of New York grew from two hundred thousand in 1830 to nearly three hundred twelve thousand by 1840 and half a million by 1850, one of the steepest growth rates in the world.[23] By 1845, immigrants accounted for 36 percent of the city's residents, while in the years between 1820 and 1860 the immigrant

---

19. On the Irish and their relationship to antebellum New York's drinking culture, see McGowan. 20. Kingsdale, 269–72. 21. Stott, 212–13. 22. Wilentz, 110. 23. Stott, 111; Wilentz, 109.

population between the ages of sixteen and forty-five rose to 57 percent.[24] Although most immigrants did not come from cities (the exception being those from England), fewer than a quarter in any year were farmers by trade, the majority being artisans from middle-class backgrounds who could afford the passage to the United States.[25]

The dramatic increases in the immigrant workforce changed the nature of labor in the United States.[26] While the European artisan economy still relied on exclusive and often long-term apprenticeships, in New York such arrangements were often made for quick gain, rather than to learn a lifelong career. One might be struck, reading *Franklin Evans*, by the rapidity with which its protagonist changes professions, working in a short period of time for a merchant, a banker, and a lawyer. This occupational mobility was in reality quite common: boys frequently held multiple apprenticeships, allowing them to move between trades, as the increasing division of labor within individual trades made broad knowledge unnecessary. By the 1850s, such practices allowed employers to rely on workers outside of their shop, known as "outworkers." This system especially hurt German immigrants, who came to the country as trained artisans, as the Irish took up unskilled labor for substandard wages.[27]

Faced with such conditions, laborers organized to gain shorter work days and better wages. In 1843, the Laborers' Union Benevolent Association, organized by Irish construction workers, became the first and largest mutual-aid society for the city's unskilled laborers.[28] While strikes were not uncommon, particularly in the mid-1830s and throughout the 1850s, many considered unions—associated with European Catholicism and believed to challenge traditions of industrious self-improvement—to be un-American.[29] James Harper, elected mayor of New York in 1844, expressed the nationalist sentiments of many: "Poverty, crime, immorality, and pauperism could never spring from any sickness of the American soul; the disease must have been imported by Catholics, the 'base mercenary hirelings and Priests' of European monarchies, aided by unvirtuous, selfish politicians."[30]

Throughout the 1830s and 1840s, increased commerce and manufacturing in the lower wards of New York drove wealthier residents uptown, leaving the districts around the Bowery for workers (and, for the less fortunate, the notori-

---

24. Stott, 72–74. 25. Stott, 74–75. 26. Wilentz, 110. 27. Wilentz, 113, 118–19.
28. Wilentz, 353. 29. Stott, 156; Wilentz, 302, 319–20. 30. Quoted in Wilentz, 320.

Map of Manhattan, 1842. *Courtesy of the Tanner Library, University of Texas, Austin.*

ous Five Points district in Ward Six).[31] Much of the action in *Franklin Evans* takes place in the lower wards of Manhattan, including Chatham Square, the Bowery, and the wharves along the East River.

Whitman's journalism from the 1840s represents New York in a state of transition. Whitman depicts urban neighborhoods functioning in a barter

31. Stott, 188, 192.

economy reminiscent of small rural villages. Describing Chatham Square, for instance, Whitman writes, "In the middle are dray carts, coaches, and cabs: on the right, loom up small hills of furniture, of every quality, with here and there an auctioneer, standing on a table or barrel top, and crying out to the crowd around him, the merits of the articles, and the bids made for them."[32] The nostalgia of this picture complements Whitman's anxiety about the social mobility enabled by a changing economy. "Among those things calculated to depreciate mechanics," Whitman writes in 1840, "none is worthy of greater apprehension than the effort to be fashionable, or what is sometimes called 'living genteelly.' The endeavors of working-men's families to keep up what they call town style . . . have made hundreds to feel the bitter pangs of insult, the mortification of being dunned, the fever of anxiety; and, in cases not a few, have brought on bankruptcy and ruin." Making a worker "ashamed of his calling," upward mobility "is totally at war with every thing in his proper habits, and his legitimate sphere of life."[33] Such bad habits are, for Whitman, at the root of all deplorable forms of excess — "The dissipation and miserable vanity of the ton, the puerile conceitedness of the dandy, and the empty heartlessness of the fashionable female" — ending, as they so often do in *Franklin Evans*, in alcoholic intemperance.[34]

While Whitman represented laborers as victims of bourgeois affectations, when he turned to *immigrant* workers he saw predators rather than prey. Little of the democratic populism of *Leaves of Grass* is apparent in Whitman's anti-Catholic journalism, which was aimed particularly against the recently arrived Irish in New York, whose increasing political power Whitman, like many urban "nativists," watched with apprehension. "Having no prejudices against foreigners, because they are such," Whitman hedged, "we yet feel that they are coming altogether too domineering among us."[35] Describing the disruption of a political rally by a crowd of disgruntled Irish workers, Whitman wrote in 1842:

> Bands of filthy wretches, whose very touch was offensive to a decent man; drunken loafers; scoundrels whom the police and criminal courts would be

---

32. *New York Aurora* (March 8, 1842). *WWJ*, 45.   33. Sun-Down Papers, *The Hempstead Inquirer* (March 28, 1840). *WWJ*, 16.   34. Sun-Down Papers, *The Hempstead Inquirer* (March 28, 1840). *WWJ*, 16–17.   35. *New York Aurora* (March 17, 1842). *WWJ*, 58.

ashamed to receive in their walls; coarse, blustering rowdies; blear-eyed and bloated offscourings from the stews, blind alleys and rear lanes; disgusting objects bearing the form human, but whom the sow in the mire might almost object to as companions—these were they who broke into the midst of a peaceful body of American citizens—struck and insulted the chosen officers of the assemblage, and with shrieks, loud blasphemy, and howling in their hideous native tongue, prevented the continuance of the customary routine. We saw Irish priests there—sly, false, deceitful villains—looking on and evidently encouraging the gang who created the tumult.[36]

Whitman calls on his countrymen (not, apparently, including Catholic citizens) to resist the "Jesuitical knaves,"[37] lest "democracy yield" to "these dregs of foreign filth—refuse of convents—scullions from Austrian monasteries." "The foreign riffraff once yielded to in this case," Whitman warned, "and there will be no end to their demands and their insolence." The Catholic invasion, Whitman wrote, could lead only to the "bulwark of truth—the 'unterrified democracy'" finding itself "ruled by a tattered, coarse, unshaven, filthy Irish rabble" led by "a gang of false and villainous priests, whose despicable souls never generate any aspiration beyond their own narrow and horrible and beastly superstition."[38]

Writing in 1846 for Henry C. Murphy's *Brooklyn Eagle*, a paper with strong ties to the Democratic Party and its Irish membership, Whitman appears to have changed his tune. "Let us (for not all even of we democrats are free from a taint of this 'foreign' prejudice) let us lift our minds out from the silly disposition to find fault with the foreigner," Whitman encouraged, "because he is not perfection and is derelict in some things." Contradicting his early anti-Catholicism, Whitman extols the virtues of the immigrant laborer:

For our own part when, at political meetings or elsewhere, we have seen a mortar-stained laborer coolly taking his prominent part in the proceedings, or lifting his voice even among the loudest, we have been filled with a far different feeling from the contempt and disgust which start in very many minds. We have felt proud at the budding in a fellow-creature's long darkened breast, of

---

36. *New York Aurora* (March 17, 1842). *WWJ*, 57. 37. *New York Aurora* (March 17, 1842). *WWJ*, 58. 38. *New York Aurora* (April 7, 1842). *WWJ*, 102.

the seas of freedom, and of a knowledge of his own rights — and have gloried to see their action (in however an awkward manner) even in the despised hod-carrier — to see the dawning of a brighter light within, and the promise of a growth which Heaven intended to be.[39]

"Ah, Mr. Native, or Mr. Whig, you are true to your instincts, we see. The Irish laborers are ignorant in book-lore we grant — and perhaps uncouth in manners. But they are *men* like us," Whitman attests, "and have wants and appetites, affections for their offspring, and anger for all kinds of tyranny. . . . And still we have the blasphemous presumption to think that the great God made this fair and ample continent merely for *our* limited use . . . ? Shall we suppose, because we came here a few years before them, that they have therefore no claim on the limitless and as yet not one thousandth part developed capacities of America for human happiness, not to say sustenance? Away with such a miserly and monstrous doctrine!"[40] Whitman became a particular advocate for fair wages, arguing in "Oppress Not the Hireling!" that "87 ½ cents per day is all the Brooklyn laborer asks — and we do say (and we only wish our remarks were sure to take effect in the right quarters) that the man, or set of men, who refuses to give that price, show a most heartless meanness, and that if the curse of ill gotten profits does not attach to their wealth, it will not be because it is undeserved! Just a little over $5 a week! And that with children to support, as most of them have!"[41]

Whatever Whitman's views of the Irish, working-class neighborhoods generated new urban institutions in the 1840s and 1850s, hybrids of European customs and American usages. The historian Richard Stott describes how large numbers of young men, often single and with disposable incomes, generated new forms of association in lower Manhattan, chief among them the boardinghouse, the saloon, and the theater, all central to the plot of Whitman's novel.[42] *Franklin Evans* attests to the carefree comforts of the boardinghouse (as opposed to the stressful debts of home ownership, which Franklin experiences in his first marriage), the alluring camaraderie of the tavern, the imagination-stirring encounter with the exotic and the foreign on the stage, all of which were generated by a new industrializing economy divorced from

39. *Brooklyn Eagle and Kings County Democrat* (April 3, 1846). *WWJ*, 315. 40. *Brooklyn Eagle and Kings County Democrat* (April 3, 1846). *WWJ*, 315. 41. *Brooklyn Eagle and Kings County Democrat* (April 3, 1846). *WWJ*, 315. 42. Stott, 212–13.

long-term apprenticeship and family oversight or obligations. In both its positive and negative attitudes toward New York, *Franklin Evans* offers valuable insight into a time when American cities were gaining national power and influence, and in the process changed notions of who Americans are, how they behave, and what appetites they are entitled to indulge.[43]

When Franklin arrives in New York, his first order of business is to find a place to live: a clean, respectable boardinghouse where families with children might reside. Whitman noted in a March 18, 1842, column for the *Aurora* that more than half the residents of New York board, including respectable families and single people of all classes.[44] The majority of such establishments, however, housed young and single working men, who paid "somewhat less than three dollars" a month.[45] Although guidebooks warned immigrants about conniving landlords and thieving co-residents, many boarders found, as Stott writes, that living "with a roommate or two, eating three meals a day, and sharing such activities as indulging 'in beer and short pipes' on the roof in summer, helped generate, despite very high turnover, strong feelings of camaraderie."[46]

Boardinghouse fellowship expanded in the inclusive sociability of the taverns and grog shops, established centers of urban life by the 1840s, leading one historian to characterize them as the first "working-class institution."[47] While bar-rooms prove the downfall of many in *Franklin Evans*, historically they served as important community centers, particularly for immigrants seeking comfort and connections in an otherwise hostile environment. Taverns provided public toilets, cashed checks and loaned money, and provided mailing addresses for patrons who moved frequently; they offered space for labor and political meetings, recreation (cards, pool, darts), sex (prostitutes were sometimes allowed to rent back rooms in which to entertain customers), and even sleep.[48] As industrialization organized workers' days in relation to time clocks and dull, repetitive, and isolating labor, taverns were a space without time limits, and that encouraged self-expression and fellowship.[49] Patrons treated tavern-goers to drinks, making the bar-room an ideal place for new immi-

43. Leslie Fiedler locates *Franklin Evans* in "the main line of American city novels . . . through Crane's *Maggie* up to the fiction of Dreiser and the 'muckrakers'" (*Love and Death*, 484). 44. *New York Aurora* (March 18, 1842). *WWJ*, 61. 45. *New York Aurora* (March 18, 1842). *WWJ*, 61. 46. Stott, 215–16. 47. Stott, 217. 48. Kingsdale, 258–62. 49. Kingsdale, 259.

grants to integrate into urban communities and to preserve native cultural practices and alliances.[50] The bar-room became a particularly important setting for working-class politics, where information could be shared, strategies debated, and voting blocs consolidated.[51] The historian Timothy Gilfoyle, building on the research of W. J. Rorabaugh, contends that the group intoxication common in antebellum bar-rooms "endowed the participants with feelings of liberty and independence while inducing a sense of equality. The group drinking binge was an ideological inebriation; to be drunk was to be free."[52] Generating both the psychological predisposition toward freedom *and* the institutional means to direct that predisposition toward specific political ends, the bar-room understandably made many politicians anxious, contributing to the impetus for temperance reform in the 1840s and 1850s. In New York, for instance, upstate Whigs pushed for laws prohibiting the sale of alcohol in order to impede the political power growing in urban taverns.[53] More subtly, temperance societies attempted to appropriate the buoyant sociality of the tavern, recreating songs, poems, and activities that, as Sean Wilentz observes, were "almost obsessive in their exuberance."[54]

When Franklin and his drinking buddies wander from taverns to theaters, they are typical of many urban dwellers of the 1840s, who found a wide variety of inexpensive entertainment for working people: summer gardens, concerts, lectures, operas, German language plays, and "blood and thunder" melodramas.[55] George Templeton Strong noted the immense throngs of all classes lured to the opera in Castle Garden in the 1850s. "Everyone goes, and nob and snob, Fifth Avenue and Chatham Street, sit side by side fraternally on the hard benches."[56] The entertainment offered in such theaters took place in the back rows as well as onstage. Franklin is shocked when the beautiful actress he admires in a play turns out to be a sordid hussy offstage. Actresses often worked overtime as prostitutes, and theaters, which sometimes permitted prostitutes to work in the uppermost tiers, became, as one reporter wrote in 1842, "assignation houses . . . for bawds and their victims" and "lust places."[57] Not surprisingly, theaters were often found next door to houses of prostitution as well as to taverns.[58]

Franklin Evans remains silent about prostitution in New York, although

50. Stott, 219. 51. Stott, 239. 52. Gilfoyle, 81. 53. Stott, 239. 54. Wilentz, 309. 55. Gilfoyle, 109. 56. Quoted in Gilfoyle, 109. 57. Gilfoyle, 67. 58. Gilfoyle, 112.

Whitman was well aware of its pervasive presence, particularly along the docks and wharves where he, like Franklin, would have disembarked from the Brooklyn ferry. Some of the poor women who populate the pages of Whitman's novel might well have supplemented their low wages by selling sex, as did many servants, chambermaids, seamstresses, and milliners.[59] In 1846, the *Tribune* claimed that three-quarters of the sexual relations in New York were "venal, licentious, and adulterous."[60] Sex trade flourished in the slums of Five Points, around the ferry docks on the East River, and within the theaters and saloons of Chatham Square and the Bowery, which Gilfoyle describes as "a bourse for sex."[61] Mobs of citizens, outraged by the often quite public displays of naked and copulating bodies, attacked brothels nearly seventy times between 1820 and 1860.[62]

If *Franklin Evans* has little to say about prostitution—or indeed about female labor in any form—that is because the novel takes place in an almost exclusively masculine world, reflecting the intense male camaraderie and competition that characterized urban working-class culture in the 1840s.[63] The same-sex camaraderie of the taverns and boardinghouses, along with what Stott calls "attention to physique, and the lively horseplay of grabbing and slapping,"[64] suggests a ubiquitous homoeroticism—if not an overt homosexuality—in working-class and immigrant urban culture, a fact that, as George Chauncey shows, allowed early gay subculture to arise within the relatively tolerant, freewheeling world of the Bowery theaters, saloons, and dancehalls.[65] Readers of *Franklin Evans* will not fail to note the quick, intense, and often erotic relationships that develop between Franklin and the men he encounters in New York. Over the course of the novel, Franklin's relationships with other men become more solidly economic (relationships of employment and, finally, of inheritance) and also more private and domestic, enacted in the family circles within privately owned homes rather than in the public spaces of taverns or theaters. In this respect, *Franklin Evans* accurately depicts the increased importance to antebellum reformers of bourgeois conventions of intimacy (of affection over physicality, conjugal and familial attachment over broader social or class affiliations) over the more raucous—and often subversive—working-class camaraderie available in Whitman's New York.

---

59. Stansell. 60. Gilfoyle, 104. 61. Gilfoyle, 39, 49–50. 62. Gilfoyle, 40, 78. 63. Stott, 256. 64. Stott, 255–56. 65. Chauncey, 33–45.

THE PRINT WORLD OF *FRANKLIN EVANS*

"It is almost impossible," Whitman wrote in 1842, "to calculate the numbers of papers that are printed in the city of New York."[66] Frank Luther Mott estimates that between 1825 and 1850, the number of periodicals in the United States increased from one hundred to nearly six hundred, most of which ran for an average of two years.[67] Whitman expressed a good deal of ambivalence about the proliferation of print in antebellum New York. In March 1842, for instance, he complained, "Very few really good papers are published in New York," the majority being "bound up in partisanship or prejudice, and . . . incapable of taking enlarged and comprehensive views of matters and things." In particular, Whitman lamented the "control of foreigners" who, "though possessing some marks of ability, are not imbued with any wholesome American spirit" and therefore lack "that fiery enthusiasm in the cause of truth and liberty — that vigor of advocacy — that energy and boldness and frankness which will ever mark the apostle of the new system — the system which teaches far different doctrine from the rusty, cankered, time-honored, anti-democratic philosophy that looms up in Europe, and is planting its poisonous seeds too widely among us."[68] Foreigners were not solely responsible for bad journalism, however, as Whitman acknowledged: "We have in America many literary quacks. Persons possessing some little tact at stringing together sentences, and a very great tact of imprudence, conceit, and brazen assumption, now and then rise up among us, and push their fancied merits into notoriety. If they are lucky enough to get into the chair editorial," Whitman charged, they "puff themselves great airs, and imagine themselves very important characters in the drama of life."[69] Whitman even called his own employer and publisher, Park Benjamin, a "vain, pragmatical nincompoop."[70] Narrow-minded foreigners and egotistical nincompoops notwithstanding, Whitman also praised certain papers, especially those for which he was working, as when he characterized the *Aurora*, in its own pages, as "fearless, open, and frank in its tone — brilliant and sound, pointed without laboring after effects, ardent without fanaticism, humorous without coarseness, intellectual without affectation —

66. *New York Aurora* (March 29, 1842). *WWJ*, 81. 67. Mott, 341–42. 68. *New York Aurora* (March 24, 1842). *WWJ*, 82. 69. *New York Aurora* (March 24, 1842). *WWJ*, 68. 70. *New York Aurora* (March 24, 1842). *WWJ*, 69.

and altogether . . . the most entertaining mélange of latest news, miscellaneous literature, fashionable intelligence, hits at the times, pictures of life as it is, and every thing else that can please and instruct."[71] Whatever his opinions of his peers and their abilities, Whitman devoted his early life to the world of print.

Nor did Whitman distinguish between *belles lettres* and the more "practical" prose of newspaper journalism. Newspapers, in Whitman's day, were responsible for establishing and maintaining literary careers. In 1841, the *New World* published two of Whitman's poems, as well as a story, and the following year it published two more poems, "Stanzas" (October 22) and "A Sketch" (December 10), as well as *Franklin Evans*. Most of the leading literary figures of Whitman's youth were involved with these periodicals as editors and authors. Edgar Allan Poe was literary and contributing editor of *Graham's Magazine* for fifteen months in 1841–42, where he published the work of America's most renowned periodical writer, Nathaniel Parker Willis. Fifteen pieces by Nathaniel Hawthorne appeared in Joseph T. Buckingham's *New-England Galaxy* in Boston. New York's *Knickerbocker*, begun in 1831, published work by Hawthorne, Willis, Henry Wadsworth Longfellow, John Greenleaf Whittier, Oliver Wendell Holmes, James Fenimore Cooper, Washington Irving, and William Cullen Bryant, while the popular *Ladies' Magazine*, founded in Boston by Sarah Josepha Hale in 1828, and the long-lived *Godey's Ladies Book*, which enjoyed a circulation of forty thousand in 1849, published leading male and female authors.[72] The renowned journalist and social reformer Horace Greeley, with his brother-in-law Jonas Winchester, began publishing *The New-Yorker* in 1834 and the *New York Tribune* in 1841.[73]

One of the most striking journalistic innovations of the 1840s was the so-called "mammoth paper," featuring serialized fiction that ranged from the sensational to the now-canonical. Park Benjamin and Reverend Rufus Wilmot Griswold launched *Brother Jonathan* in 1839, with two editions — a folio selling for two dollars per annum and a quarto edition for three — that enjoyed a combined circulation of nine thousand.[74] Soon Benjamin and Griswold left *Brother Jonathan* to join Jonas Winchester at the *New World*, which issued its first number on June 6, 1840. The folio paper was four feet long and eleven

71. *New York Aurora* (March 29, 1842). *WWJ*, 81.   72. Mott, 344–46, 514.   73. Mott, 358. 74. Mott, 359.

columns wide, leading Griswold to call it a "Leviathan" sheet, and by the end of 1840 began appearing as a quarto edition as well.[75]

These periodicals issued separately printed "extras," often featuring entire literary works. *Franklin Evans* first appeared as such an extra, where it occupied thirty-one double-columned pages. Most "extras," however, were reprints of British and other foreign works. To compete with book publishers, who sent messengers to the steamships to pick up new editions of British works by authors such as Charles Dickens and Bulwer-Lytton and rush them to press, the *New World* and *Brother Jonathan* also sent agents to the docks to purchase British works, which the "extras," set in print overnight, could issue through a score of newsboys.[76] Such cheap "extras" were characterized as "papers" so as to achieve the lower postage rates reserved for newspapers, thereby keeping subscription prices, five dollars a year, relatively low; as the *New World* advertised, they could "be forwarded to all parts of the country at a single newspaper postage." This loophole closed in April 1843, when a post office order subjected "extras" to the much higher pamphlet postage, and in June of the same year British copyright regulations prevented their sale in Canada.[77]

A look at the *New World* over the course of 1842 provides a sense of both the literary and print culture contexts in which *Franklin Evans* appeared. The paper described itself as "A Weekly Journal of Popular Literature, Science, Music, and the Arts, Containing the latest works by Distinguished authors, sermons by eminent divines, original and selected tales and poetry, &c. &c." and the epigraph frankly expressed the paper's nationalist and even imperialist ambitions: "No pent-up Utica contracts our powers; For the whole unbounded continent is ours."[78] Authors published in the course of 1842 included Frances E. Osgood, Eliza Pratt, Catharine M. Sedgwick, and Henry Wadsworth Longfellow. The most heavily advertised work of the year was Dickens's *American Notes for General Circulation*. The paper also printed numerous short news items, lists of marriages and deaths, and advance notice of lectures by such luminaries as Richard Henry Dana, Orestes Brownson, George Bancroft, and Ralph Waldo Emerson. The *New World* was not wholly apolitical, as evinced by its series of editorials decrying the arrest of its agent in

75. Mott, 359–60. 76. Mott, 360. 77. Mott, 361. 78. See *New World* cover facsimile, p. xxxix.

Charleston for distributing a copy of the paper that contained William Ellery Channing's oration on West Indian independence. Going from the sublime to the ridiculous, it also included a list of people who owed the paper money. Other "extras" advertised in 1842 in the *New World* included volumes on *Animal Chemistry* and *Agricultural Chemistry; The Western Captive, or Ties of Tecumseh* (touted as "an original novel, by Mrs. Seba Smith"); *The Conspirator* ("an original American Novel, founded on the Conspiracy of Aaron Burr . . . written by a lady"); and Bulwer-Lytton's *Godolphin*.

In short, Whitman's *Franklin Evans* appeared in a cultural space where authors now considered undeniably literary published alongside now-forgotten popular writers, where prosaic news jostled with serious poetry and fiction. It also appeared at a time when debates over literary nationalism were in full swing. The extras' focus on British and other foreign authors brought them in for criticism by those hoping to establish a homegrown literary tradition. The *New World* probably did not succeed in quelling such objections when it advertised its publication of Alexandre Dumas's *Pauline: A Tale of Normandy* and Dickens's *American Notes* under the heading "Original American Novels." Park Benjamin claimed in 1835 that no literary talent existed in the United States, complaining, "With the exception of those whom Fortune has placed beyond the necessity of exertion, there are no authors by profession [in America]. The efforts of American writers are, for the most part, made in hours of leisure, set aside from business."[79] By 1841, however, Mathew Carey complained to William Gilmore Simms that American authors suffered from a literary market "glutted with periodic literature, particularly the mammoth weeklies."[80] Whitman was more pointed in his criticism, asserting that American writers were "more miserably paid" than writers anywhere, because of the absence of copyright laws; "most of our writers," he complained, "are frittering away their brains for an occasional five dollar bill from the magazine publishers."[81] In the face of this criticism, in 1842 Godey and Graham increased their pay rates for American contributors: Graham paid between four and twelve dollars a page for prose, and ten to fifteen dollars per poem. Hawthorne was offered five dollars a page in 1842, as was Poe.[82] Despite better pay for contributors, however, the "extras" remained cheap and widely read:

79. Mott, 494. 80. Mott, 495. 81. *Brooklyn Evening Star* (February 5, 1846). *WWJ*, 252. 82. Mott, 506–7.

as one New York journalist noted, " 'They have a way in this city of publishing spicy weekly newspapers at two cents a copy and bestowing upon them a circulation of ten, twenty, and thirty thousand a week.' "[83]

In characterizing the "mammoth papers" as "spicy," this reporter echoes a common charge that their sensationalist prose, often focused on crime and licentiousness, appealed to the base appetites of an untutored readership. Often critics were less polite, as when a writer in the *Tribune* condemned "the Satanic press."[84] In response to such criticism, the editors of the *New World* claimed that their "ample pages are unsoiled by profane or improper jests, vulgar allusions, or irreligious sentiments."[85] Early in 1842, the editors expanded their defense of their paper's respectability, writing, "The best contributors have been engaged. A correspondence with the most interesting parts of the world has been established. In short, the best arrangements have been made to publish an independent literary journal, acceptable to all classes of readers. The editor can think of nothing which has been left undone to enhance the value and to elevate the character of the New World."[86]

In short, the story-papers repeatedly found themselves defending both their patriotism and their respectability. It is little wonder the editors chose to advertise *Franklin Evans* as "written expressly for the NEW WORLD, by one of the best Novelists of this country, with a view to aid the great work of Reform, and rescue Young Men from the demon of Intemperance." In the same year, they added to their list of "Books for the People" another unquestionably American work, *Life and Public Services of Henry Clay*; but even in the "extra" of *Franklin Evans* itself the *New World* advertised another foreign work, Frederika Brewer's *The Neighbors: A Tale of Everyday Life*, translated from the Swedish.

Whitman's contribution in 1842 to the controversy over literary nationalism was perhaps *Franklin Evans* itself, but he also continued to discuss questions of sensationalism and respectability in literature. He wrote in *Brother Jonathan* in February to defend the depictions of the wide array of human experiences, high and low, found in one of his favorite works, Dickens's *Oliver Twist*. Anticipating later defenses of realism and naturalism, Whitman argued:

---

83. Mott, 361. 84. Quoted in Mott, 361. 85. Mott, 361. 86. *New World* (January 1, 1842). *WWJ*, 18.

The mere fact of a man's delineating human character in its lowest stages of degradation, and giving it unbounded scope in every species of wickedness, proves neither his "democracy" nor its opposite. If it be done in such a way, as that a kind of charm is thrown all the time around the guilty personage described—in such a way that excuses and palliations for his vice are covertly conveyed, even now and then—such writings, most assuredly, would have no fair claim to rank among "the literature of democracy." But when the specimens of naked, ragged deformity, as ignorant as wicked, are drawn out before us, and surrounded with their fit accompaniments, filth and darkness, and the deepest discomfort—when crime is pourtrayed [*sic*] never so that by any possibility the reader can find the slightest temptation to go out and do likewise—when we can see how evil doing is followed by its sure and long and weary punishment—when our minds are led to the irresistible conclusion that iniquity is loathsome, and by the magic of the pen-painter, have his pictures so stamped upon them that we ever after associate desperate actions with lowness and the very vulgarity of pollution—in such cases, I say, the delineations of life in its lowest aspects, and even characterized by grossest ignorance and brutality, do not militate against their author's claim for admiration from all true democrats.[87]

Such fiction, for Whitman, provided a useful social pedagogy. "Among newspapers," he proclaimed, "the penny press is the same as common schools among seminaries of education. They carry light and knowledge in among those who most need it. They dispense the clouds of ignorance; and make the great body of the people intelligent, capable, and worthy of performing the duties of republican freedmen."[88] Not only the urban poor read the weeklies, however, as Whitman was well aware; the penny papers, Whitman claimed, teach wealthy readers abut the degradations of poverty. "The rich cannot taste the distresses of want from their own experiences," Whitman reasons; "it is something if they are made to do so through the power of the pen." "A good parent or teacher sometimes has to lay before those whom he would reform," he concludes, "the strong, naked, heinous truth."[89]

Perhaps the dissemination of such truths was what Whitman had in mind

---

87. *Brother Jonathan* (February 26, 1842). *WWJ*, 36.   88. *New York Aurora* (March 26, 1842). *WWJ*, 74.   89. *Brother Jonathan* (February 26, 1842). *WWJ*, 38.

when, in September 1840, he flirted with the idea of writing fiction. "I see no reason why we should let our lights shine under bushels," he declared. "Yes: I *would* write a book! And who shall say that it might not be a very pretty book? Who knows but that I might do something very respectable?"[90] Whether *Franklin Evans* is either "pretty" or "respectable" has often been debated. What is certain is that it would not have appeared were it not for the proliferation of print in 1840s New York. It was the conjunction of that new print culture and another nineteenth-century social phenomenon — the movement for social reform — that made *Franklin Evans* possible.

WHITMAN AND SOCIAL REFORM

Due largely to Whitman's capacity for self-mythologizing, readers today may know more about the events leading to the writing of *Franklin Evans* than about the novel itself. Park Benjamin and his assistant, James Aldrich, visited Whitman to request that the young writer compose a temperance novel for the *New World*.[91] Temperance tales were coming into vogue at the time, especially among the working-class readers who subscribed to papers like Benjamin's.[92] James Hart reports that over 12 percent of American novels published during the 1830s were temperance fictions; "though they were mostly brief tracts disguised as fiction and distributed free," Hart writes, "they had a great circulation."[93] Temperance fiction was highly formulaic, abounding with sensational scenes of sin, corruption, and violence. "Bloated corpses with staring eyes were common around the drunkard's house in a temperance novel," Hart reports, "though an occasional body just exploded into nothingness by spontaneous combustion."[94] While temperance tales titillated audiences with immorality, they carefully concluded with predictable morals, the drunkard either repenting or dying a grisly death. The survivors in temperance tales "were such prigs," Hart quips, "as to make Little Eva seem a hoyden by comparison."[95]

While surely formulaic, temperance tales in fact varied widely, especially in the proportions they devoted to sensationalism as opposed to a more respectable sentimentalism. But when Whitman looked back on his early novel over

---

90. *Long-Island Democrat* (September 29, 1840). *WWJ*, xlvix. 91. Winwar, 73.
92. Winwar, 73. 93. Hart, 108. 94. Hart, 108. 95. Hart, 109.

forty years later, temperance fiction's reputation as repetitive and sub-literary
was so well established that it comes as no surprise that Whitman vehemently
disavowed *Franklin Evans* in an 1888 conversation with Horace Traubel:

> I doubt if there is a copy in existence: I have none and have not had one for
> years; it was a pamphlet. Parke Godwin and another somebody (who was it?)
> came to see me about writing it. Their offer of cash payment was so tempting —
> I was so hard up at the time — that I set to work at once ardently on it (with the
> help of a bottle of port or what not). In three days of constant work I finished
> the book. Finished the book? Finished myself. It was damned rot — rot of the
> worst sort — not insincere, perhaps, but rot, nevertheless: it was not the busi-
> ness for me to be up to. I stopped right there: I never cut a chip off that kind
> of timber again.[96]

Whitman again distanced himself from the temperance cause later in 1888,
telling Traubel that profit alone led him to write *Franklin Evans*. When Whitman offers Traubel wine, his guest teases the poet that he will be thrown out of
the temperance society. "They can't," Whitman responds; "I never was in."
When Traubel asks, "But didn't you write a temperance novel once?" Whitman responds, "Yes, so I did — for seventy five dollars cash down. And, by
the way, that seventy-five dollars was not the end of it, for the book sold so
well they sent me fifty dollars more in two or three weeks."[97] As Alexander
Cowie observes, "the author of *Leaves of Grass* had by that time shown himself to be above fanatical organized attempts to curb human vices." "He was
a liberator," Cowie concludes, "not a judge."[98]

While Whitman may well have outgrown the pat judgments of organized
temperance, we should not accept uncritically his disavowals of either temperance or of *Franklin Evans*, especially given that his retrospective account
of the writing of the book is both inaccurate and expressed with nearly the
same vehemence with which he rejected John Addington Symonds's 1890
interpretation of *Leaves of Grass* as homoerotic.[99] After all, within months
of the appearance of *Franklin Evans* Whitman published two chapters of
something called *The Madman* (reprinted here), which seems to be the beginning of another temperance novel and which appeared in an official publi-

96. Traubel, Vol. 3, 93. 97. Traubel, Vol. 4, 323. 98. Cowie, 309. 99. Moon, 11-12.

cation of the Washingtonian Temperance Societies, the New York *Washingtonian and Organ*, under an announcement reading "By the author of 'Franklin Evans.' "[100] Furthermore, Whitman republished *Franklin Evans* in the *Brooklyn Eagle* in 1846, when he became the paper's editor, albeit with its temperance message toned down.[101] And while the poetic exuberance of *Leaves of Grass* might lead one to envision Whitman as a Bacchanalian hedonist, in fact he was only an occasional drinker who apparently never consumed to inebriation.[102] Traubel's anecdotes notwithstanding, Whitman's relationship to the reform movements that proliferated over the 1840s — to abolish slavery and alcohol consumption, improve prisons and tenement life, stamp out licentiousness, and bring women the vote — was complex and ambivalent. Indeed, of these movements, in the early 1840s temperance may well have been the one about which Whitman was *least* equivocal.

By 1846, however, Whitman was demonstrably skeptical about reformist enthusiasm. "We have had the presumption," Whitman sarcastically confessed, "for a while past, to think that *we* were somewhat of a 'reformer' in our humble way — disposed to go the length of the string, for improvements of all kinds, political, first, and others afterward. But we feel quite ashamed of ourselves for presumption, when we come to see what lofty flights some of our fellow citizens take in the same field. They leave us not only far behind, but totally out of sight."[103] Whitman remained particularly averse to reformers' frequent assertions of innate human depravity, and to the strict doctrines and demands for loyalty they developed in response. Whitman declared, "We would not be considered one of those bigots that think there is no good in humanity, except what resides in some favorite school of faith — we believe in a *general average* of good."[104] Covering Scottish labor reformer Robert Owen's speech in June 1846, before the World Convention at New York's Clinton Hall, Whitman reports being "somewhat in doubt whether to laugh at the whole thing as a humbug, or commend it inasmuch as it contained germs of a bold, though fruitless inquiry into the wrongs and evils of the world." "It is utterly chimerical and labor thrown away," he asserts, "to attempt remodeling the world on an unalloyed basis of purity and perfection. God did

100. For details, see Brasher, 240–43. 101. Holloway, *Free and Lonesome Heart*, vi. 102. Holloway, *Free and Lonesome Heart*, 28. 103. *Brooklyn Eagle and Kings County Democrat* (May 29, 1846). *WWJ*, 387. 104. *Brooklyn Eagle and Kings County Democrat* (April 22, 1846). *WWJ*, 338.

not see fit to do so, and we hardly expect the thing will be accomplished by Mr. Robert Owen."[105]

In regard to the temperance movement, Whitman expressed similar hesitation, remarking in 1840, "I am not one of those who would deny people any sense of delight, because I think it is a sin to be happy, and to take pleasure in the good things of this life. On the contrary, I am disposed to allow every rational gratification, both to the palate, and the other senses."[106] In 1846, Whitman stated his opposition to legal restraints on alcohol consumption, which he predicted would prove ineffectual (although he rather confusingly encouraged readers to vote for legislators who supported such laws).[107]

At the same time, Whitman held in contempt any anti-reform politician who was "averse to innovation, loves the old rather than the new, and will not favor any 'experiment' " and therefore is "the very opposite of reform."[108] He declared himself committed — "as who, sincere with his own heart, can fail to be?" — to "the great salutary *truth* of the temperance doctrine — of the mighty evils of drink, spreading like a deadly thing wherever it flows — or the salutary effects of the *pledge*, the charm that has reformed hundreds, and as a precautionary measure, saved thousands."[109] As early as 1840, Whitman used his journalism to inveigh against all forms of intemperance, including tobacco consumption. "Our young men," Whitman wrote, "entertain an idea that there is something very manly in having a segar stuck in the corner of their lips; or a round ball of sickening weed that a dog would not touch rolling in their mouths."[110] "Custom may, and does, enable some people to become so habituated to these things," Whitman warns, "that they produce no evident evil. But it is still not less the case that they *do* produce evil. They waken the strength of the nervous system; they alternately excite and depress the powers of the brain; and they act with constant and insidious attacks upon the health."[111]

Throughout 1842, the year Whitman wrote and published *Franklin Evans*, the author was particularly captivated by the Washingtonians, a temperance

---

105. *Brooklyn Eagle and Kings County Democrat* (June 6, 1846). *WWJ*, 405.
106. *Hempstead Inquirer* (April 28, 1840). *WWJ*, 20. 107. *Brooklyn Eagle and Kings County Democrat* (May 18, 1846). *WWJ*, 365. 108. *Brooklyn Eagle and Kings County Democrat* (April 22, 1846). *WWJ*, 338. 109. *Brooklyn Eagle and Kings County Democrat* (May 18, 1846). *WWJ*, 365. 110. *Hempstead Inquirer* (April 28, 1840). *WWJ*, 19. 111. *Hempstead Inquirer* (April 28, 1840). *WWJ*, 19.

association begun in Baltimore in 1840 with a mere six members, which claimed half a million members only two years later. Abraham Lincoln's 1842 "Address to the Washingtonian Temperance Society of Springfield, IL," reprinted here, lauds the new organization for many of the same reasons as did Whitman, and tells its history concisely. Lincoln, who was an avid Washingtonian, characterizes older, clergy-led temperance organizations such as the American Temperance Society as motivated by "a cold abstract theory." Earlier temperance movements, which assumed that "all habitual drunkards were utterly incorrigible, and therefore must be turned adrift, and damned without remedy," focused on how the pure could avoid the temptation of drink. "There is in this something so repugnant to humanity," Lincoln opined, "so uncharitable, so cold-blooded and feelingless, that it never did, nor ever can enlist the enthusiasm of a popular cause." In contrast, Washingtonian literature "adopt[s] a more enlarged philanthropy," drawing on "those who have suffered by intemperance *personally*, and have reformed" as "instruments to push the reformation to ultimate success." There was as well a class element to the shift in the temperance movement; while previous temperance drives had been led by abstemious middle-class men, often clergy, the Washingtonians were led by working men and women who were themselves suffering drinkers. The Washingtonians drew on liberalizing Christian revival rhetoric of individual salvation and human perfectibility to encourage "fallen" drinkers to reform themselves and each other, denying, as Lincoln emphasized, "the doctrine of unpardonable sin."[112] The Washingtonians also matched Whitman's ambivalence about prohibitionist laws, generally opposing such acts in favor of "moral suasion" of individual drunkards.

In 1842, sixteen thousand New Yorkers claimed to be members of the city's twenty-three Washingtonian Societies.[113] While partly resulting from the Washingtonians' broad circulation of print materials such as *Franklin Evans* and formal speeches like Lincoln's, their popularity is primarily attributed to the public gatherings known as "experience meetings"—a term and practice drawn from Methodism—at which people would be brought to tears by listening to lecturers tell stories of their own drunken pasts. Whitman reports attending such a meeting at Grand Street's Temperance Hall in March 1842.

112. Griffin, 70–73. 113. Griffin, 71.

The apartment was filled with an assemblage of both sexes. A speaker whose name we understood as Capt. Wisdom was speaking from the platform. His language seemed totally deficient in polish and in grammatical correctness; but he evidently felt what he was saying, and desired to do as much good as possible. No doubt, the method of Mr. Wisdom is far more effective for the sphere it moves in, than a more refined style.

An address by a person whose tongue had a broad foreign accent, followed Mr. W. This man gave his "experience," and descanted in enthusiastic terms on the great blessing the temperance cause had been to him. He was a very uncouth speaker. Yet, how all the boundaries of taste, all the laws of conventional usage, are leaped over, in oratory, by deep feeling and ardent sincerity. Every hearer in the room, assuredly, was thrilled to the heart by portions of this uneducated man's remarks. For our own part, we were never more interested in our life.

Then there was music. A choir, composed mainly of ladies, sang an ode — and a company of fine looking young firemen variefied the experience with a temperance glee.

As we left the house, we could not help but wondering at the mighty enthusiasm which all there, men, women, and children, seemed to be imbued with.[114]

We can only speculate on whether the "enthusiasm" of at least some of the crowd was, as it apparently was for Whitman, owing to the handsome firemen who "variefied" the meeting. Describing a Washington parade in the same month, Whitman gives a glimpse of the "adhesive" enjoyment of male beauty that would later inspire the poems of *Calamus*, and which resonates with the pageantry of the dream sequence in *Franklin Evans*.

First came a banner bearing the head of Washington, immediately after which were a body of firemen. Whether it be a whim, or from some more tangible cause, we do have a fondness for the New York firemen. They are mostly fine, stalwart, handsome young men; and in their close fitting dresses and red shirts, we never behold them, but the Roman gladiators and the Olympian games are brought to our mind. We question whether any city in the world can turn out a more manly set of young fellows. It is honorable to them, that they engage

114. *New York Aurora* (April 1, 1842). *WWJ*, 91.

in the temperance movement. With the generosity and evident devotedness of youth, they throw themselves, heart and soul, into the cause. This is a great thing gained. Once make temperance a favorite and fashionable custom among the young men of our city, and the whole conquest is over, — the enemy is vanquished![115]

Beyond the erotic "enthusiasms" they generated, the Washingtonians, with their "processions, and meetings, and orations, and festivals, and banners displayed, and music, and a grand blow out at night to cap the whole," provided a visually stimulating form of street spectacle for a public newly accustomed to theatrical entertainment. Describing one such scene, Whitman writes,

> After the firemen came an immense number of citizens, formerly intemperate men, but now worthy members of society. There was a beautiful flag representing a female figure, and on each side a gushing spring of water. Then the junior temperance societies, with a banner inscribed, "beware of the first glass!" A number of sailors followed. Then more firemen, with a beautiful hose cart, No. 18, we believe. The hatters' association made a very respectable appearance, as did also the Newark Society and the Chelsea Society. The banners had a great many quaint devices. One we noticed bearing a sheaf of grain, and the motto, "If you eat me, I am life; if you drink me, I am death."[116]

As Whitman's eyewitness account demonstrates, the public spectacles staged by the Washingtonians appropriated the icons of nationalism — flags, banners, public orations — for a citizenry who may have felt little direct involvement in the operations of government. In so doing, they helped generate an often oppositional counter-public in antebellum cities like New York.

Franklin Evans is exemplary of the newly intensified conjunction of print culture with voluntary associations bent on social reform. Literature played an increasingly important role in this conjunction, as the American Temperance Society's 1836 decision to approve the use of fiction to further its cause demonstrates. The *New World*'s publicity for *Franklin Evans* capitalized on reformers' acceptance of fiction. "Friends of Temperance, Ahoy!" it begins:

115. *New York Aurora* (March 30, 1842). *WWJ*, 87.   116. *New York Aurora* (March 30, 1842). *WWJ*, 87.

THIS NOVEL, which is dedicated to the Temperance Societies and the friends of the Temperance Cause throughout the Union, will create a sensation, both for the ability with which it is written, as well as the interest of the subject, and will be universally read and admired. It was written expressly for the NEW WORLD, by one of the best Novelists of this country, with a view to aid the great work of Reform, and rescue Young Men from the demon of Intemperance. The incidents of the plot are wrought out with great effect, and the excellence of its moral, and the beneficial influence it will have, should interest the friends of Temperance Reformation in giving this Tale the widest possible circulation.

As Michael Warner argues, Whitman's text was not simply a novel; it was a newspaper supplement, a tract, and above all, an adjunct to America's first "full-scale, mass-mediated social movement," temperance reform.[117]

In its alliances with working-class Washingtonianism, moreover, *Franklin Evans* serves as a test case, both fascinatingly problematic and in some ways paradigmatic, of Jürgen Habermas's assertion of the role of print in the formation of a bourgeois public sphere. *Franklin Evans* enlists readers' identification with fictional protagonists to align them with reforms that are simultaneously personal and social. However, *Franklin Evans* can also be seen as putting the Habermasian model to the test. The Washingtonian temperance movement's working-class basis challenges Habermas's claims that the public sphere was always an essentially bourgeois formation, and that public spheres emerging from other economic and cultural sectors were variants "suppressed in the historical process."[118] As Glenn Hendler has argued, no reading of the novel could support the Habermasian insistence that the medium of communication in the public sphere was "rational-critical discourse." The narrative itself is driven by Franklin's appetitive and even erotic excess, just as the Washingtonian movement it was meant to serve expanded through dramatic displays of male emotionality.

READING *FRANKLIN EVANS*

On November 5, 1842, the *New World* announced the forthcoming publication of *Franklin Evans* at a price of ten for a dollar and one hundred for eight dollars (individual readers could purchase the novel for twelve and a half cents,

117. Warner, 30. 118. Habermas, xviii.

but the editors were no doubt hoping for bulk purchases by Washingtonian and other temperance societies). As promised, *Franklin Evans* appeared on November 24, 1842, as a thirty-one-page octavo pamphlet, which sold approximately twenty thousand copies. The *New World* again advertised the novel, now renamed *Franklin Evans, or the Merchant's Clerk: a Tale of the Times*, on August 19, 1843, and between November 16 and 30, 1846, Whitman republished the tale as *Fortunes of a Country-Boy: Incidents in Town and His Adventures at the South*. This version, described in the *Eagle* as "A Tale of Long Island," was substantially different from the *New World* edition, notably shorter and with a far less explicit emphasis on the temperance message.[119]

The novel's publication history is thus a particularly rich example of the phenomenon Meredith McGill has dubbed "the culture of reprinting" that shaped the career and reception history of numerous nineteenth-century authors. After these iterations, however, the novel disappeared until Emory Holloway's 1929 Random House edition. Then, due perhaps to the decade's fascination with social movements or with the creative promptings of intoxication, *Franklin Evans* enjoyed a brief "revival" in the 1960s; after being included in Thomas Brasher's *Early Poems and the Fiction* volume of Whitman's *Collected Works*, it also emerged in an edition edited by Jean Downey in 1967.[120] No contemporary edition of Whitman's "collected" poetry and prose includes the novel, however, nor has any edition followed Downey's, now out of print.

While *Franklin Evans* has been virtually inaccessible to most readers since its original newspaper publications, it did not escape critical attention, most of it dismissive. Van Wyck Brooks claimed the novel "abounded in every known cliché of the moral-mongers," with "scarcely a line or a thought that suggested in any way an original mind."[121] Seeing in *Franklin Evans* only a numbingly predictable morality tale of naïve country-dwellers "making their tremulous way into the wicked Big Town, upon which they have projected all that their mothers and preachers have warned them of, and for which they ferociously long," Leslie Fiedler blamed Whitman for introducing into the American urban novel a "sentimental and lubricious" provincialism.[122] Alexander Cowie found the novel's structure "wobbly at best," and attributed

---

119. For a detailed and methodical comparison of the variations between these versions, as well as accounts of the publication history of the novel and some of its chapters, see Brasher, 124–239. 120. Brasher, 124–25. 121. Brooks, 40. 122. Fiedler, 490.

THE NEW WORLD.

PARK BENJAMIN,
EDITOR.

J. WINCHESTER,
PUBLISHER.

"No pent-up Utica contracts our powers; For the whole boundless continent is ours."

EXTRA SERIES.   OFFICE 30 ANN-STREET.   NUMBER 34

VOL. II...No. 10.   NEW-YORK, NOVEMBER, 1842.   PRICE 12½ CENTS.

Original Temperance Novel.

Entered according to Act of Congress, in the year 1842,
BY J. WINCHESTER,
In the Clerk's Office of the Southern District of New York.

FRANKLIN EVANS;

OR

THE INEBRIATE.

A TALE OF THE TIMES.

BY WALTER WHITMAN.

INTRODUCTORY.

THE story I am going to tell you, reader, will be somewhat aside from the ordinary track of the novelist. It will not abound, either with profound reflections, or sentimental remarks. Yet its moral—for I flatter myself it has one, and one which it were well to engrave on the heart of each person who scans its pages—will be taught by its own incidents, and the current of the narrative.

Whatever of romance there may be—I leave it to any who have, in the course of their every-day walks, heard the histories of intemperate men, whether the events of the tale, strange as some of them may appear, have not had their counterpart in real life. If you who live in the city should go out among your neighbors and investigate what is being transacted there, you might come to behold things far more improbable. In fact, the following chapters contain but the account of a young man, thrown by circumstances amid the vortex of dissipation—a country youth, who came to our great emporium to seek his fortune—and what befell him there. So it is a plain story; yet as the grandest truths are sometimes plain enough to enter into the minds of children—it may be that the delineation I shall give will do benefit, and that educated men and women may not find the hour they spend in its perusal, altogether wasted.

And I would ask your belief when I assert that, what you are going to read is not a work of fiction, as the term is used. I narrate occurrences that have had a far more substantial existence than in my fancy. There will be those who, as their eyes turn past line after line, will have their memories carried to matters which they have heard of before, or taken a part in themselves, and which, they know, are real.

Can I hope, that my story will do good? I entertain that hope Issued in the cheap and popular form you see, and wafted by every mail to all parts of this vast republic; the facilities which its publisher possesses, giving him the power of diffusing it more widely than any other establishment in the United States; the mighty and deep public opinion which, as a tide bears a ship upon its bosom, ever welcomes anything favorable to the Temperance Reform; its being written for the mass, though the writer hopes, not without some claim upon the approval of the more fastidious; and, as much as anything else, the fact that it is as a pioneer in this department of literature—all these will give "THE INEBRIATE," I feel confident, a more than ordinary share of patronage.

For youth, what can be more invaluable? It teaches sobriety, that virtue which every mother and father prays nightly, may be resident in the characters of their sons. It wars against Intemperance, that evil spirit which has levelled so many fair human forms before its horrible advances. Without being presumptuous, I would remind those who believe in the wholesome doctrines of abstinence, how the earlier teachers of piety used parables and fables, as the fit instruments whereby they might convey to men the beauty of the system they professed. In the resemblance, how reasonable it is to suppose that you can impress a lesson upon him whom you would influence to sobriety, in no better way than letting him read such a story as this.

It is usual for writers, upon presenting their works to the public, to bespeak indulgence for faults and deficiences. I am but too well aware that the critical eye will see some such in the following pages; yet my book is not written for the critics, but for THE PEOPLE; and while I think it best to leave it to the reader's own decision whether I have succeeded, I cannot help remarking, that I have the fullest confidence in the verdict's being favorable.

And, to conclude, may I hope that he who purchases this volume, will give to its author, and to its publisher also, the credit of being influenced not altogether by views of the profit to come from it? Whatever of those views may enter into our minds, we are not without a strong desire that the principles here inculcated will strike deep, and grow again, and bring forth good fruit. A prudent, sober, and temperate course of life cannot be too strongly taught to old and young; to the young, because the future years are before them—to the old, because it is their business to prepare for death. And though, as before remarked, the writer has abstained from thrusting the moral upon the reader, by dry and abstract requisitions—preferring the more pleasant and quite as profitable method of letting the reader draw it himself from the occurrences—it is hoped that the New and Popular Reform now in the course of progress over the land, will find no trifling help from a "TALE OF THE TIMES."

Front cover, *New World* "extra" featuring *Franklin Evans*, November 24, 1842.
Courtesy of the Newberry Library, Chicago.

"its brief contemporary vogue" to "its comparative novelty."[123] Emory Holloway, largely responsible for preserving the text from obscurity, agreed that
Franklin Evans "abound[s] in sentimental piety." "A picaresque story may
hold interest, despite the episodic handling of its incidents," Holloway continues, "if the rogue have wit and courage; but Whitman's central character, if
he may be called a character at all, is necessarily a weak-willed youth, destined
to get the worst in every encounter, not only with the demon drink, but with
every man and woman he meets."[124] Full of "wooden stereotypes," the novel,
in Holloway's critical judgment, is simply "too subjective, too sentimental,
too preachy."[125] Even one of the novel's most astute critics, Frances Winwar,
laments, "Never a humorist, [Whitman] saw that not the faintest glowworm
flitted through his Inebriate's dismal swamp."[126]

While *Franklin Evans* is hardly as formulaic or predictably moralistic as
most critics have asserted, it is without doubt a "wobbly" text. Incorporating
thinly veiled autobiography (Franklin's early carriage ride into Manhattan reflects Whitman's own arrival in the city from West Hills with his grandfather
Van Velsor[127]), interpolated literary materials Whitman had on hand or con-
ceived to fill out space in the narrative (Whitman used his story, "The Child
and the Profligate," as the source for chapter 8, for instance, while he seems
to have written the tales of "Unrelenting" and of "little Jane" for publication
elsewhere[128]), and Washingtonian rhetoric, *Franklin Evans* can hardly be said
to present a "coherent" style or plot line. Rather than assuming, as have critics following Whitman's own lead, that the "incoherence" of *Franklin Evans*
arises from Whitman's drunken lack of commitment, it might be more pro-
ductive to assume that the novel's ruptures reflect central cultural ideologies
that, in the state of emergence, were themselves "incoherent," even conflicted.
As Michael Denning cautions about other literature of the 1840s addressed to
the "masses," "questions about the sincerity of their purported beliefs or the
adequacy of their political proposals are less interesting than questions about
the narrative embodiment of their political ideologies."[129] Three central mo-
tifs in *Franklin Evans* — speculative economics and social reform, gender and
the sexualized transmission of capital, and racial nationalism — are just such

123. Cowie, 308. 124. Holloway, *Free and Lonesome Heart*, 29. 125. Holloway, *Free
and Lonesome Heart*, 29–30. 126. Winwar, 76. 127. Brooks, 140. 128. Holloway, *Free and
Lonesome Heart*, vii; Brasher, 125–26. 129. Denning, 103.

flashpoints for narrative (and hence ideological) disruption in *Franklin Evans* and its world.

While *Franklin Evans* is usually called a "novel," in his introduction Whitman situates it "somewhat aside from the ordinary track of the novelist." Even granting that its explicit agenda to bring about social change distinguishes *Franklin Evans* from many novels, one can still ask what kind of social change Whitman hoped the tale would generate. Despite his later disavowals, in 1842 Whitman articulated revolutionary aspirations for *Franklin Evans*, which he dedicated to "THE PEOPLE," boldly asserting, "In all ages, a revolution for the better, when started, has found its advocates among the poorest classes of men" (112). At the same time, Whitman assuages readers potentially alarmed by such revolutionary claims: "I am too strongly armed in the honesty of my intentions, to suppose that there can be any doubt as to the propriety of the *moral* intended to be conveyed—or to fear" (111). A revolution from which one has nothing to fear isn't much of a revolution (as Whitman's character Bourne, whose father fled France to escape the "terrors" that followed the French Revolution, might have told him). Promising both revolution and reform, Whitman represents in *Franklin Evans* the tensions that arose when potentially disruptive criticisms of the uneven distributions of wealth in industrializing America transformed into the self-regulating habits of a reformist culture in which "character," not class, determined one's social position.

At the time he wrote *Franklin Evans*, Whitman was keenly aware of the corrosive effects class stratification had on democracy in America. Whitman's February 28, 1842, column in the *Aurora* pointedly asks "Can This Be Justice?"

> Whether the mass of our citizens know it or not, New York, and not only New York, but each large American city—swarms with rascals of rank. The law, instead of punishing, encourages them. Society's choice circles give them the free pass. They are received pleasantly wherever they go; and even though their evil doings become at length too glaring for concealment, they, either by their wealth, or by identifying themselves with some political clique, and rallying it to their support—laugh to scorn the complaints of justly indignant public opinion.[130]

130. *New York Aurora* (February 28, 1842). *WWJ*, 39.

Whitman could be describing here the corrupt lawyer Demaine, who in *Franklin Evans* uses his class position to avoid prosecution for swindling widows and orphans, while the poor, whose only crime is drinking, die humiliated in the street.

Although Franklin abandons his degraded friends Denis and Colby to pursue the life of wealth and privilege represented by Demaine, Whitman proved more loyal to the audience to whom he dedicates the tale: "the weak — the nervous; to those who feel the want of some artificial aid to raise their spirits in society to what is no more than the ordinary pitch of those around them" (55). The poor are, for Whitman, better readers because, knowing the degradations to which poverty can lead, they don't judge; if more people acknowledged the "horrid dreams" harbored in their own bosoms, Whitman claims, "scorn would be changed to pity." "It is not well to condemn men for their frailness," Whitman contends, urging readers, "Let us rather own our common bond of weakness" (56). Here Whitman echoes the more sympathetic ethos of the Washingtonians, but there are broader implications of his empathy. If he represents human character as a gothic compendium of "horrid dreams," he also makes suffering the basis of an alternative ethic, based not on shared virtue, but on the pain occasioned by a deeply flawed economy.

Such a counter-ethic is precisely what is at stake in the choice between revolution and reform, as becomes clear in a telling editorial "correction" Jean Downey made to *Franklin Evans* in her 1967 edition. Asserting, "Such must fly the convivial class [glass?] in the first instance, if they do not want to sell themselves, for their term of life, to misery" (106 in Downey, 55 in this edition), Whitman suggests the emergence of a *class* of persons — the miserable — given the ability to read their affiliation as a "class" differently. Downey's substitution of "glass" for "class" as the evil to be avoided reflects the shift in focus from economic intemperance to self-management by the "weak" of their own appetites, a shift that obscures why the weak are hungry in the first place.

The self-management (or, as it would have been called in the 1840s, "self-culture") required by reform consisted of a series of codified stages. Prompted by an unexpected act of sympathy, often from a stranger who can legitimately claim to have been in a comparable state of weakness and abjection, one first acknowledges certain inviolable laws. These are not legal statutes but rather laws of the same human "nature" that enable the stranger's act of sympathetic identification. Deviations from such laws result in self-inflicted shame, recti-

fied only by repetitive actions that instill new habits, desires, and moral cen-
sors. Finally, the success or failure of reform is judged by a "public" to whom
one displays one's character in repeated rituals of confession and emotional
"cleansing." The Washingtonian "experience meetings," in which inebriates
confessed their lapses from the laws of healthful restraint, tearfully acknowledged their shame, and signed pledges that established more sober habits,
are typical of the changing patterns of reform in the 1840s.

The laws that reform purported to uncover in human nature not only established sobriety and other forms of self-restraint; they also created a "human
nature" fitted to the needs of industrial labor. In his 1844 *Education and Self-
Improvement*, for instance, the phrenologist and social reformer O. S. Fowler
asserts that each reader must undertake reform *"for himself*, and do it, not
'here a little and there a little,' but HABITUALLY."[131] In order "to be produc-
tive of happiness," Fowler continues, "every faculty must be exercised upon
with its *legitimate object*, and in accordance with its *normal function*"; only
under those conditions can the human faculties "be trained all to work *har-
moniously* with each other, and never be allowed to *conflict* or *quarrel* with
each other."[132] Fowler's theory seems innocuous, yet his description of habitual actions directed at a "legitimate object" inscribes as inviolable nature
a new model of labor requiring repetitive exertion (on assembly lines, for instance) centered on a single skill, producing a single object, which became
the totality of workers' "legitimacy" within mass production. Rather than an
artisan who contained an entire craft in his or herself, an industrial laborer
must coordinate his or her singular skill with those of others, without "conflict or quarrel," in order to produce, if not happiness, at least profit. In his
program for reform, Fowler, who influenced Whitman's thinking, makes a
form of labor that Marx famously described as alienated appear, not enforced
upon workers, but the result of their own desire to be normal. In "choosing"
to engage in self-managing reform, in other words, self-alienation becomes,
paradoxically, the most self-fulfilling act: willed consent. The penal reformer
Charles Caldwell demonstrates this succinctly in his 1829 tract, *New Views on
Penitentiary Discipline, and Moral Education and Reform*. "It is not enough,"
Caldwell warns would-be reformers, to change a criminal's "outward action,
by making him labour against his will. That whim which dictates action must

131. Fowler, 138. 132. Fowler, 155, 157.

be changed . . . not by coercion rendered hateful by the scourge, but by education and discipline, made acceptable, at least, if not desirable, by reason, principle, and firmness, united to a benevolent and earnest wish, in the teacher, to bestow a benefit, by rescuing a fellow-being from the dominion of vice."[133]

Beyond codifying the laws of human nature, reform generated categories of deviant personhood — "perversions" — based on a presumably shared (but flawed) character. Perversion — like "addiction," a concept that Michael Warner argues was "virtually invented by the temperance movement" — became as deeply rooted a part of human nature as virtue, leading reformers to coin terms ("addict," "alcoholic," "psychopath," "con man," "hoodlum," and "pornographer") that turn actions (drinking alcohol, making pornography, stealing) into identities. Despite their emergence in reform contexts, these identities were believed to be inalterable ("incorrigible," "intransigent," "recalcitrant," and "irredeemable" were also reform coinages).[134] In an age of economic speculation reliant on future payoffs, perverse people were thought to lack a contractual frame of mind; characterizing them in terms of ephemerality, immediate gratification, nostalgia, and wastefulness, reform imagined such people to be incapable of evaluating consequences, and therefore of sexual, social or economic reproduction. Not surprisingly, in *Franklin Evans* moments of reform coincide with instances of investment, in which speculators put a down payment on a profitable future made possible by the vigilant self-management of the tale's reformed protagonist. Franklin must give up current gratification, sacrificing momentary pleasures to purchase an upwardly mobile future made possible, not by his nature (Franklin's inclinations always lead him astray), but by repetitive *habit*, a word that appears obsessively in *Franklin Evans*. "*Once thoroughly regenerated*," Whitman writes, sounding like Fowler or Caldwell, "the remembrance of his old deformation will stand before his eyes like a pillar of fire, and warn him back from any farther indulgence in his vicious courses" (56).

One can never become thoroughly regenerated, however, at least not in *Franklin Evans*, which — like many other temperance narratives — is more a tale of backsliding than one of reform. Despite his innocent hope, "Perhaps if I had filled up my time with active employment, I might have kept to my resolution, and even in the end totally reformed" (54), Franklin must be serially

133. Caldwell, 2. 134. Mintz, 10.

reformed, his craving for alcohol repeatedly rekindled by other forms of addiction generated by modern capital. When Franklin tries to leave New York and its temptations, for instance, he quickly tires of the countryside's "monotony" (52), having become addicted to the variety of the city. Even the repeated ritual of confessing and being "reformed" becomes addictive for Franklin. Whitman seems to have understood that, despite his conventional moral ("I would advise every young man to marry as soon as possible, and have a home of his own" [111]), "normalcy" has no narrative: if Franklin were ever to become "thoroughly regenerated," the desire of readers for more trouble—for more tale—would be frustrated, and they would stop buying papers. Like narrative, then, profit relies, not on reform and the restraint of appetite, but on the generation of more hunger, more desire.

Franklin Evans repeatedly links economic speculation and addiction, often in subtle ways. The story of the crooked speculator, Andrews, is a case in point: Andrews "died of grief at the failure of some stock-jobbing operations, wherein a cunning fellow-broker overreached him" (110). Economic appetites rarely stay within the limits of legitimate profit, but fail from overextension or give rise to excesses ("overreaching") of greed. With economic speculations, as with drinking, no one seems to desire moderately. Whitman again links drinking and investment in the story of the schoolteacher, Fanning, who falls into ruin both because he "invested in stocks" (57) and, at the same moment, began drinking excessively. In the novel, economic greed and alcoholism become versions of the same intemperance, capital being the strongest source of excessive appetite, and the most destructive.

Just as alcoholics in *Franklin Evans* conceal their drunkenness, the economically intemperate are also skilled actors and deceivers. After Andrews' death, his properties "were found to be as fallacious as the basis on which they had been reared" (110). The greedy Demaine cheats while "keep[ing] up appearances" (110), and hence Whitman compares him to a stage illusion, "as far removed from true gentlemen, as the gilded sun, in stage melo-dramas, from the genuine source of light himself" (110). The problem, for readers of *Franklin Evans* no less than for characters in the text, is how to discern real from feigned virtue. When Whitman describes the Marchions as "among the most respectable and respected families in the city" (110), the proximity to Demaine's story casts doubt on how Marchion acquired *his* wealth or how well-deserved his respectability is. Little wonder that when he finally inherits

Stephen Lee's fortune, Franklin admits that, despite his joy in the windfall, "I could not help wondering at the method of it" (107).

In a world of deceptive appearances, where the economy relies on greater and less controllable desires and therefore no reform is final, trust is a complicated affair, almost bound for failure. The future behaviors of people, like those of stocks and markets, are highly unpredictable, yet contracts, even "moral" ones like the temperance pledge, require just such predictability. When Lee decides to leave his estate to the young and virtually unknown Franklin, he claims he is convinced, based on inquiries made without the boy's knowledge, that Franklin's wild oats have all been sown. Such a conviction, as Lee acknowledges, cannot be based on empirical fact, but on "whim" and "fancy." "Whim," however, is close kin to "impulse," as is "fancy" to "desire." One *never* gets over a certain speculative "wildness" in *Franklin Evans*, not even the patriarchal Lee. In the end, then, Franklin has to acknowledge himself, despite his habitual reform, as a bad "return" on the investment (68).

Soon after his arrival in New York, Franklin begins what proves a tragic pattern. Fleeing the life of dissipation he has been introduced to by his pal Colby, Franklin marries a young and innocent woman who soon dies as a result of his drunken neglect. Despondent over the death of his wife, Evans begins to drink more, loses his job, associates with criminals, and is arrested when a robbery goes bad. While in jail, he is sought out by a benefactor, Marchion, who secures his freedom and persuades him to take the Old Pledge, which forbade the drinking only of hard liquor. Just as his life begins to improve, Evans backslides further into trouble. In the hope of starting a new life away from the city, he moves to Virginia, where, while drunk, he marries a slave woman. Once sober, he regrets his marriage, leading him to ignore his loving wife and take a white mistress, which turns the former slave into a homicidal maniac, who kills the mistress and then herself. Having failed to escape temptation in the country, Evans returns to New York, where his friend and mentor, Stephen Lee, on his deathbed tells Evans the sad tale of the death of his children as a result of his wife's drunkenness, prompting Evans to sign the total abstinence pledge, as Lee leaves all his money to him.

In each episode in this synopsis, Franklin takes a moralistic stance in relation to the city (a cesspool of sin), women (full of corrupting excess), and above all liquor. Over time, however, Franklin experiences desire for increasingly rich men, causing panic, usually manifested as a drinking spree. The panic is resolved when Franklin displaces his desire for men (always also a desire for capital) onto women, who become embodiments of whatever excess aroused Franklin's desire in the first place. The women become more unruly as the novel progresses, dying in increasingly violent ways, while Franklin styles himself, in relation to these criminal women, as rational and judicious in the manner of his male mentors. Desire is thus displaced through disavowed identification with women, but in ways that show how capital operates by exciting the desire of young men who profit by reforming perversion into professionalism.

The most striking instance of this pattern occurs in the eighth chapter, which tells of an impoverished and besotted mother, whose death Franklin witnesses after he accompanies home a bedraggled child who begs money to buy alcohol for his mother. The chapter immediately follows Franklin's first alcoholic crisis, in which he allows an important errand assigned to him by his employer, Stephen Lee, to go undone while he carouses in theaters and saloons with his drinking-mates. In the scene of the mother's death, then, Franklin projects *his* shame at having disappointed his "father figure" onto a "bad" mother. The poor woman has her own interpretation of her situation, however: "It was as if around the room, and peering down from the upper corners of the wall, the death-stricken outcast fancied she saw faces, bodiless, and working with strange grins of mockery" (45-46). Recognizing that she is mocked by "bodiless" figures who are—and the verb is telling—"working," the delirious woman brings to the surface the economic shame at the heart of Franklin's projection. Franklin's appetites have led him away from Lee's transcendent ideal, which the mother turns from a bodiless abstraction into a gothic horror. Retransforming Franklin's purported benevolence into a cruel mockery, the mother's interpretive power over Franklin's projections turns him from an objective witness into the abject/object he attempts to make *her*: "I was half petrified as her look was directed toward me, and the child at my feet. I stood as still as a statue" (46). When she takes her foul and tattered rags and throws them at Evans, he "half shriek[s] with fear" (46). If Franklin attempts to generate a sense of his own wholeness as a benevolent and relatively self-managing male in opposition to a neglectful mother who is ruled by her ungovernable appetites, he is only partially successful (the odd phrase, "half shrieked," is one of several instances in this chapter in which Franklin describes himself as divided or "halved"). However identified with abstract virtue he may be, the appetite-ridden Franklin is never as disembodied as he wishes to believe.

An earlier episode in the novel similarly shows Franklin "divided" in ways that challenge his status as objective narrator. In chapter 5, in which Evans describes his disgust at finding his coworker Denis drunk, *Franklin Evans* departs for the first time from its first-person narration. Whitman contrasts Denis's downfall and arrest with the elaborate swindles perpetrated by Demaine and Andrews, the latter of which Franklin couldn't have witnessed firsthand. Objective omniscience, in this juxtaposition, gives way before shame-induced dissociation. Both drinking and swindling generate intemperance and secrecy, representing two sides of Evans: he is given over both to the dissipation of pleasure and the *desires* of upward mobility (this chapter occurs as Franklin is about to leave Andrews' employ to work for Lee, thereby doubling his salary). The juxtaposition of the two stories makes visible the relation between the two desires, both of which Franklin must disavow in order to gain the omniscient goodness necessary for reform and for the "honest" profit associated with Lee (the source of whose wealth is never named). Only by disavowing desire and pleasure (we might say "experience") can Franklin achieve the disinterestedness required by virtue. Yet how can he narrate without experience? Even as the text warns against experience, its Washingtonian faith in first-person testimony (and its dedication to the "weak" who read well because of their experiences) pulls in the opposite direction. Chapter 5 contains both forms of narration—first-person and omniscient, experience and virtue—in ways that continue to trouble the divided protagonist.

While Franklin cannot resolve this conflict in relation to Denis and Demaine, gender difference, in the form of intemperate women, seems to allow him some resolution. Franklin begins chapter 9 by reasserting his distance from the accusing mother: "There is a sacredness in some of our sorrows, which prevents them from being fit subjects for the rude and common gaze" (47). The very fact that Franklin will go on narrating, he suggests, demonstrates his separation from the "sorrows" that consign the mother to invisibility and silence. Yet Franklin cannot quite leave this poor woman alone. His statement of difference at the start of chapter 9 leads immediately to the story of his first wife, Mary (47), also the name of the dead woman's daughter. The doubling of Mary transforms the victimizing mother, whose intemperate thirst destroys a household, into a victimized wife whose household is destroyed by economic intemperance. "We never purchased until we saw the means of payment," Franklin begins his tale of ideal marriage. "But about a year after our marriage," he continues, "the serpent came into our little Eden. Ambition—the poison that rankles in the hearts of men, and scorches all peace, and blights the bloom of content—ambition entered there" (48). Engaging in speculative investments to earn money to build a house, Franklin goes bankrupt and begins drinking (49). Realizing she has "bound her fortunes to a *drunkard*" (49), Mary, forsaken and forlorn, soon sickens and dies. While Franklin is unable to escape blame in both stories, he does escape punishment, which falls to women, his worse or better halves.

Perhaps to disavow this unjust punishment, Franklin ultimately turns women from victims of intemperance into deceptive embodiments of ungovernable desire. Franklin begins his account of his love triangle with Margaret and Mrs. Conway, "The course of my narrative needs now that another character should be introduced upon the stage" (83), and describes the slave woman as having "a most difficult part to play" (86) and Mrs. Conway as having "acted the part of a most unqualified coquet" (86). Given the association in *Franklin Evans* of acting with dishonesty, indecency, and, above all, intemperance, we can guess that Margaret and Mrs. Conway will soon become agents of intemperate desire and rage, of which Franklin will be the guileless victim, led into an "extasy of passion" (86). Having asserted the relationship between intemperance and women, Franklin can claim that alcohol most dangerously turns healthy men "effeminate" (114).

Despite his efforts to escape effeminacy, however, the weak-willed and desiring Franklin proves the prototype of his characterization of women. While he attempts to distance himself from Margaret and Mrs. Conway, he is, like them, "an ingrate, a criminal, a fool and all but a murderer."[135] Intemperate passion turns Franklin into "an actor who plays a part" (85), just as it does Margaret and Mrs. Conway. If women's desires for men make them intemperate, and Franklin, too, suffers from persistent intemperance, can we assume that he experiences desires for men? Emory Holloway astutely observes, "Passionate desires which are under conscious control" in waking hours "come tumbling forth under pressure of time and the stimulation of alcohol, but in disguise."[136] The saloon, as Leslie Fiedler notes, was a dis-

---

135. Holloway, *Free and Lonesome Heart*, 29.   136. Holloway, *Free and Lonesome Heart*, 30.

tinctly homosocial space, "for a long time felt as the anti-type of the home, a refuge for escaping males nearly as archetypal as the wilderness and the sea."[137] Franklin's experiences of homosocial bonding and alcoholism are not limited to the saloon, however: every time Franklin establishes contact with a powerful man, he immediately goes on a drinking spree. One might well wonder why his various benefactors—Lee, Marchion, Bourne—take such a sudden interest in the young man from the country. If *Franklin Evans* as a reform tale insists that improvement comes through diligent effort (Whitman, significantly, seems to have named his protagonist for the originator of such rags-to-riches self-improvement tales, Benjamin Franklin), the tale's events contradict that moral, showing that whims, accidents, and ill-defined attractions leave Franklin, as Holloway observes, "rewarded with a fortune he in no way deserves."[138] Does the fact that these transactions take place over exchanges of cash suggest that capital, in *Franklin Evans*, is a queer business?

Franklin's life of urban dissipation begins with a queer invitation: his new friend Colby invites him to "go out and cruise a little" (27). The intoxication that will give him so much trouble comes to Franklin, then, in the form of the urban *flâneur*, whom Walter Benjamin describes as "someone abandoned in the crowd" who "is not aware of the special situation, but this does not diminish its effect on him and it permeates him blissfully like a narcotic that can compensate him for many humiliations." As Benjamin observes, "The intoxication to which the *flâneur* surrenders is the intoxication of the commodity around which surges the stream of customers."[139] The connection Benjamin draws between urban anonymity, intoxication, and commodification establishes Franklin Evans as one of American literature's first *flâneurs*, moving through crowded city streets, taverns, and theaters in ways that fill him with intoxicating sensation while also enabling the transfer of desires cleansed of the taint of embodiment. As Mark Turner observes, the *flâneur* is also the prototype of the modern homosexual, moving "unseen" through the cityscape as both the embodiment of desire and the commodified object of exchange (between, for instance, the lawyers and policemen who populate the pages of *Franklin Evans*). For Turner, Whitman's *Leaves of Grass* is the great text of queer *flâneur* culture in America. Whitman's newspaper columns about wandering through New York City were prose prototypes for this *flâneur* and the modern urban homosexual. So, in a way, was *Franklin Evans*.

137. Fiedler, 258. 138. Holloway, *Free and Lonesome Heart*, 29. 139. Benjamin, 55.

Even in such a nascent form, this development could not occur without a certain amount of shameful disavowal, part of which can be seen in Franklin's anxious treatment of women and of femininity in the tale. Franklin's relationships with men, however, are also fraught. Despite his self-satisfied claim, "I was never the person to forget a friend" (109), he does, in fact, forget many friends, beginning with the man with whom he first cruises New York, Colby, whom Franklin leaves drunk on the street. To honor one's past with other men is to acknowledge one's intoxication by alcohol, the city, and desire, all of which leave "a stigma for the future." A "few hours' casual gratification," after all, can render youth "useless," and Franklin, whose investments in futurity promise great things, cannot risk such a taint. "Desire," he ambiguously asserts, "had no farther room for wishing." Above all, to acknowledge one's desires, to become embodied in the presence of other men, is to risk one's national belonging, as Franklin makes clear in his description of Bourne, the French expatriate — perhaps a slaveholder originally from Haiti? — and Southern plantation owner. "I rather thought, from his accent and manner," Franklin reports, "that he was not an American. In the course of our talk, I learned that he was a bachelor" (77). To be a "bachelor" is to be un-American, a double alienation from normality that Franklin risks in his extended sojourn as Bourne's guest and drinking buddy.[140]

If homoeroticism risks national alienation, race re-integrates Franklin into the comforts of national belonging. The construction of national identity in the post–Revolutionary War United States often involved attributing contrasting and less desirable traits to African and Native Americans, in contrast to whom white Americans could conceive themselves as rational, industrious, and virtuous. Showing nationalism to be deeply tied to land speculation and exploited labor, which required the often violent "vanishing" of Native Americans and the enslavement of African Americans, *Franklin Evans* narrates national identity formation in opposition to certain discredited and victimized bodies. In so doing, *Franklin Evans* makes the struggle between self-management and intemperance a racial dynamic.

As a journalist, Whitman encouraged benevolent acts of "memorialization" that asserted the disappearance of Indian nations still engaged, in the 1840s, in active warfare to protect their lands from imperial invasion. In two columns from July 1846, Whitman urged Congress to buy George Catlin's

---

140. On nineteenth-century American bachelors, see Bertolini; Chudacoff; Snyder.

photographs of Native Americans and his collection of "Indian artifacts" for the Smithsonian. Claiming that Indians "are truly melting away like the snows of spring,"[141] Whitman expresses apprehension that, "unless Government act promptly, we shall never again have the opportunity of restoring to our country these paintings and memorials, so emphatically American, and of such decided importance to Art and to our national History."[142] Establishing Native American culture as (white) America's "past," as a primitive stage in a natural progression toward mature nationalism, Whitman helps bring about the very disappearance he seeks to commemorate.

Like the United States in Whitman's journalistic account, *Franklin Evans* begins with the "vanishing" of Indians. As a wagon load of passengers travels from the countryside to New York, Stephen Lee, a self-proclaimed antiquarian, tells the story of the Indian chief, Unrelenting. As a young warrior, Unrelenting kills a Kansi warrior, but spares a young boy to tell the story of Unrelenting's triumph. Years later, that boy, now a grown warrior, comes to the dwelling of Unrelenting and his only son, Wind-Foot, who offer the stranger lodging. When Unrelenting sets off "on some public business for his tribe" (14), the Kansi warrior kidnaps Wind-Foot. The fleeing men are pursued by the enraged father, who kills his enemy just moments after the warrior kills Wind-Foot. With these deaths, Lee's story implies, two native tribes tragically "vanish," without a white person entering the tale. As survivors and inheritors, whites, like Lee, serve only to memorialize inevitable loss.

Lee transforms the aggressive appropriation of Indian lands by white settlers into a tale of a "race" vanquished by its own natural intemperance. While Lee promises a story about the impact on Indian life of "the greatest curse ever introduced among them," namely "the curse of *rum!*" (10), neither Unrelenting nor the Kansi warrior ever drinks, for the presence of alcohol would implicate white settlers in these "vanishings." Indian intemperance is not as simple as one swig too many from the rum bottle, an act that, Washingtonian rhetoric contended, they could be led to forswear. Rather, theirs is intemperance of *affect*, so deeply a part of their natures as to be ineradicable. Indians, in Lee's tale, are victims of their own intemperate aggression, rage, and desire for vengeance. Sounding very much like the drunkard of temperance

---

141. *Brooklyn Daily Eagle and Kings County Democrat* (July 9, 1846). *WWJ*, 457.
142. *Brooklyn Daily Eagle and Kings County Democrat* (July 22, 1846). *WWJ*, 476.

literature, Unrelenting "trembled with agitation" in telling his story, during which he "wrought himself up to a pitch of loudness and rage" (13), while the Kansi warrior's violent emotions are displayed through "two fiery orbs, rolling about incessantly, like the eyes of a wild beast" (14). The struggle between whites and Native Americans, Lee suggests, is more properly understood as the latter's battle with ungovernable emotion, their unlucky fate sealed in and by their own turbulent nature.

Despite its assertion of essential racial difference, however, Lee's tale is haunted by moments of cross-racial identification. Lee "survives" to tell Unrelenting's tale, just as the Kansi boy does, and like Unrelenting, who narrates his story to his young son, Lee tells the same tale to his surrogate son, Franklin. Like his traveling mate Colby, Franklin had grown bored listening to a female passenger describe her daughter's wedding, which the boys find "totally uninteresting" (8). Just as the speech act of Lee's narration creates an all-male alternative to the domestic sentimentality of the mother's, so the tale itself conjures an almost exclusively male world (Wind-Foot has no mother; the only woman in Lee's story comes to tell Unrelenting of the abduction) in danger of extinction. The tale is animated by fears of effeminacy: Unrelenting claims the Kansi warrior has a "coward arm [that] warrest with women and children" (17), while the warrior in turn torments Wind-Foot by calling him a girl (16). If male homosociality disappears in America's past due to intemperance, the same force, arising in taverns and boardinghouses, resurrects it as Franklin's future. Even as Lee warns Franklin against such sites of temptation, his tale disavows his own "unrelenting" paternalism and family duty. Just as intemperance dissolves family ties (and hence obligations) in the tale of Unrelenting, so alcohol gives Franklin a way to resist *his* obligations to the persistent (if not unrelenting) Lee.

If race "vanishes" at the outset of *Franklin Evans*, it returns, midway through Whitman's text, in Franklin's account of the slave woman, Margaret, which displaces hostility and desire between men onto the savage appetites of women. At the start of chapter 15, Franklin leaves New York for Virginia on a journey "partly of business, and partly of pleasure" (77). He soon meets the plantation owner Bourne, with whom, after many shared bottles of wine, Franklin takes up residence. If Franklin is threatened by the excess of liquor, same-sex desire, and capital, all of which keep him in Virginia, he is elevated, through the most violent displacement in the novel, to a position of adjudication and hence of cultural superiority. Threatened with becoming less than a "real man," in other words, Franklin is saved by becoming more than a "mere slave." A "Creole" field slave, Margaret, threatened by a licentious overseer, has "lifted the instrument of labor she had been using, and felled him to the earth with a heavy blow" (80).[143] When Margaret is brought before her master and Franklin, the latter becomes infatuated with the Creole, intercedes with Bourne on her behalf, and ultimately marries her. In becoming her advocate, Franklin reverses his own disempowerment in the previous episode of his tale, in which, having been arrested for robbery, a humiliated Franklin is convicted by a judge. Displacing his "guilt" onto Margaret, Franklin accomplishes his desired identification with the lawyer Marchion, who gets Franklin released from prison, giving the younger man funds to invest in the South. In marrying Margaret, moreover, Franklin distinguishes his own lustful interest from that of the distasteful overseer. Yet the violence inflicted on Margaret by Franklin turns out to be even more devastating, and less open to resistance: when Franklin abandons his Creole wife for a white woman, Mrs. Conway, Margaret kills her rival and herself. Before she dies, however, Margaret makes the overseer and Franklin hear her confession together. Putting the two men in parallel positions, Margaret reveals the kinship of benevolence and violence and unmasks the questionable innocence on which Franklin's (racial) self-representations depend.

Midway through his narration of Margaret's downfall, Franklin interrupts himself to relate an "imaginative mania" that gave "full scope to my fancy." Franklin imagines a city in a "mighty and populous empire" "almost without boundary," a seaport "filled with rich navies, and with the products of every part of the earth, and with merchants, whose wealth was greater than the wealth of princes" (94–95). His is a fantasy of American imperialism, in which the "products" brought into port might have included slaves. In the

---

143. The meaning of the term "creole" in this context is obscure, though it carried some implication of racial mixing. It had one meaning in Haiti, and another in New Orleans where Whitman may have first encountered it. At the time Whitman wrote, the term was not commonly used in Virginia. Whitman later became fascinated with creoles during an 1848 sojourn in New Orleans, where he met a "great Creole mulatto woman (I believe she weighed 230 pounds)" whom he associated with drinking wine, coffee, and "French brandy." He "deeply regretted" "the chance of better knowledge of French and Spanish Creole New Orleans people." *Complete Writings* Vol. 3, 210.

fantasy, however, such "business" as slavery "seemed to be suspended" (95), transformed into a spectacle of reform's service to the state: on this day, the last inebriate will sign the pledge, literalizing the nation's symbolic emblem: the flag depicts a white woman crushing the snake of temptation beneath her heel. If imperialism generates slavery and the racialized appetites that result in Margaret's death, in Franklin's "mania" abstract whiteness is the solution to the nation's internal flaws. If Margaret cannot be saved by temperance, the dutiful followers of the triumphant white woman will be. As a banner in Franklin's imagined city declares, "The Last Slave of Appetite is Free" (98).

Margaret haunts this fantasy, however, as the reformed inebriate declares to the assembled crowd, "I throw off the chains, and take upon myself the pleasant bondage of good" (97). The chains of the slave fail to turn "freedom" into an unbounded state, for imperial ambitions require intemperate appetites. The persistence of enslavement, even in proclamations of liberty, highlights the inconsistency between America's idealized political rhetoric and the legal protection of chattel slavery. Franklin's host, Bourne, lives in America rather than in his native France because he loves "liberty" (78), yet he participates in what Whitman characterized as "that most abominable of all man's schemes of making money."[144] In response to such charges, Bourne might claim, as many plantation owners did, that Africans, being innately servile and ignorant, are well suited for slavery, which makes slaves happier than they would be in freedom. While Whitman resisted this particular racial logic, he did not challenge a divinely inspired difference between the races. "It is not ours to find an excuse for slaving, in the benighted conditions of the African," he wrote in 1846; "Has God not seen fit to make him, and leave him so?"[145]

Despite such assertions of innate racial difference, however, *Franklin Evans* is populated with exiles, immigrants, and creoles representing not pure but mixed identities. Mrs. Conway, Phillips, the northerner-turned-overseer, and Franklin Evans himself disrupt the regional divide between North and South, just as Bourne does between native and alien, or Margaret does between white and black. Whitman's characterization of Margaret may have come from Whitman's visits to see "negro minstrels"—white performers in

144. *Brooklyn Eagle and Kings County Democrat* (March 18, 1846). *WWJ*, 288.
145. *Brooklyn Eagle and Kings County Democrat* (March 18, 1846). *WWJ*, 289.

blackface—in New York. Whitman reports, "I often saw Rice, the original 'Jim Crow' at the old Park Theatre filling up the gap in some show bill— and the wild chants and dances were admirable—probably ahead of anything since."[146] Performing racial "mixing," blackface minstrels bring forth, in Whitman's imagination, not essential racial difference, but the theatricality of race. Margaret, too, is a skillful actress, able to disguise her unruly passions with the appearance of temperate calm. This aspect of her character makes Margaret, for Frances Winwar, "the most complete and satisfactory portrait [Whitman] had so far painted of a woman."[147]

At the center of *Franklin Evans*, its eponymous protagonist "is fatally fascinated by the exotic sensuality of a Creole slave."[148] That "fascination" was perhaps itself a mixing, of identification (in an earlier episode, Franklin, discovering that a business partner has swindled him, goes "mad with resentment and agitation" and strikes the man "to the earth" [61], just as Margaret does to Phillips) and desire (for the vengeance she, like Unrelenting and the Kansi warrior, enacts against an enforced choice between resignation and rage, domesticity and adventure, virtue and pleasure, all of which ultimately get coded as a difference between disembodied whiteness and a hyper-embodied "race").

This racialization of the cultural logic of temperance reform is played out not just in the interactions between differently raced characters; it traverses the very body of the drunkard. Nor is this intersection of race and temperance merely an idiosyncrasy of Whitman's. Franklin Evans follows the same racial trajectory as the protagonists of many other temperance tales, fictional and nonfictional. The drunkard, at his lowest point, is often described as a man who has figuratively and often literally lost his whiteness, whose skin has taken on an "unnatural redness" or still darker tones. Having so lowered himself, due to drinking, that he has become "a miserable object," Franklin Evans experiences his abjection as a change of skin color: "My face, I felt, was all dirty and brown, and my eyes bleared and swollen. What use had I for life?" (62). Once they have escaped from "the forces of the Red Fiend," inebriates are almost always whitened, not only by the clear water associated with sobriety, but also by the restoration of their "natural" color (112).[149]

---

146. *Complete Writings* Vol. 4, 53. 147. Winwar, 78. 148. Holloway, *Free and Lonesome Heart*, 30. 149. For different accounts of this trajectory, see Murphy, Hendler.

As the persistent mixings in the plot of *Franklin Evans* demonstrate, purity is hard to maintain, the efforts necessary to defend the borders of the pure body exhausting, if not futile. The difficulties *Franklin Evans* and its hero have in maintaining inviolable distinctions between races, genders, or classes, between capital and desire, even between narrative coherence and digression, suggest much about the inconsistent ideologies framing American life in the 1840s. *Franklin Evans* is a particularly important historical document precisely for the reason critics and editors have left it unread for decades: it is an incoherent and often aesthetically dissatisfying text. In its incoherence, *Franklin Evans* demonstrates not only the inconsistency of material effects (while some get richer, many get poorer; while some feel freer, many are enslaved), it more importantly makes visible the affects — anxiety, rage, frustration, desire — produced in the minds and bodies of citizens by the contradictory demands of self-management and self-expression, of appetite and self-denial. Encouraged to restrain the emotions continually stirred by modern life, Franklin Evans is not so different from the figures of failed reform that populate American media today: those who cannot stop eating, cheating, or defrauding stockholders. We turn to such figures — often against our better judgment — in the continued hope that they might provide some insight into how to balance appetite and virtue, want and wait. The twenty-first century promises to bring many more spectacles of failed reform, of unconquerable appetite, of fearful disavowal and shamed identifications. If that is the case, then Whitman's novel has much to teach us, especially if, as the author hoped would be the case, we feel a twinge of sympathy — even empathy — with his never-quite-reformed hero.

We have transcribed the text directly from the original 1842 *New World* publication of *Franklin Evans*, consulted at the American Antiquarian Society in Worcester, Massachusetts. Where that text was smudged or torn, we leaned on the magisterial 1963 scholarly edition of the novel in *Walt Whitman: The Early Poems and the Fiction*, edited and annotated extremely helpfully by Thomas L. Brasher.

FRANKLIN EVANS, OR THE INEBRIATE
A Tale of the Times

FRANKLIN EVANS;

OR

THE INEBRIATE.

A TALE OF THE TIMES.

BY WALTER WHITMAN

INTRODUCTORY

THE story I am going to tell you, reader, will be somewhat aside from the ordinary track of the novelist. It will not abound, either with profound reflections, or sentimental remarks. Yet its moral—for I flatter myself it has one, and one which it were well to engrave on the heart of each person who scans its pages—will be taught by its own incidents, and the current of the narrative.

Whatever of romance there may be—I leave it to any who have, in the course of their every-day walks, heard the histories of intemperate men, whether the events of the tale, strange as some of them may appear, have not had their counterpart in real life. If you who live in the city should go out among your neighbors and investigate what is being transacted there, you might come to behold things far more improbable. In fact, the following chapters contain but the account of a young man, thrown by circumstances amid the vortex of dissipation—a country youth, who came to our great emporium to seek his fortune—and what befell him there. So it is a plain story; yet as the grandest truths are sometimes plain enough to enter into the minds of children—it may be that the delineation I shall give will do benefit, and that educated men and women may not find the hour they spend in its perusal, altogether wasted.

And I would ask your belief when I assert that, what you are going to read is not a work of fiction, as the term is used. I narrate occurrences that have had a far more substantial existence, than in my fancy. There will be those who, as their eyes turn past line after line, will have their memories carried to matters which they have heard of before, or taken a part in themselves, and which, they know, are *real*.

Can I hope, that my story will do good? I entertain that hope. Issued in the cheap and popular form you see, and wafted by every mail to all parts of this vast republic; the facilities which its publisher possesses, giving him the power of diffusing it more widely than any other establishment in the United States; the mighty and deep public opinion which, as a tide bears a ship upon its bosom, ever welcomes anything favorable to the Temperance Reform; its being written *for the mass*, though the writer hopes, not without some claim upon the approval of the more fastidious; and, as much as anything else, the fact that it is as a pioneer in this department of literature — all these will give "THE INEBRIATE," I feel confident, a more than ordinary share of patronage.

For youth, what can be more invaluable? It teaches sobriety, that virtue which every mother and father prays nightly, may be resident in the characters of their sons. It wars against Intemperance, that evil spirit which has levelled so many fair human forms before its horrible advances. Without being presumptuous, I would remind those who believe in the wholesome doctrines of abstinence, how the earlier teachers of piety used parables and fables, as the fit instruments whereby they might convey to men the beauty of the system they professed. In the resemblance, how reasonable it is to suppose that you can impress a lesson upon him whom you would influence to sobriety, in no better way than letting him read such a story as this.

It is usual for writers, upon presenting their works to the public, to bespeak indulgence for faults and deficiences [*sic*]. I am but too well aware that the critical eye will see some such in the following pages; yet my book is not written for the critics, but for THE PEOPLE; and while I think it best to leave it to the reader's own decision whether I have succeeded, I cannot help remarking, that I have the fullest confidence in the verdict's being favorable.

And, to conclude, may I hope that he who purchases this volume, will give to its author, and to its publisher also, the credit of being influenced not altogether by views of the profit to come from it? Whatever of those views may enter into our minds, we are not without a strong desire that the principles here inculcated will strike deep, and grow again, and bring forth good fruit. A prudent, sober, and temperate course of life cannot be too strongly taught to old and young; to the young, because the future years are before them — to the old, because it is their business to prepare for death. And though, as before remarked, the writer has abstained from thrusting the moral upon the reader, by dry and abstract disquisitions—preferring the more pleasant and quite as profitable method of letting the reader draw it himself from the occurrences—it is hoped that the New and Popular Reform now in the course of progress over the land, will find no trifling help from a "TALE OF THE TIMES."

<hr />

CHAPTER I

The tree-tops now are glittering in the sun;
Away! 'tis time my journey was begun.

—R. H. DANA

ONE bright cool morning in the autumn of 183-, a country market-wagon, which also performed the office of stage-coach for those whose means or dispositions were humble enough to be satisfied with its rude accommodations, was standing, with the horse harnessed before it, in front of a village inn, on the Long Island turnpike. As the geography of the reader may be at fault to tell the exact whereabouts of this locality, I may as well say, that Long Island is a part of the State of New York, and stretches out into the Atlantic, just southeastward of the city which is the great emporium of our western world. The most eastern county of the island has many pretty towns and hamlets; the soil is fertile, and the people, though not refined or versed in city life, are very intelligent and hospitable. It was in that eastern county, on the side nearest the sea, that the road ran on which the market-wagon just mentioned was going to traverse. The driver was in the bar-room, taking a glass of liquor.

As the landlord, a sickly-looking, red-nosed man, was just counting out the change for the one dollar bill out of which the price of the brandy was to be taken, a stranger entered upon the scene. He was a robust youth, of about twenty years; and he carried an old black leather valise in his hand, and a coarse overcoat hanging on his arm. The proprietor of the vehicle standing outside, knew, with the tact of his trade, the moment this young man hove in sight, that he probably wished to take passage with him. The stranger walked along the narrow path that bordered the road, with a light and springy step; and as he came toward the tavern, the personages who noticed him, thought they saw him brushing something from his eyes—the traces of tears, as it were. Upon the valise which he carried in his hand, was tacked a small card, on which was written, "*Franklin Evans.*"

Reader, I was that youth; and the words just quoted, are the name of the hero of the tale you have now begun to peruse. Flattered shall I feel, if it be interesting enough to lead you on to the conclusion!

"What, Frank, is it you?" said the landlord's wife to me, coming in from an adjoining room at this moment. "Surely you cannot be going from the village? How are all your uncle's folks this morning? Baggage with you, too! Then it must be that you leave us, indeed."

"I am bound for New York," was my brief answer to the somewhat garrulous dame, as I opened the old-fashioned half-door, and entered the house. I threw my valise upon a beach, and my overcoat upon it.

The good landlady's further inquisitiveness was cut short, by my taking the driver out to his wagon, for the purpose of making arrangements and settling the price of my passage. This was soon concluded, and my rather limited stock of traveling gear was safely deposited on the top of some baskets of mutton in the rear of the vehicle.

"Come, youngster," said he who owned the mutton; "come in with me, and take a drop before we start. The weather is chill, and we need somewhat to keep us warm."

I felt no particular wish either to drink or refuse: so I walked in, and each of us drank off a portion of that fluid, which has brought more wo into society than all the other causes of evil combined together.

The landlord and his family were old acquaintances of mine, from the fact that we had for several years resided in the same village. It was not, therefore, without some little feeling of displeasure with myself, that I repulsed all the good-natured inquiries and endeavors of him and his wife, to discover the object of my journey. I had known him as a worthy man in times past, previous to his keeping the tavern. Young as I was, I could well remember the time, when his eyes were not bleared, and his face flushed with unnatural redness, and his whole appearance that of a man enfeebled by disease: all of which characterized him now. Ten years before, he had been a hale and hearty farmer; and with his children growing up around him, all promised a life of enjoyment, and a competency for the period of his own existence, and for starting his sons respectably in life. Unfortunately, he fell into habits of intemperance. Season after season passed away; and each one, as it came, found him a poorer man than that just before it. Everything seemed to go wrong. He attributed it to ill luck, and to the crops being injured by unfavorable weather. But his neighbors found no more harm from these causes than in the years previous, when the tippler was as fortunate as any of them. The truth is, that habits of drunkenness in the head of a family, are like an evil influence—a great dark cloud, overhanging all, and spreading its gloom around every department of the business of that family, and poisoning their peace, at the same time that it debars them from any chance of rising in the world.

So, as matters grew worse, my hapless friend narrowed down the operations of his farm, and opened his dwelling as a country inn. Poor fellow! he was his own best customer. He made out to glean a scanty subsistence from the profits of his new business; but all the old domestic enjoyment and content, seemed fled for ever. The light laugh, and the cheerful chuckle with which he used to toss his infant child in his arms, when returned at evening from his labor, were heard no more. And the cozy and comfortable winter fireside— the great wide hearth, around which they used to cluster when the hail pattered against the small windows from without—where was its comfort now? Alas! while the hearth itself remained in its old place, the happy gatherings were passed away! Many a time, when a young boy, I had stolen from my own home of an evening, to enjoy the vivacity and the mirth of that cheerful fireside. But now, like an altar whose gods and emblems were cast down and forgotten, it was no more the scene of joy, or the spot for the pleasantness of young hearts. The fumes of tobacco, and the strong smell of brandy and gin, defiled its atmosphere; while its huge logs, as they blazed upward, lighted the faces of pallid or bloated inebriates!

The farmer's sons, too, had left him, and gone to seek their living in a more congenial sphere. Intemperance is the parent of peevishness and quarrels, and all uncharitableness. Every day brought new causes of grievance and of dissention. Sometimes, the father was unreasonable, and demanded of his children far more than was consistent with justice. Sometimes, they forgot the respect due from son to parent; for whatever may be the faults of those who give us birth, there is little excuse for thankless ones, whose disobedience to the parental will, is indeed sharper than the serpent's tooth. And so the grown up children went away from the family residence, and were thenceforward almost as strangers.

I have been led into an episode. Let me return to the matter more immedi-

ately in point to the plot of my narrative. Upon getting into the vehicle, I found
that it already had four occupants, whom I had not seen before; as the canvas
top had concealed and sheltered them, and they had remained silent during
my conversation with the driver and the people of the tavern. Some part of
what I learned about these personages in the course of our journey, I may as
well state here.

There was a young man about four or five years older than myself. His
name was John Colby. He was a book-keeper in a mercantile establishment
in the city, and from his lively, good-tempered face, one might easily judge
that fun and frolic were the elements he delighted in. Colby sat on the same
seat with myself, and not many minutes passed away before we were on quite
sociable terms with one another.

Back of us sat an elderly country woman, who was going to visit a daughter.
Her daughter, she took occasion to inform us, had married a very respectable
citizen about three months previous, and they now lived in good style in the
upper part of a two-story house in Broome-street. The woman was evidently
somewhat deficient in perception of the ridiculous—as she herself was concerned; but still, as she *was* a woman, and a mother, and her conversation
was quite harmless—no one thought of evincing any sign of amusement or
annoyance at her rather lengthy disquisitions upon what, to us, were totally
uninteresting topics.

At her side was a middle-aged gentleman, named Demaine. He was dressed
with such exceeding neatness, that I could not but wonder how he came to
ride in so homely a conveyance. Of his character, more will be learned in the
subsequent pages.

On the back seat of all, and crowded among a heterogenous [*sic*] mass of
'market truck,' sat a gentleman, the last of my four companions. I could occasionally hear him humming a tune to himself, which was proof that he did
not feel in any other than a pleasant mood. He was dressed plainly, though I
thought richly; and I understood by my friend, the driver, at one of the stopping places, that his rear passenger had come with him from an obscure village,
whence there was no other conveyance, and where he had been for sporting
purposes.

~~~~~~~

CHAPTER II

There stood the Indian hamlet, there the lake
Spread its blue sheet that flashed with many an oar,
Where the brown otter plunged him from the brake,
And the deer drank; as the light gale flew o'er,
The twinkling maize-field rustled on the shore;
And while that spot, so wild, and lone, and fair,
A look of glad and innocent beauty wore,
And peace was on the earth, and in the air,
The warrior lit the pile, and bound his captive there.

Not, unavenged—the foeman from the wood
Beheld the deed.

—BRYANT

THE journey on which we were all bound, (each of us was going to New-York,) might have been rather monotonous, were it not that after a few miles we most of us allowed the reserve of strangers to melt away, and began to treat one another as familiar acquaintances. My neighbor by the side of the country woman, was the only exception to this. He preserved a stiff pragmatical demeanor, and evidently thought it beneath him to be amused, and quite indecorous to join in the laugh at our little witticisms. Colby and I, however, chatted away, occasionally interchanging a remark with the gentleman on the back seat, whom we found to be quite a fine fellow, according to our notions. Though there was a species of dignity about him which forbade too near an approach of familiarity, there was nothing of that distant haughtiness which characterized our other male passenger.

With the disposition of cheerful hearts, we found a source of pleasure in almost everything. The very slowness and sleepiness of the pace with which our horses jogged along, was the text for many a merry gibe and humorous observation. Entering into the spirit of our gayety, the sportsman in the further seat entertained us with numerous little anecdotes, many of them having reference to scenes and places along the road we were passing. He had, he told us, a fondness for prying into the olden history of this, his native island; a sort of antiquarian taste for the stories and incidents connected with the early settlers, and with the several tribes of Indians who lived in it before the whites came.

I could see, indeed, that the gentleman was quite an enthusiast on the subject, from the manner in which he spoke upon it. He dwelt with much eloquence upon the treatment the hapless red men had received from those who, after dispossessing them of land and home, now occupied their territory, and were still crowding them from the face of their old hunting-grounds.

"The greatest curse," said he, growing warm with his subject — "the greatest curse ever introduced among them, has been the curse of *rum!* I can conceive of no more awful and horrible, and at the same time more effective lesson, than that which may be learned from the consequences of the burning firewater upon the habits and happiness of the poor Indians. A whole people — the inhabitants of a mighty continent — are crushed by it, and debased into a condition lower than the beasts of the field. Is it not a pitiful thought? The bravest warriors — the wise old chiefs — even the very women and children — tempted by our people to drink this fatal poison, until, as year and year passed away, they found themselves deprived not only of their lands and what property they hitherto owned, but of everything that made them noble and grand as a nation! Rum has done great evil in the world, but hardly ever more by wholesale than in the case of the American savage."

We could not but feel the justice of his remarks. Even our driver, whose red nose spoke him no hater of a glass of brandy, evidently joined in the sentiment.

As we crossed a small creek over which a bridge was thrown, he who had spoken so fervently in behalf of the Indians, pointed us to [look] over the fields in the distance, where we could see quite a large inland sheet of water. He told us it was a lake about two miles broad, and gave us a long and unpronounceable word, which he said was the Indian name for it.

"There is an old tradition," said he — and we could perceive that he was now upon a favorite hobby — "there is a very old tradition connected with this lake, which may perhaps diversify our journey, by the relation."

We all professed our pleasure at the idea of hearing it, and without further preliminary the antiquarian began:

Among the tribes of red men that inhabited this part of the world three hundred years ago, there was a small brave nation, whose hunting-grounds lay adjacent to the eastern shore of that lake. The nation I speak of, like most of its neighbors, was frequently engaged in war. It had many enemies, who sought every means to weaken it, both by stratagem and declared hostility. But the red warriors who fought its battles were very brave; and they had a chief, whose courage and wonderful skill in all the savage arts of warfare, made him renowned through the island, and even on no small portion of the continent itself. He was called by a name which, in our language, signifies "Unrelenting." There were only two dwellers in his lodge—himself and his youthful son; for twenty moons had filled and waned since the chieftain's wife was placed in the burial-ground of her people.

As the Unrelenting sat alone one evening in his rude hut, one of his people came to inform him that a traveller from a distant tribe had entered the village, and desired food and repose. Such a petition was never slighted by the red man; and the messenger was sent back with an invitation for the stranger to abide in the lodge of the chief himself. Among these simple people, no duties were considered more honorable than arranging the household comforts of a guest. Those duties were now performed by the chief's own hand, his son having not yet returned from the hunt on which he had started, with a few young companions, at early dawn. In a little while the wayfarer was led into the dwelling by him who had given the first notice of his arrival.

"You are welcome, my brother," said the Unrelenting.

The one to whom this kind salute was addressed was an athletic Indian, apparently of middle age, and habited in the scant attire of his race. He had the war-tuft on his forehead, under which flashed a pair of brilliant eyes. His rejoinder to his host was friendly, yet very brief.

"The chief's tent is lonesome. His people are away?" said the stranger, after a pause, casting a glance of inquiry around.

"My brother says true, that it is lonesome," answered the other. "Twelve seasons ago the Unrelenting was a happy ruler of his people. He had brave sons, and their mother was dear to him. He was strong, like a cord of many fibres. Then the Spirit Chief snapped the fibres, one by one, asunder. He looked with a pleasant eye on my sons and daughters, and wished them for himself. Behold all that is left to gladden my heart!"

The Unrelenting turned as he spoke, and pointed to an object just inside the opening of the tent.

A moment or two before, the figure of a boy had glided noiselessly in, and taken his station back of the chief. The new-comer seemed of the age of fourteen or fifteen years. He was a noble youth! His limbs never had been distorted by the ligatures of fashion; his figure was graceful as the slender ash, and symmetrical and springy as the bounding stag. It was the chief's son—the last and loveliest of his offspring—the soft-lipped nimble Wind-Foot.

With the assistance of the child, the preparations for their simple supper were soon completed. After finishing it, as the stranger appeared to be weary, a heap of skins was arranged for him in one corner of the lodge, and he laid himself down to sleep.

It was a lovely summer evening. The moon shone, and the stars twinkled, and the million voices of a forest night sounded in the distance. The chief and his son reclined at the opening of the tent, enjoying the cool breeze that blew fresh upon them, and idly flapped the piece of deer-skin that served for their door—sometimes swinging it down so as to darken the apartment, and then again floating suddenly up, and letting in the bright moonbeams. Wind-Foot spoke of his hunt that day. He had met with poor luck, and in a boy's impatient spirit, he peevishly wondered why it was that other people's arrows should hit the mark, and not his. The chief heard him with a sad smile, as he remembered his own youthful traits: he soothed the child with gentle words, telling him that even brave warriors sometimes went whole days with the same ill success as had befallen him.

"Many years since," said the chief, "when my cheek was soft, and my limbs had felt the numbness of but few winters, I myself vainly traversed our hunting-grounds, as you have done to-day. The Dark Influence was around me, and not a single shaft would do my bidding."

"And my father brought home nothing to his lodge?" asked the boy.

"The Unrelenting came back without any game," the other answered; "but he brought what was dearer to him and his people than the fattest deer or the sweetest bird-meat. His hand clutched the scalp of an accursed Kansi!"

The voice of the chief was deep and sharp in its tone of hatred.

"Will my father," said Wind-Foot, "tell ——"

The child started, and paused. A sudden guttural noise came from behind them. It seemed between a prolonged grunt and a dismal groan, and proceeded from that part of the tent where the stranger was lying. The dry skins which formed the bed rustled as if he who lay there was changing his position, and then all continued silent. The Unrelenting turned to his son, and proceeded in a lower tone, fearful that their talk had almost broken the sleep of their guest.

"Listen!" said he; "You know a part, but not all of the cause of hatred there is between our nation and the abhorred enemies whose name I mentioned. Longer back than I can remember, they did mortal wrong to your fathers, and your fathers' people. The scalps of two of your own brothers hang in Kansi tents; and I have sworn, boy, to bear for them a never-sleeping hatred.

"On the morning I spoke of, I started with fresh limbs and a light heart to search for game. Hour after hour I roamed the forest with no success; and at the setting of the sun I found myself weary and many miles from my father's lodge. I lay down at the foot of a tree and sleep came over me. In the depth of the night, a voice seemed whispering in my ears—it called me to rise quickly—to look around. I started to my feet, and found no one there but myself; then I knew that the Dream Spirit had been with me. As I cast my eyes about in the gloom, I saw a distant brightness. Treading softly, I approached. The light, I found, was that of a fire, and by the fire lay two figures. Oh, my son, I laughed the quiet laugh of a deathly mind, as I saw who they were. Two of our hated foes—I knew them well—lay sleeping there; a Kansi warrior, and a child, like you, my son, in age. I felt of my hatchet's edge—it was keen as my hate. I crept toward them as the snake crawls through the grass—I bent over the slumbering boy—I raised my tomahawk to strike—but I thought that, were they both slain, no one would carry to the Kansi tribe the story of my deed. My vengeance would be tasteless to me if they knew it not, so I spared the child. Then I glided to the other. His face was of the same cast as the first; so my soul was gladdened more, for I knew they were of kindred blood. I raised my arm—I gathered my strength—I struck, and cleft his dastard brain in quivering halves!"

The chief's speech trembled with agitation. He had gradually wrought himself up to a pitch of loudness and rage; and his hoarse tones, at the last part of his narration, rang croakingly through the lodge.

At that moment the deer-skin at the door was down, and obscure darkness filled the apartment. The next, the wind buoyed the curtain aside again; the rays of the moon flowed in, and all was a halo of light. Spirits of Fear! what sight was that back there! The strange Indian was sitting up on his couch; his ghastly features glaring forward to the unconscious inmates in front, with a look like that of Satan to his antagonist angel. His lips were parted, and his teeth clenched; his neck stretched forward—every vein of his forehead and temples bulged out as if he was suffocating—and his eyes fiery with a look of demoniac hate. His arm was raised, and his hand doubled; each nerve and sinew of them in bold relief. It was an appalling sight, though it lasted only for a moment. The Unrelenting and his son saw nothing of it, their faces being to the front of the tent: in another instant the Indian had sunk back, and was reposing with the skins wrapped round him, and motionless. It was now an advanced hour of the evening. Wind-Foot felt exhausted by his day's travel; so they arose from their seat at the door, and retired to rest. In a few minutes the father and son were fast asleep; but from the darkness which surrounded the couch of the stranger, there flashed two fiery orbs, rolling about incessantly, like the eyes of a wild beast in anger. The lids of those orbs closed not in slumber during that night.

Among the primitive inhabitants who formerly occupied this continent, it was considered very rude to pester a traveler or a guest with questions about himself, his last abode or his future destination. He was made welcome to stay, until he saw fit to go—whether for a long period or a short one. Thus, the next day, when the strange Indian showed no signs of departing, the chief entertained little surprise, but made his guest quite as welcome; and indeed felt the better pleased at the indirect compliment paid to his powers of giving satisfaction. So the Indian passed a second night in the chieftain's tent.

The succeeding morn, the Unrelenting called his son to him, while the stranger was standing at the tent door. He told Wind-Foot that he was going on a short journey, to perform which and return would probably take him till night-fall. He enjoined the boy to remit no duties of hospitality toward his guest, and bade him be ready there at evening with a welcome for his father. As the Unrelenting passed from the door of his tent, he was surprised to witness a wildness in the stranger's bright black eyes. His attention, however, was given to it but for a moment; he took his simple equipments, and started on his journey.

It was some public business for his tribe that the Unrelenting went to transact. He travelled with an elastic step, and soon arrived at his destined place. Finishing there what he had to do, sooner than he expected, he partook of a slight refreshment and started for home. When he arrived in sight of his people's settlement, it was about the middle of the afternoon. The day, though pleasant, was rather warm; and making his way to his own dwelling the Unrelenting threw himself on the floor. Wind-Foot was not there; and after a little while, the chief rose and stepped to the nearest lodge to make inquiry after him. A woman appeared to answer his questions:

"The young brave," said she, "went away with the chief's strange guest many hours since."

The Unrelenting turned to go back to his tent.

"I cannot tell the meaning of it," added the woman, "but he of the fiery eye bade me, should the father of Wind-Foot ask about him, say to the chief these words: '*Unless your foe sees you drink his blood, that blood is not sweet, but very bitter.*'"

The Unrelenting started, as if a snake had stung him. His lip quivered, and his hand involuntarily moved to the handle of his tomahawk. Did his ears perform their office truly? Those sounds were not new to him. Like a floating mist, the gloom of past years rolled away in his memory, and he recollected that the words the woman had just spoken, were the very ones himself uttered to the Kansi child, whom he had spared in the forest, long, long ago—and sent back to his tribe to tell how and by whom his companion was killed. And this stranger? Ah, now he saw it all! He remembered the dark looks, the mystery and abruptness that marked his guest; and carrying his mind back again, he traced the same features in his face and that of the Kansi boy. Wind-Foot then was in the hands of this man, and the chief felt too conscious for what terrible purpose. Every minute lost might be fatal! He sallied from his lodge, gathered together a dozen of his warriors, and started in search of the child.

All the chief's suspicions were too true. About the same hour that he returned to his village, Wind-Foot, several miles from home, was just coming up to his companion, who had gone on a few rods ahead of him, and was at that moment seated on the body of a fallen tree, a mighty giant of the woods, that some whirlwind had tumbled to the earth. The child had roamed about with his new acquaintance through one path after another, with the heedlessness of his age; and now, while the Indian sat in perfect silence for many minutes, the boy idly sported near him. It was a solemn place: in every direction around, were the towering fathers of the wilderness—aged patriarchs, that grew up and withered in those solitudes, and shaded underneath them the leaves of untold seasons. At length the stranger spoke:

"Wind-Foot!"

The child, who was but a few yards off, approached at the call. As he came near, he started, and stopped in alarm; for his companion's features were wild, and bent toward him like a panther, about to make the fatal spring. Those dreadfully bright eyes were rolling, and burning with a horrid glitter; and he had the same fearful appearance that has been spoken of as occurring on the first night he spent in the chief's tent. During the moment that passed while they were thus looking at each other, terrible forebodings arose in the child's mind.

"Young warrior," said the Indian, "you must die!"

"The brave stranger is in play," said the other, "Wind-Foot is a little boy."

"Serpents are small at first," the savage replied, "but in a few moons they have fangs and deadly poison. Hearken! branch from an evil root. I am a Kansi! The boy whom your parent spared in the forest, is now become a man. Young warriors of his tribe point to him and say, 'his father's scalp crackles in the dwelling of the Unrelenting, and the tent of the Kansi is bare.' Offspring of my deadliest foe! Ere another sun has traveled over our heads, your blood must fatten the grave of a murdered father."

The boy's heart beat quickly, but the courage of his race did not forsake him.

"Wind-Foot is not a girl," he said. "The son of a chief can die without wetting his cheek by tears."

The savage looked on him for a few seconds with a malignant scowl. Then producing from an inner part of his dress, a withe of some tough bark, he stepped to the youth, to bind his hands behind him. It was useless to attempt anything like resistance, for besides the disparity of their strength, the boy was unarmed; while the Indian had at his waist a hatchet, and a rude stone weapon, resembling a poniard. Having his arms thus fastened, the savage, with a significant touch at his girdle, pointed to Wind-Foot the direction he was to travel—himself following close behind.

When the Unrelenting and his people started to seek for the child, and that fearful stranger whom they dreaded to think about as his companion, they were lucky enough to find the trail which the absent ones had made. None except an Indian's eye would have tracked them by so slight and round-a-bout a guide. But the chief's vision seemed sharp with paternal love, and they followed on, winding and on again—at length coming to the fallen tree on which the Kansi had sat. Passing by this, the trail was less devious, and they traversed it with greater rapidity. Its direction seemed to be to the shores of a long narrow lake, which lay between the grounds of their tribe and a neighboring one. So onward they went, swiftly but silently; and just as the sun's red ball sank in the west, they saw its last flitting gleams dancing in the bosom of the lake. The grounds in this place were almost clear of trees—a few scattered ones only being interspersed here and there. As they came out from the thick woods, the Unrelenting and his warriors swept the range with their keen eyes.

Was it so, indeed? Were those objects they beheld on the grass some twenty rods from the shore, the persons they sought? And fastened by that shore was a canoe. They saw from his posture, that the captive boy was bound; and they saw, too, from the situation of things, that if the Kansi should once get him in the boat, and start for the opposite side of the waters, where very possibly some of his tribe were waiting for him, the chances for a release would be hopelessly faint. For a moment only they paused; then the Unrelenting sprang off, like a wolf deprived of her cubs, uttering loud and clear the shrill battle-cry of his nation.

The rest joined in the terrible chorus, and followed him. As the sudden sound was swept along by the breeze to the Kansi's ear, he jumped to his feet, and with that wonderful self-possession which distinguishes his species, was aware at once of the position of the whole affair, and the course he had best pursue. He seized his captive by the shoulder, and ran toward the boat, holding the person of Wind-Foot between himself and those who pursued, as a shield from any weapons they might attempt to launch after him. He possessed still the advantage. They, to be sure, being unencumbered, could run more swiftly; but he had many rods the start of them. It was a fearful race; and the Unrelenting felt his heart grow very sick, as the Indian, dragging his child, approached nearer to the water's edge.

"Turn, whelp of a Kansi!" the chief madly cried. "Turn! thou whose coward arm warrest with women and children! Turn, if thou darest, and meet the eye of a full-grown brave!"

A loud taunting laugh of scorn was borne back from his flying enemy, to the ear of the furious father. The savage did not look around, but twisted his left arm, and pointed with his finger to Wind-Foot's throat. At that moment, he was within twice his length of the canoe. The boy whom he dragged after him, heard his father's voice, and gathered his energies, faint and bruised as he was, for a last struggle. Ah! vainly he strove: the only result was, to loosen himself for a moment from the deathly grip of the Kansi; and his body fell to the ground—though it was useless, for his limbs were bandaged, and he could not rescue himself from his doom. That moment, however, was a fatal one for the Kansi. With the speed of lightning, the chief's bow was up to his shoulder—the cord twanged sharply—a poison-tipped arrow sped through the air—and, faithful to its mission, cleft the Indian's side, just as he was stopping

to lift Wind-Foot in the boat. He gave a wild shriek—his life-blood spouted
from the wound—and he staggered and fell on the sand. His strength, however, was not yet gone. Hate and measureless revenge—the stronger, that they
were baffled—raged within him, and appeared in his glaring countenance.
Fiend-like glances shot from his eyes, glassy as they were beginning to be with
the death damps; and his hand felt to his waist-band, and clutched the poniard handle. Twisting his body like a bruised snake, he worked himself close
up to the bandaged Wind-Foot. He raised the weapon in the air—he shouted
aloud—he laughed a laugh of horrid triumph—and as the death-rattle shook
in his throat, the instrument (the shuddering eyes of the child saw it, and shut
their lids in intense agony) came down, driven too surely to the heart of the
hapless Wind-Foot.

When the Unrelenting came up to his son, the last signs of life were quivering in the boy's countenance. His eyes opened, and turned to the chief; his
beautiful lips parted in a smile, the last effort of innocent fondness. On his features flitted a transient lovely look, like a passing ripple of the wave—a slight
tremor shook him—and the next moment, Wind-Foot was dead!

CHAPTER III

Thine is the spring of life, dear boy,
  And thine should be its flowers;
Thine, too, should be the voice of joy,
  To hasten on the hours:
And thou, with cheek of rosiest hue,
  With winged feet, should'st still
Thy sometime frolic course pursue,
  O'er lawn and breezy hill.
Not so! what means this foolish heart,
  And verse as idly vain?
Each has his own allotted part
  Of pleasure and of pain!
                              —HENRY PICKERING

WE were so interested in the legend of the antiquary, that we did not notice
how time passed away while it was being related. For some minutes after its

conclusion, there was silence among us; for the luckless death of the poor Indian boy, seemed to cast a gloom over our spirits, and indispose us for conversation.

As it was now past noon, we began to feel as though we should be none the worse for our dinner. Accordingly, in good time, our driver drew up at a low-roofed public house, and proceeded with great deliberation to ungear his horses, for the purpose of giving them a temporary respite from their labors.

Glad of being able to get out in the open air, and upon our legs once more, myself and Colby (for we had become quite cronies) sprang lightly from the vehicle, and bouncing along the little door-yard, felt quite refreshed at stretching our cramped limbs on the low porch which ran along in front of the house. Demaine got out very leisurely, and with a cool disdainful look, stood by the front wheels of the wagon, eyeing the house and the people of the place, some of whom now made their appearance. The country woman also made a movement forward. She was a fat and somewhat clumsy dame; and we thought the least Demaine could do, would be to offer her some assistance in getting down upon the ground. He stood in such a position himself, that he effectually precluded any one else from offering that assistance. But he continued his contemptuous stare, and paid, apparently, not the least attention to what was going on around him.

Turning around a moment to look at Colby, who called my attention in the room, the next minute my hearing was assailed by a quick cry; and upon looking toward the wagon, I saw that the woman had entangled her dress, and was on the point of falling. A little longer, and she might have been down upon that part of the vehicle just behind the horses, or even under their feet; and yet Demaine, with his arrogant look, offered her no assistance! I sprang toward her; but before I could reach the place, the antiquary had rapidly jumped out upon the ground, and was safely landing her beside him. The incident was a trifling one; but I don't know that I ever, merely from one item of conduct, took such a dislike to any man as I did to Demaine, from that occurrence.

I thought I noticed during our dinner, that the antiquary regarded Demaine with peculiarly cool and distant demeanor. To us, he was affable and pleasant, and polite in his attentions to the old lady; but though not rude, I am sure the same feelings which took root in my own mind, started in his also.

Upon resuming our journey, the same vivacity and fund of anecdote, which

had so agreeably entertained us, from our companion in the back seat, was
again in requisition. I don't know how it was, but I felt confident that the antiquary was more than he seemed. His manners were so simple, and at the same
time so free from anything like coarseness, that I said to myself, if I should
aspire to be a *gentleman*, here would be my model. There was nothing in his
conduct from which it might be inferred that he wished to demand your respect; on the contrary, he was quite friendly, and talked about plain things in
plain language. Yet he had the stamp of superior station, and an indescribable
air of something which told us that he would have been quite as much at home,
and quite as unassuming, in the parlors of the richest people of the land. In
the course of conversation, it came to be mentioned by me, that I was going to
the city for the first time since I was a little child, and that I intended making
it my future residence. Whether the antiquary was interested in my remarks,
or whether he merely spoke from his natural good-will, I do not know; but he
addressed me somewhat after this fashion:

"You are taking a dangerous step, young man. The place in which you are
about to fix your abode, is very wicked, and as deceitful as it is wicked. There
will be a thousand vicious temptations besetting you on every side, which the
simple method of your country life has led you to know nothing of. Young
men, in our cities, think much more of dress than they do of decent behavior.
You will find, when you go among them, that whatever remains of integrity
you have, will be laughed and ridiculed out of you. It is considered 'green' not
to be up to all kinds of dissipation, and familiar with debauchery and intemperance. And it is the latter which will assail you on every side, and which,
if you yield to it, will send you back from the city, a bloated and weak creature, to die among your country friends, and be laid in a drunkard's grave; or
which will too soon end your days in some miserable street in the city itself.
It is indeed a dangerous step!"

The kindness of the motives of the speaker, prevented any displeasure I
might have felt at being thus addressed by a perfect stranger. Colby whispered
to me, that the antiquary was undoubtedly a good fellow, but somewhat too
sour in his judgments; which may have been the case, in truth. The subsequent pages, however, will prove the wisdom of his warning upon the subject
of intemperance.

As the afternoon waned, and the sun sank in the west, we drew nigher
and nigher to our destination. The increasing number of carriages, the houses

closer to one another, and the frequent sight of persons evidently just out from the city for a ride, admonished us that we were on the point of entering the great emporium of our western world.

When at last we came upon the paved streets, I was astonished at the mighty signs of life and business everywhere around. It was yet sometime ere sunset, and as the day was fine, numbers of people were out, some of them upon business, and many enjoying an afternoon saunter.

The place at which our conveyance stopped was in Brooklyn, near one of the ferries that led over to the opposite side of the river. We dismounted; glad enough to be at the end of our journey, and quite tired with its wearisomeness. Our passengers now prepared to go to their several destinations. The antiquary took a little carpet-bag in his hand, and politely bidding us adieu, made his way for the boat near by. Demaine was more lengthy in his arrangements. He had not much more to carry than the antiquary, but he called a porter, and engaged him to take it down to the landing. The country woman, also, hurried away; eager, no doubt, with parental fondness, to see her child.

Before Colby let me, we spoke for several minutes together. Though we had never seen each other until the morning of that day, a kind of friendship had grown up between us; and as I was in a strange place, with hardly an acquaintance in all its wide limits, it may be imagined I felt in no disposition to dissolve the bands of that friendship. Colby gave me the street and number where I could find him. The place of his business was in Pearl-street; his boarding-house further up town.

"I shall always be glad to see you," said he, "and as you seem to be unused to the town, perhaps you may find me of some advantage. Call and see me to-morrow."

"You may expect me," I answered, and we parted.

And now I was in the city. Here I had come to seek my fortune. What numbers had failed in the same attempt!

It may not be amiss to let the reader into the few simple incidents of my former history. My father had been a mechanic, a carpenter; and died when I was some three or four years old only. My poor mother struggled on for a time—what few relations we had being too poor to assist us—and at the age of eleven, she had me apprenticed to a farmer on Long Island, my uncle. It may be imagined with what agony I heard, hardly twenty months after I went to live with my uncle, that the remaining parent had sickened and died also.

The cold indifference of the strangers among whom she lived, allowed her to pass even the grim portals of death before they informed me of her illness. She died without the fond pressure of her son's hand, or the soothing of a look from one she loved.

I continued to labor hard, and fare so too; for my uncle was a poor man and his family was large. In the winters, as is customary in that part of the island, I attended school, and thus picked up a scanty kind of education. The teachers were, however, by no means overburthened with learning themselves; and my acquirements were not such as might make any one envious.

As I approached my nineteenth year, my uncle, who was an honest and worthy man, evidently felt that he was hardly justifiable in keeping me at work in an obscure country town, to the detriment of my future prospects in life. With a liberality therefore, of which many a richer person might be glad to be able to boast, he gave up the two last years of my apprenticeship — and the very two, which perhaps, would have been of more value to him than all the others. He called me to him one day, and addressing me in the kindest terms, informed me, what he felt he ought to do for his brother's child — but which his poverty prevented him from doing. He gave me my choice — whether to go to New York, and see what I could do there for a living, or to remain a while longer with him; not to labor, but to attend school, and perfect myself in some more valuable parts of education. Probably, it would have been far better had I chosen the latter of the two alternatives. But with the anxious and ambitious heart of youth, I immediately determined upon the former.

The matter thus settled, arrangements were soon made — my little stock of clothes packed up in the old valise already introduced to the reader — and receiving with thankfulness from my uncle a small sum of money, which I felt sure he must have cramped himself to bestow on me, I made my adieus to my aunt and my sorrowful cousins, and went my way. The first day of my leaving home, found me at evening, as the reader knows, on the borders of that great city, where I was to take up my abode.

Yes, here I had come to seek my fortune! A mere boy, friendless, unprotected, innocent of the ways of the world — without wealth, favor, or wisdom — here I stood at the entrance of the mighty labyrinth, and with hardly any consciousness of the temptations, doubts, and dangers that awaited me there. Thousands had gone on before me, and thousands were coming still. Some had attained the envied honors — had reaped distinction — and won princely estate; but how few were they, compared with the numbers of failures! How many had entered on the race, as now I was entering, and in the course of years, faint, tired, and sick at heart, had drawn themselves out aside from the track, seeking no further bliss than to die. To die! The word is too hard a one for the lip of youth and hope. Let us rather think of those who, bravely stemming the tide, and bearing up nobly against all opposition, have proudly come off victorious—waving in their hands at last, the symbol of triumph and glory.

What should be *my* fate? Should I be one of the fortunate few? Were not the chances much more against me than they had been against a thousand others, who were the most laggard in the contest? What probability was there, that amid the countless multitude, all striving for the few prizes which Fortune has to bestow, *my* inexperienced arm should get the better of a million others?

Oh, how good a thing it is that the great God who has placed us in this world—where amid so much that is beautiful, there still exists vast bestowal among men of grief, disappointment, and agony—has planted in our bosoms the great sheet-anchor, Hope! In the olden years, as we look back to our former life, we feel indeed how vain would have been our strife without the support of this benignant spirit.

To be sure, thousands had gone before me, in the struggle for the envied things of existence, and *failed*. But many others had met with *success*. A stout heart, and an active arm, were the great levers that might raise up fortune, even for the poor and unfriended Franklin Evans. In our glorious republic, the road was open to all; and, my chance, at least, was as good as that of some of those who had began with no better prospects.

CHAPTER IV

Stay, mortal, stay! Nor heedless thus,
　　Thy sure destruction seal;
Within that cup there lurks a curse
　　Which all who drink shall feel.
Disease and death, for ever nigh,
　　Stand ready at the door;
And eager wait to hear the cry,
　　Of "Give me one glass more!"

　　　　　　　—WASHINGTON MINSTREL

WHEN I arose the next morning, and thought over in my mind what it would
be better for me to do first, I saw that it was necessary to provide myself with a
boarding-house. After breakfast, I crossed the ferry, and purchasing a paper
of one of the news-boys, for a penny, I looked over to the column containing
advertisements of the places similar to what I wished. I was somewhat surprised to find that every one had the most "airy, delightful location," the very
"best accommodations," with "pleasant rooms," and "all the comforts of a
home." Some of them informed the reader that there were "no children in the
house." These I passed over, determining not to go there; for I loved the lively
prattle of children, and was not annoyed as some people pretend to be, by
their little frailties.

Noting down upon a memorandum several that I thought might suit me,
I started on my voyage of discovery. The first place that I called at was in
Cliff-street. A lean and vinegar-faced spinster came to the door, and upon my
inquiring for the landlady, ushered me into the parlor, where in a minute or
two I was accosted by that personage. She was as solemn and sour as the spinster, and upon my mentioning my business, gave me to understand that she
would be happy to conclude a bargain with me, but upon several conditions. I
was not to stay out later than ten o'clock at night — I was to be down at prayers
in the morning — I was never to come into the parlor except upon Sundays —
and I was always to appear at table with a clean shirt and wristbands. I took my
hat, and politely informed the lady, that if I thought I should like her terms,
I would call again.

I next made a descent upon a house, which in the advertisement, was described as offering good conveniences on "very reasonable terms." This I
supposed meant that it was a cheap boarding-house. The mistress took me
up into an open attic, where were arranged beds of all sorts and sizes. She
pointed me to a very suspicious looking one, in a corner, which she said was
not occupied. She told me I could have that, and my meals, for three dollars
a week, payable punctually on every Saturday night. I did not like the look of
the woman, or the house. There was too little cleanliness in both; so I made
the same remark at parting, as before.

A third and fourth trial were alike unsuccessful. The fifth, I liked the house
very well, but upon being informed that all the boarders were men, I determined upon making another trial. I desired to obtain quarters where the society was enlivened with ladies.

Quite tired at length with my repeated disappointments, and more than half suspicious that I was myself somewhat too fastidious, I determined that my next attempt should bring matters to a conclusion. Fortunately, the place I called at, had very few of the objections I found with the others. The landlady seemed an intelligent, rather well-bred woman, and the appearance of the furniture and floors quite cleanly. And here it will perhaps be worth while for me to state, that this item of cleanliness was one which I could not forego, from the effects of my country life. I had been used to see, amid much poverty, the utmost freedom from anything like dirt, dust, or household impurity. And without it, I could not be comfortable in any situation.

I concluded an arrangement with the woman, and told her I should come that very day. I was to have a snug little room in the attic, exclusively for my own use, and was to pay three dollars and a half per week.

Soon after leaving this place, which I gave a good look at when I got outside, lest I might forget it, I went down in Pearl-street to call upon Colby. He was glad to see me, but as it was now the business part of the day, and I saw he had plenty to do, I did not stay but a few minutes. I gave him the street and number of my new residence, and he engaged to call and see me in the evening, when his employments were over.

Who should I meet, as I was coming up from the ferry after having been over to Brooklyn for my valise, but my friend of the day before, the antiquary. He expressed his pleasure at seeing me by a smile, and a few kind words.

"And how do you like the city?" said he.

"I have hardly had an opportunity of finding out much about it yet, sir. But I dare say I shall know more by-and-by."

"Too much," he rejoined, shaking his head—"too much, perhaps. There are a thousand things here, my young friend, which no man is the better for knowing."

He paused, and I knew not exactly what reply to make.

"May I ask what you intend doing in New-York," said he, at length.

"I hardly know myself, sir," I answered; "I have come here with the intention of getting employment. What that may be, will depend a good deal upon my luck. I shall not mind much what I turn my hand to, so that I gain an honest living by it, and a fair chance of bettering myself as I grow older."

"That is a strange way," said my companion, evidently with some interest. "People are not apt to get any employment worth having in this city, if they come here in the way I understand you to say you come."

"I am determined to do my best. Perhaps," I added, for I thought the anti-

quary showed quite a friendly disposition—"perhaps, sir, you could suggest
something to me in the way of getting a situation?"

My friend looked down upon the ground awhile, and smiling good-
humoredly as he raised his face, replied,

"Well, Evans, I possibly may do something for you. Look you: I do not
wish to conceal that I am somewhat interested in your case. When but a little
older than you, I came to this city, in pretty much the same way that you come
now. I was not poor, but was without acquaintances or friends, as you say
you are. And though I had money, I received, God knows, but little friendliness from those who might have shown at least some kindness to me: but
whose dispositions were not as large as their means, for they were rich. I have,
however, lived long enough to do without their friendship, and I don't know
what reason there is that I should not give you a helping hand. Perhaps what
I may do for you may not be much, and may not cost me anything. So much
the more scope for your own exertions, and honor to you if you hew out your
fortune for yourself. Here is my card," and he handed it to me: "come to me
to-morrow morning at eleven. I am punctual, and shall expect you to be the
same; and perhaps you will not regret the chance acquaintance you made in
the market-wagon. Good day."

I could hardly return the salutation, so pleased was I at the turn events were
taking. To be sure, I did not know the nature of the business my friend would
employ me in, but it *was* employment, and that was the first stepping-stone to
the heights that lay above. I looked at the card; upon it was written, "*Stephen
Lee,*—, Exchange Place." I carefully deposited it in my breast pocket, and
with a lighter step wended on to my new boarding-house.

Whether it was that I had gained confidence since my interview with
Mr. Lee, or from some other cause, I felt myself very little abashed at sitting
down, for the first time in my life, at dinner with some twenty well-bred ladies
and gentlemen. Though many of the observances were somewhat new to me,
and one or two of my nearest neighbors, plainly saw, and felt amused, at my unsophisticated conduct in some respects; I believe I came off, upon the whole,
with tolerable credit.

I had an opportunity, too, of seeing who were the really well-bred people
of the house. For those possessed of the truest politeness will never deign
to wound the feelings of one in their company, by showing that they notice
his deficiencies, and are entertained at his ignorance and awkwardness. On

the contrary, they would rather do like that greatest of rakes, and of gentle-men, George IV; who, when some court ladies, at tea, simpered at a couple of unfashionable companions for pouring their tea in their saucers, instead of drinking it from their cups; poured his also into the saucer, and thus com-mended it to his royal lips, that they might not be mortified by the mirth of the rude ones.

At night, Colby, according to his promise, paid me a visit. He was much pleased when I told him of my encounter with Lee, and of his promise to me. He told me, when I showed him the card, that he had frequently heard of that personage, who was a merchant of much reputation and no small wealth. Colby congratulated me on my luck, and jokingly told me, he should not be surprised to see me one day the owner of warehouses and the head of great business.

"But come," said he, "this is dull fun here. Let us go out and cruise a little, and see what there is going on."

"Agreed," said I. "I shall like it of all things."

So we took our hats and sallied forth from the house.

After strolling up and down one of the most busy streets several times, I be-came a little more used to the glare of the lamps in the windows, and the clatter and bustle which was going on around me. How bright and happy everything seemed! The shops were filled with the most beautiful and costly wares, and the large, clear glass of the show-windows flashed in the brilliancy of the gas, which displayed their treasures to the passers-by. And the pave was filled with an eager and laughing crowd, jostling along, and each intent on some scheme of pleasure for the evening. I felt confused for a long time with the universal whirl, until at length, as I said, the scene grew a little more accustomed, and I had leisure to think more calmly upon what I saw.

In a little while, Colby asked me if I did not wish to hear some fine music and drink a glass of wine. I assented, and we entered a beautifully furnished room, around which little tables were placed, where parties were seated drink-ing and amusing themselves with various games. We took our station at the first vacant seats, and called for our drinks. How delicious everything seemed! Those beautiful women—warbling melodies sweeter than ever I had heard before, and the effect of the liquor upon my brain, seemed to lave me in hap-piness, as it were, from head to foot!

Oh, fatal pleasure! There and then was my first false step after coming in the borders of the city—and *so soon* after, too! Colby thought not, perhaps, what he was doing—but still he was very much to blame. He knew I was young, fond of society, and inexperienced; and it would have been better for me had he ushered me amid a pest-house, where some deadly contagion was raging in all its fury.

I tremble now as I look back upon the results which have sprung from the conduct of that single night, as from one seed of evil. Over the lapse of ten years I gaze, and the scene comes back to me again in the most vivid reality. I can remember even the colors of the chequer-board, and the appearance of the little table, and the very words of some of the songs that were sung. We drank—not once only, but again and again.

Yes, with a singular distinctness, the whole appearance of the room, and of the men with their hats on and cigars in their mouths, that sat all about, are as plain before my eyes as though they were painted in a picture there. It was all new to me then. A hundred more exciting scenes have passed over my head since, and have left no impression, while this is marked as with a steel pencil upon the tablets of my memory.

I remember being struck with the appearance of one poor fellow in a corner. He probably was not much older than myself; yet his face was bloated, his eyes inflamed, and he leaned back in that state of drowsy drunkenness which it is so disgusting to behold. I presume his companions—those who had made merry with him until he was brought to this stage of degradation—had left him in scorn; and there he sat, or rather supported himself in the corner, not half awake, and the subject of many a gibe and light laugh. Was it not a warning to me? And yet I was not warned.

After a time, some of the white-aproned subordinates of the place came to him, roughly broke his slumbers, and put him forth from the place. Miserable man! Without doubt, he now sleeps the sleep which no jostle can awaken, and which no curl of the lip, or gibe of the scoffer, can start from its dark repose. He must have died the death of the drunkard!

Colby saw at length that he had been too heedless with me. Used as he was to the dissipation of city life, he forgot that I was from the country, and never in my life before engaged in such a scene of *pleasure*.

With some difficulty preserving the steadiness of my pace, as we left the room, I took his arm, and he walked with me toward my residence. Indeed, if he had not done so, I question whether I should have reached it; for my head

swam, and the way in the night was somewhat difficult to find. Leaving me at
the door, my companion bade me good night, and departed.

I entered, took a light from a number which were left upon a table in the
hall for the use of the boarders, and slowly ascended the stairs to my room. My
slumbers were deep and unbroken. So were those of the preceding evening,
and yet the nature of the two was widely different. The former was the repose
of health and innocence — the latter, the dull lethargy of *drunkeness* [*sic*].

CHAPTER V

All is not gold that glitters.
— OLD PROVERB

THE reflections which operated in my mind the next morning, are not a sufficiently tempting theme for me to dwell upon. I can hardly say that shame
and remorse possessed me to such a degree, as to counterbalance the physical
discomfort which weighed painfully upon every part of my frame.

In the course of the forenoon, I visited my antiquarian merchant friend,
Mr. Lee. He had not forgotten me, but was as good as his word. His own
establishment, he said, already employed a sufficiency of clerks and attendants
whom he could not turn out without doing them injustice. He had made inquiries, and informed me that a Mr. Andrews, a gentleman doing business in
Wall-street, with whom he was slightly acquainted, might be able to give me
a situation.

My patron wrote a note, addressed to Andrews, which I carried to that
personage. I found him in a handsome granite edifice, in a back room furnished sumptuously, out of which opened another, fronting on the street. It
was a bank. Numerous people were constantly coming and going, upon business; everything was transacted with a quiet easy air, and without much bustle,
though I could see that the matters which were discussed involved the value
of thousands.

What conceivable situation Mr. Lee could have had in view for me there, I
could not imagine; but I was soon undeceived. Mr. Andrews looked over the
note, and called me to him. He was a thin, black-eyed, rather delicate-looking
man, and had a completely professional appearance. He told me he was a lawyer, and that his connection with the institution in which I now saw him did

not prevent him from attending to his other avocations. He wanted some one as a kind of clerk, porter, and errand boy — three in one — to take care of his office while he was absent. The office was in an upper part of the same street.

I readily agreed to accept the terms which Andrews proposed, and he desired me to commence my duties on the morrow. As I took my departure from the place, who should I see in front, with a quill behind his ear, but my market-wagon acquaintance, Demaine. I accosted him with the salutation of the day, but he made a very slight and cool answer; and as I did not care much about his good-will, I went forth without further parley.

Somewhat at a loss what to do with myself, I walked down to Colby's place of business, and made him promise to call upon me again that evening, as he had the preceding one.

"And how have you felt to-day?" said he, smiling mischievously; "you country boys cannot hold up under a few glasses, like us of the city."

I blushed, as I brought to mind the folly I had committed, and internally thought I could never be guilty of it again.

"I know," answered I, "that there are many things in which you will find me rather awkward. But my very visit here, to ask you again to-night, proves that I am willing to get knowledge."

Knowledge! Better would it have been for me had I remained in ignorance through the whole course of my life, than attained to *such* knowledge.

When Colby came in the evening, and we started out to walk as before, I felt determined not to go in the musical drinking-house again. But I don't know how it was, the very first proposition my companion made to that effect, found me a willing listener. We entered, and called for our drinks.

It was indeed a seductive scene. Most of the inmates were young men; and I noticed no small number quite on the verge of boyhood. They played the same as the rest, and tossed off glasses of liquor, without apparently feeling any evil effects from it. Little as I knew of the world, I felt that there was something wrong here. The keeper of the house was not an American. He made his appearance now and then among the company, smiling and bowing, and highly pleased, no doubt, that shillings were pouring into his pockets with such profitable rapidity.

And the music again! How sweet it sounded out, combined with the fascinating looks of the females who sang. I was completely enthralled, and drank deeper even than the night before.

In the course of the evening some little incidents happened, which served as a proof of the truth of the old proverb, which declares that glittering things may not be of the value they seem. It happened thus. Colby and myself, accompanied by a friend of my friend's, whom we met at the drinking-room, determined to go to the theatre that evening, and accordingly did so. The house was crowded. Beautiful women and elegant men — moustached dandies and lively youth — brilliant fashionables of all varieties, combined to render the scene exhilarating and splendid. And the music from the orchestra, now soft and subdued, now bursting out with notes of thunder — how delicious it glided into the ear! The curtain drew up and the play began. It was one of those flippant affairs, that pretend to give a picture of society and manners among the exclusive. The plot worse than meager — the truthfulness of the scene a gag, which ought not to have excited aught but ridicule — the most nauseous kind of mock aristocracy tinging the dialogue from beginning to end — yet it was received with applause, and at the conclusion, with vociferous and repeated cheers! The manager had printed upon his bills that London was pleased with it, and that one of the scenes represented life as in the private parlor of an English Duke — with the curtains, carpets, and drapery of the parlor, as good as real! I blushed for the good sense of my countrymen.

In the farce which followed, one of the characters was a wild hoyden of a girl. It was done very agreeably by one of the actresses, whose beauty excited my admiration to no small degree. So much indeed was I fascinated with her, that I expressed my opinion in terms which the liquor I had drank just before by no means contributed to render less strong. I vowed that if I could see her, side by side, and speak to her, I would give the world. Mitchell, the one who made the third of our party, listened to me for some time with a kind of sober surprise; and then, giving a wink to Colby, told me he was acquainted with the actress who had pleased me so much, and would introduce me to her that very evening, if I desired. I thanked him a thousand times.

In the interval between the acts, my eyes were attracted by the figure of a young gentleman in the stage-box, (we sat in the pit,) who seemed to me a perfect pattern of perfection in his dress and manners — in fact, a gentleman of the highest order. I saw Mitchell looking at him also.

"Do you know him?" said I.

"Yes," he answered.

"A fine looking fellow," said I.

He assented.

When the play was over, we went out. Along by the theatre, there were the glaring gaslights of several fashionable refectories.

"Gentlemen," said our companion, "suppose we go down here, and get some oysters."

We agreed, and down we went.

While waiting in our little box, Mitchell called one of the men in attendance:

"John, bring us a bottle of Port."

The wine was brought.

"Mr. Evans," said Mitchell to me, "do you know I have a fancy always to be served by a particular individual in this refectory? Just notice the man's face, now, and tell me what you think of my taste."

When the waiter came again, in obedience to our companion's call, he held him in talk several minutes about some trivial details respecting the cooking of the articles we had ordered. When he went out, I looked up in Mitchell's face—

"Why," said I, "that—that—that man is the very fellow!"

"What very fellow?"

"He is the picture of the gentleman we saw in the boxes at the theatre!"

"I dare say he is the person; in fact, I know he is."

I changed the subject, and we finished our oysters.

"And now," said Mitchell to me, "if your friend Colby will wait here five minutes, I will introduce you to the actress."

My mistake in regard to the *fashionable gentleman*, had taught me a lesson, and my country life had taught me also to keep better hours. So I would have excused myself, but Mitchell seemed anxious that I should go with him.

"It's but a step," said he.

So we walked round the block, into a dirty alley leading to the rear of the theatre. Mitchell told me he had the *entrée* there (to the theatre, I mean, not the alley) and in we walked.

I pass over my stares of wonder, and my running aslant dungeon walls, castles, and canvas palaces. We reached an open space, on one side, where there were quite a number of persons idling. At a little table sat a woman, eating some cheese and thick bread, and drinking at intervals from a dingy pewter mug, filled with beer. She was coarse—her eyes had that sickly bleared appearance, which results from the constant glitter of strong light upon them;

her complexion was an oily brown, now quite mottled with paint, and her feet and ancles were encased in thick ill-blacked shoes.

Mitchell went up to the table, (I leaning on his arm,) and engaged in chit chat with the delectable creature. He introduced me. I was thunderstruck! *She* was my charmer, of the hoyden in the farce! Her voice was coarse and masculine, and her manners on a par with her voice.

After ten minutes conversation, we bade the lady good night, and wended our way back to Colby, whom we found waiting for us. Neither myself nor Mitchell alluded to the subject, and Colby, no doubt understanding how matters stood, did not mention it either.

The occurrences of the night, I may as well confess, taught me to question the reality of many things I afterward saw; and reflect that, though to appearance they were showy, they might prove, upon trial, as coarse as the eating-house waiter, or the blear-eyed actress. I lost also, some of that reverence, and that awkward sense of inferiority, which most country folk, when they take up their abode in this brick-and-pine Babel, so frequently show — and which, by the way, is as amusing to the observers, as it is unfair to themselves.

CHAPTER VI

"Strange that such difference there should be
'Twixt tweedle-dum and tweedle-dee."

In the course of a few weeks I became quite at home in my new situation, in the office of Andrews. He treated me very civilly always, though of course he never made any approach to friendliness. I could not expect it, in the situation I occupied.

Under the auspices of my friend Colby, I became pretty well used to city life; and before the winter passed away, I could drink off nearly as much strong liquor as himself, and feel no inconvenience from it. My employer, Mr. Andrews, had become so well satisfied with my performance of my duties, that he advanced me somewhat above my original situation. I had now none of the more menial services to perform. An Irishman, named Dennis, was engaged to act as porter, and to make the fires, open and shut the office, and so on. Andrews occasionally employed him to do business also for the financial institution of which he was an officer.

There is hardly much need that I should detain the reader with a minute account of this part of my career. Though I knew it not at the time, it was the downward career of a drunkard! I concealed from Andrews, as a matter of course, my habits of intemperance, and attended with tolerable carefulness to my duties during the day. Through Colby's means, I soon obtained a wide circle of acquaintance, mostly young men in the same walk of life with ourselves, and having the same habits. We used frequently to go round of nights from place to place, stopping every now and then at some bar-room, and taking a drink all round. This we used to call a 'red circle.' How appropriate a name that was, the reader can judge for himself.

And about this time (I had lived nearly six months in my situation with Andrews) an incident occurred, which had an important bearing upon my future course of life. Though I saw my good benefactor, Mr. Lee, but seldom, I was not ungrateful for the kindness he had shown me, and often wished that there might be some way of repaying it. One evening, when I had finished my supper, and was going up to my room to prepare for a visit to the theatre, which I had engaged to attend that night with Colby and a party of friends, the landlady handed me a note, which had been left for me during the day. Quite curious to know who could have written to me, and what about, I opened it hastily, and read the following:

" — EXCHANGE PLACE, TUESDAY MORNING,

"DEAR YOUNG FRIEND,

"The interest I have taken in your welfare, has by no means grown cold, though of late I have not seen you, or had any opportunity of showing my good will. The particular reason of my writing is, that one of my clerks has lately left me; his situation, I think would be an agreeable one for you, and if you choose to accept it, it is at your service. The salary is $800 per year.

"Give your present employer a couple week's [sic] notice, before you leave him, in order that he may have an opportunity of getting some one in your place. At the end of that time come to me, and I will induct you in your new duties. If this proposition meets your approval, write me to that effect as soon as convenient.

"STEPHEN LEE."

I was quite overjoyed! Not only was the stipend offered me by my old friend more than twice as much as that I received from Andrews, but then I should be in the service of a man I loved, instead of one whom, at best, I could look upon with no stronger feeling than indifference. I sat down immediately, and indited a grateful acceptance of Mr. Lee's offer.

My duties at Andrews', of late, had not been, to tell the truth, of the most pleasant description. We found out, after Dennis had been with us awhile, that he had an unfortunate habit of tippling, which sadly interfered with his efficiency at work. For my own part, I could not conscientiously find fault with him, and therefore concealed his mistakes as much as possible. But they became so glaring at length, that they could not be hidden, and Andrews discharged him. Dennis frequented a little drinking-shop, which was in one of the streets on my way home, and there I often saw him afterward. So that my own labors were now as heavy as when I first commenced them.

Besides, I occasionally saw things which looked very suspicious, in connection with Andrews' business arrangements. I heard rumors too, in my intercourse with the neighboring clerks, which by no means increased my opinion for my employer's honesty. Those who were supposed to be at home in such affairs, more than hinted that he would before long be summarily removed from his station in the moneyed establishment, before alluded to in these pages. It was asserted also, that Andrews had lately used immense sums of money, the origin of which no one could tell. So I felt not at all grieved at the idea of finding another master, and gave the notice premonitory which Mr. Lee desired, with but ill-concealed gratification.

Some days after, as I was passing down to the office from my breakfast, I saw Dennis, the discharged porter, come out of the little groggery I have mentioned. He stepped forward, and stood upon the curb-stone, looking down upon the ground, very miserable to all appearance. Dennis had gone from bad to worse, until he was now at the very lowest stage of degradation. Though I saluted him, I could hardly conceal my disgust at his filthy and bloated looks. How little did I think, that one day might find me so little removed from his present condition! Perhaps it will not be without a wholesome moral, if I finish this chapter with the relation of poor Dennis's subsequent conduct that day, and an off set of the doings of another personage, who has figured somewhat in my narrative — as those occurrences subsequently came to my knowledge.

At the early hour I saw him, Dennis was passing through the agonies which mark the period immediately after a fit of intoxication. Pain and hunger racked him in the corporeal frame; despair, mortification and disgust with himself burnt in his heart. He felt that he was a degraded man. With an unwonted bitterness, thoughts of many chances neglected — of weeks spent in riot — of the scorn of the world — and the superciliousness of those called respectable — cut at his heart with a sharp grief. Heaving an inward groan, he started off, and passed down a by-street, to walk away, if possible, such fearful reflections.

Nearly an hour, he rapidly traversed, at hap-hazard, the narrowest and darkest ways he could pick; for he did not wish to be seen. Then his appetite became acute, and he wished for food. Wishing, merely, was vain; and he had not a single cent. Poor creature! In the preceding two days, he had not eaten a single meal. Should he beg? Should he ask for work? His suspicious appearance might subject him to denial; besides, the emergency was one not to be postponed. In an evil moment Dennis yielded to the tempter. He saw, in a small grocery, some bread piled upon a barrel top. He entered, and while the owner was busy at a back shelf, the ravenous man purloined a loaf and made off with it. The keeper of the grocery saw him as he went out, discovered the theft, and pursued the criminal. He was brought back, a police officer called, and the bread found upon him.

So the thief was taken off to prison, and being arraigned a few hours afterward, was summarily convicted, and sentenced to the customary place, just out of the city; there to remain for several days, at hard labor and confinement.

During the same hour wherein these things were being transacted, in another and distant part of the town, sat a gentleman in a parlor. The carpet was very rich, the curtains glossy silk, and the chairs heavy mahogany. The person who sat there was Andrews, my master. On a table before him lay some written papers. By the opposite side of the table, and just about to depart, stood a second gentleman, elegantly attired, and with a lofty look, which spoke of pride within.

"The time is as favorable now," said Andrews, in reply to something his companion had spoken, "as it ever was. Besides, we must make hay while the sun shines. Who knows whether we shall have the chance, five days from this?"

"And yet you are not willing to take the bold steps," rejoined the other; "the transfer ought to have been made a week ago."

"Are you sure it can be made without the others knowing it?" said Andrews.

"As easy as speak," was the answer; "they never examine."

"But they *might* examine."

"I tell you, only pay them a handsome dividend, and they'll rest easy any length of time."

Andrews put his finger under his chin, and looked down a moment abstractedly.

"Have you not determined yet?" asked the person standing.

"Long ago, sir—long ago," was Andrews' reply. "But it is a dangerous game, and should be played cautiously."

"Well; shall we take this step, or no?"

Andrews raised up his head; his dark eye twinkled as it met the glance of his companion, and the two looked at each other a minute. There was evil fraternity in that look. Then Andrews bent his head two or three times without speaking. The other understood him. He smiled, and turning, left the apartment.

A person looking on as they parted, would hardly have thought them to be aught else than two respectable citizens—yet were they two most consummate scoundrels. It was indeed too true—the host of rumors I had heard about my employer's honesty. The situation he occupied, he turned to account, by schemes which were nothing more or less than swindling; and his well-dressed companion was of kindred spirit with himself. He had now come to have a private conference with Andrews, and the subject of that conference was a scheme for making a splendid fortune jointly, by means of the peculiar facilities for cheating possessed by both. A long time ago, the plan had been marked out; and now the hour was nigh, to strike the finishing stroke.

It would be painful to describe, as it would also be to read, all the villainy, the deceit, the underhand swindling, and the imposition which these two wicked men had followed, and were on the eve of closing. In all their rascality, however, they acted warily—with the wisdom of the serpent. They knew that whatever might be the execrations of people, the *law* could not touch them. Opinions, too, might be bought: defence and character might be bought. And what, that it was possible to buy, might they not purchase?

In the course of the succeeding week, the conspiracy worked its way out. The bubble burst! The master hands had arranged things well, and they triumphed.

Yet was the tempest a terrible one. Widows, left with a narrow competence; young children; sick people, whose cases were hopeless, but who might languish on for many years; sailors, away upon the ocean; fishermen, whose earnings were scant and dearly bought; mechanics; young men just commencing business; economical doctors and clergymen in their novitiate; all these, and

hundreds more, had either deposited sums of money in the institution, or
were sufferers by its bankruptcy in other ways. Many lost their all. There was
one woman, a widow, an energetic country trader, the mother of a large family,
which she supported by her business habits, who had come to the city with
what was for her quite a large sum—all she was worth, and some borrowed
funds besides. Her intent was to purchase a heavy stock of goods, for sale the
subsequent season. For security, she had her money placed in the vaults of
the institution—and lost every cent!

It would be almost an endless effort to tell who was injured. All classes, all
ranks, all occupations, felt more or less of the withering blight.

But the tempest blew over at last. The two men who had provoked it, went
out still among their fellow-men, with forms erect, and with smooth smiles.
He of the dark eye was just finishing, a few miles from the city, a palace-like
residence, of great size and beauty. Now he had it furnished with the most
sumptuous luxury. Cost and pains were not spared, until Desire had no further room for wishing. Here this rich man settled himself; and here, when he
had become a little used to his grandeur, so that it did not sit awkwardly upon
him, he determined to give a superb entertainment. Preparations were accordingly made; scientific cooks were engaged; foreign delicacies purchased, and
the most exquisite dishes prepared.

The hour and the company arrived; and the master of the feast looked
around with a smile, as each one seated himself at his appointed place. They
ate, and drank, and made merry. Delight, and Friendliness, and Content,
seemed the presiding spirits of the banquet.

After awhile, when their glasses were filled with rich wine, it was proposed
that they should have a toast. So a benevolent-looking elderly gentleman rose,
and after speaking a few minutes, to the purport that he felt sure those present
would all cordially join him, he raised his glass aloft—his example being followed by the others, and said—

"*Even-handed laws*—which, in our glorious republic, dispense to all im-
partially their due."

When the revelers heard this sentiment, they clinked their glasses together,
and raised a peal which made the lofty ceiling ring again. Then a second, and
then a third—which was a louder and a gladder peal than either of the others.

And at the same moment that the echoes died away, there was, about a mile
off, a human soul writhing in its final struggle. It was that of the poor drunk-

ard Dennis, who stole the loaf in his hunger, and had been sent to expiate his crime in toil and imprisonment. The dissipation of years had made him weak; and he could not bear up against the exposure, joined with hard work. But his task-master was merciless; and as long as the wretched man could stand, he was kept laboring. At last, he fell very ill. Who would medicine a rascally jail bird? He went on from bad to worse, and was soon in a dying condition.

Before the splendid dinner party returned to their homes that night, the corpse of the *convicted* thief lay cold and clayey upon the prison floors.

<hr />

CHAPTER VII

"Look not upon the wine when it is red!"

AFTER I had been a while in my situation at Mr. Lee's store, I thought I might safely indulge myself in adding a little to my expenses. I made improvements both in my style of living, and in my dress. The new boarding-house in which I took up my quarters, was in the upper part of the town. Colby came to see me quite often, as usual. The reader probably, by this time, has gained no small insight into the character of my friend. He was by no means a bad man; and yet his early habits, and giving way to temptation, had brought him to be anything else but a fit companion for a country youth, just beginning life in the city.

One morning, while I was attending to my usual duties in the counting-room, a stranger, with a dark and swarthy complexion, came in and asked for Mr. Lee. He was not in at the time; and thinking that the business of the dark-faced personage was very likely some trifling affair, I told him that my employer was away, but would probably return in a half-hour, or less. The stranger paused a moment, with a troubled expression upon his countenance; then drew from his breast pocket a couple of sealed documents, and handed them to me.

"Give these papers," said he, "to your master, the moment he arrives. They are of more consequence than you know, and I would that I could have delivered them to his own hands."

"I will do as you desire," said I, laying the papers up in a little partition on the desk.

A few minutes afterward, I learned from one of my fellow-clerks, that

Mr. Lee had gone out that morning, leaving word that he would not be back till the close of the day. I thought of the stranger's parting injunction; but he was gone some time, and could not be informed how the fact really was. After all, perhaps, the documents might be of no weighty moment, and I reflected no more upon the subject.

On my way down from dinner, Colby met me in the street.

"This is lucky," he exclaimed, seizing me by the hand. "We have made up a fine party for the play to-night, and you must promise to be one of us."

"With pleasure," was my reply; "nothing could delight me more."

So it was arranged, that when the hour arrived, they should call upon me, and we would all go together.

We did not close our store as early as usual that evening, in consequence of our master's absence. Though doing an extensive business, he was a man very careful of the details, and was in the practice of being in his counting-room until the last moment. We waited therefore until the very evening, and the neighbors all around had shut up, and left us quite solitary. As the porter was making the usual arrangements of closing, Mr. Lee returned. He looked around him a moment, remarked that he did not know as his presence there was necessary, and was on the point of departing. So selfish was I, that though at that moment the remembrance of the swarthy stranger, and his letters, came to my mind, I debated a moment whether I should give them to Mr. Lee, as that would detain us some minutes longer. I was in haste to get home, that I might be ready in time for our visit to the theatre. Happily, however, duty triumphed.

"I had nearly forgot, sir," said I, "these papers were left here this morning, by a man who desired that you might get them as soon as possible."

Mr. Lee took them, and opened them. The very moment he began to read, I could see that he was deeply interested. After finishing one, he perused the other with the same eagerness. And thus a second time, with a slower and more careful manner, he read over both the letters again, from beginning to end.

"It's a lucky thing, Evans," said he, "that you did not miss giving me these. Not for half my fortune would I have been without them this very evening."

He then explained to me, that he had of late been engaged in some mercantile speculations at the south, which proved a failure. Some traders with whom he had intercourse there, were becoming alarmed, and demanded certain moneys, or their value, which Mr. Lee was bound to pay; but which, it had been the understanding, were to remain uncalled for, for several months yet. A statement of this sudden demand was forwarded by Mr. Lee's agent, with a sorrowful acknowledgment that he had not the wherewithal to meet it, and asking directions for his conduct. The swarthy southerner, who was a planter, come to the north on business, was going to leave the city the next morning, at an early hour, and prompt action was therefore necessary.

Mr. Lee immediately sat down and wrote to his agent, directing where and how he could obtain the needed funds. He enjoined him to pay the liabilities the moment they were called for, as he would rather be at the expense of them, twice over, than have his reputation and fair name as a merchant put in danger. Having made up and endorsed his reply, he gave it into my hands, with the address of the planter, who was to take it on, telling me to call at his hotel in the course of the evening, and place it in his hands. I promised to do so, of course, and went home to my supper.

As it was now quite in the evening, I had hardly finished my meal before my companions came, according to arrangement, to take me with them to the play. I debated a little while whether I had not better postpone my evening's enjoyment, as I had the planter's letter to carry. But I feared they would suspect that I did not like their companionship; and determined, in my own mind, to go out between some of the earlier acts of the piece, and convey my message.

I went to the theatre. We enjoyed ourselves highly, for the performances were creditable, and each of us naturally fond of that species of amusement, and moreover, in great spirits. As the first piece was one I had long wished to see acted, I concluded not to go until that was finished. Then there was to come a dance, which one of my companions praised so highly that I was determined to stay and see that also. And then the intermission was so very short that, before I knew it, the curtain was up, and the actors on in the after-piece. Feeling that I was not doing right, I made a bold push, and bade my companions good night, if I should not see them again, telling them that I had some business to transact for my employer. They laughed at me, stating the improbability of such a thing, at that time of night. If ever there was anything that annoyed me, it was to be suspected of trying to sneak out from the truth by a kind of back-door, as it were. Accordingly, when they promised that if I would wait until the end of the first act, they would all go with me, I sat down again by them. I knew I was culpable, and yet I had not resolution of mind enough to break away.

We went from the theatre. On our way to the hotel, we were to pass one of our favorite drinking-places, where, as we came off against the entrance, we heard the inmates stamping and applauding at a great rate. There was evidently something more than usual going on, so one of our party insisted that we should step in and have a look.

"Only one moment," said he, "and then we will walk on with Evans."

But the moment stretched on to minutes, and the minutes to almost half an hour; at the end of which time we were snugly seated round a table, imbibing fragrant liquors through long glass tubes. And with the contents of the first glass, came a total disregard of anything but the pleasure of drink. Forgetful of my own duty — of my master's honor, and the crisis which would turn against him, if I continued sitting there a little while longer, I drank, and drank, and drank; until, as the night advanced, lost to the slightest vestige of remembrance with regard to the pacquet, I was the wildest and most exhilarated of the party.

What fire burnt in my brain! I laughed, and with garrulous tongue, entertained those about me with silly stories, which the quantity of liquor they had taken, alone prevented them from being nauseated with. All around us were the scenes which belonged to such a place, and which I have partly described before. The music went on, but we heard it no longer. The people talked, and the dice rattled, but we heeded them not. The Demon of Intemperance had taken possession of all our faculties, and we were his alone.

A wretched scene! Half-a-dozen men, just entering the busy scenes of life, not one of us over twenty-five years, and there we were, benumbing our faculties, and confirming ourselves in practices which ever too surely bring the scorn of the world, and deserved disgrace to their miserable victims! It is a terrible sight, I have often thought since, to see *young men* beginning their walk upon this fatal journey! To reflect that those faculties which have been given us by God, for our own enjoyment, and the benefit of our fellows, are, at the very outset rendered useless, and of not so much avail as the instinct of the very beasts. To know that that [*sic*] the blood is poisoned, and that the strength is to be broken down, and the bloom banished from the cheek, and the luster of the eye dimmed, and all for a few hours' sensual gratification, now and then — is it not terrible! If there were no other drawback, the mere physical prostration which follows a fit of drunkenness were enough. But to the young, it saps the foundations, not only of the body's health, but places a stigma for the future on their worldly course, which can never be wiped out, or concealed from the knowledge of those about them.

~~~~~~

CHAPTER VIII

Yet sense and passion held them slaves,
    And lashed them to the oar,
Till they were wrecked upon their graves,
    And then they rose no more.
Oh! God of mercy, make me know
    The gift which thou hast given;
Nor let me idly spend it so,
    But make me fit for Heaven!

—CHRISTIAN EXAMINER

READER, I am coming to the dark and cloudy part of my fortunes. I would that I had not to tell what you will see in the following pages—but a sentiment of good-will for my fellows, prompts the relation. I think that by laying before them a candid relation of the dangers which have involved me, and the temptations which have seduced me aside, the narrative may act as a beacon light, guiding their feet from the same fearful hazards.

There is no need that I should pause here to dwell on my meeting with my benefactor Lee, and the shame with which I acknowledged my guilt, and gave him back his letter. But great as was my fault, I was hardly prepared for his storm of anger. I did not know how much he worshipped his good name among the mercantile world, or I might have been better prepared for it. He had jealously guarded his professional honor, as the apple of his eye; and now there was no escape. The mails to the distant place were very irregular; and besides, a letter to that town where his agent resided, would not reach it in time, now, if there were no impediment.

Though conscious of my remissness, the irritability, which is one of the results of intemperate habits, caused me in the course of our interview, to attempt an excuse for my conduct. High words arose—in the end I was insolent, and Mr. Lee bade me leave the place and never enter it again! I departed, telling him he should be obeyed.

Dearly, during that day, and many subsequent ones, did I repent my folly. How often did I curse that miserable weakness of my mind, which led me to yield to the slightest opening of temptation!

And what was to be done now, for a living? Some employment must be had—I could not starve. Though my salary had been quite liberal, I had spent every cent, and with the exception of a small sum, due me on a back account, I owned not a dollar in the world. Will it be believed, that, in this strait, I was besotted enough to run into the very jaws of the lion? I accidentally learned that the proprietor of a second-rate hotel, where I had in times past been in the habit of going, was in want of a bar-keeper. I made application for the place, and, after some demur, was accepted. But the scenes which I witnessed there, and the duties my situation obliged me to perform, were too repulsive, even for my callous heart: and at the end of a fortnight I left my place.

During my avocations there, I saw many an occurrence, which, had I possessed true judgment, might have served as a sufficient warning to me, of the curses of intemperance. There was one of the customers at our bar, quite a small boy, who came almost every evening with a little jug, which he had filled with brandy. I never asked the child—but I knew the principal part of his story from his actions. He had a drunken parent! Their dwelling was nigh the tavern. I had occasion, two or three times, to show some little kindness to the boy, when he was rudely treated by the inmates of our place; who exhibited, at times, all those various phases of temper which brandy can produce.

One evening, I had a respite from my employment, and amused myself by my favorite recreation, the theatre. As I was returning quite late, and was passing through a narrow, dirty street, a boy asked me for some pennies, in a piteous tone. He said he wanted them to buy bread. I thought the voice was familiar—and scanning the lad's features, discovered my little acquaintance who had so often brought the jug. Of late, however, I had missed his accustomed visits to the bar. I spoke kindly to him—and the poor fellow, no doubt unaccustomed to such treatment, burst into tears. More and more interested, I inquired of him what distress had sent him forth at that hour; and he acknowledged that, instead of wanting the pennies to buy bread, he wished to purchase liquor—and for his *mother!*

"I don't know what ails her," said the little wretch, "but she acts more strange to-night, than I ever saw her before."

"Where does she live?" said I.

"Not a block off," answered the boy. "Wouldn't you just step and see her, sir? She has been ill for a long time."

I thought it no wonder, when, as the child turned to go on before, and show me the way, I caught sight of the little red jug, under his jacket. He led me up a dirty rickety stoop, into a dark entry of the same description; and it was not without considerable risk of my personal safety, that I arrived at last at the door of a room in the attic, where, he said, his mother was lying. He opened the door, and we entered. Never before had I been in so miserable a place. The furniture of the apartment, what there was of it, would have been scouted from a negro hovel. The bed on which the woman herself lay in one corner, was a filthy thing of feathers and soiled rags. Another corner was tenanted by a little girl, the sister of the boy who had conducted me: she was asleep. There was no fire — hardly any light; for the flickering of a half-burned tallow candle on the hearth-stone, only served to cast strange, shadowy hues around, making the place drearier and still more desolate. I stood and looked upon the scene — then, approaching the woman, I gazed down upon her, and the very first glance I gave in her face, saw that she was dying! Horror-struck, I stepped away from the bed, and for several minutes was silent and motionless with awe.

Every little while, the woman would turn uneasily, and raise herself somewhat from the bed, and look about — oftenest looking at the spot where her girl slumbered. My little guide crouched down close by my feet — it may be that the knowledge of the presence of death was upon him. Again the woman raised herself — then sank wearily back again, her faint groans sounding through the apartment. Poor creature! She was very wretched — and no doubt she had been as guilty as she was wretched; and thoughts of remorse might be the cause of that restlessness which I saw depicted in her countenance. But amid all her agony — amid the dark remembrances that came trooping up there, like fiends in the silence of midnight, to torment her — amid her doubts and fears about the Dim Beyond — amid faintness, and thirstiness, and pain — one controlling thought was mightier than all the rest — motherly love. She called in a hoarse whisper,

"Mary!"

There was no answer. A second time she called, and sank down her head, and held very still, to listen if she was heard. The quiet, regular breathing of the sleeping girl, was the only sound that broke that terrible stillness — for we were mute with dread. Again, the whisper sounded out with even a ghastlier tone than before,

"My daughter!"

The hoarse sound seemed to be reëchoed from other voices. It was as if around the room, and peering down from the upper corners of the wall, the death-stricken outcast fancied she saw faces, bodiless, and working with strange grins of mockery. She sat up in the bed—horror giving her strength—and stared wildly about. I was half petrified as her look was directed toward me, and the child at my feet. I stood as still as a statue. With a feeble hand, she drew from its place, the rag-heap used for her pillow; she tightened and bound it with her trembling fingers—I looking on in wonder the while—and then she threw it toward *me!* I half shrieked with fear.

The woman was plainly losing her senses, as the dread moment came nigh.

"Oh, Jack!" she exclaimed, as she saw her boy near me, "come to your poor mother!"

I raised the child, and bade him obey her. He was frightened at her fearful wildness, and crept toward the bed with trembling steps.

"Dear one, lean to my face!" she said.

The poor lad speechlessly obeyed the injunction. The girl slept on. And now the dying woman lay, her mouth partly open, drawing in the breath at intervals with a convulsive movement of the jaws. Her face was livid, and covered with large drops of sweat, and her eyes turned upward. It was evident, that she struggled with the Grim Messenger.

To me, the fearful novelty of the scene almost took away all power of speech or action. What I have narrated was done in the space of but few seconds. Indeed, I was not in the room, from first to last, more than ten or twelve minutes. The woman's arm, numb as it was getting to be, wound itself around her child, and pressed him closer. Something like a smile—a most deathly one—settled upon her features. She tried to speak—but just then her sinking powers forbade the effort. It seemed from her looks and faint gestures, that she would have had the boy rouse his sister, and bring her there also. Then she probably felt conscious how very short were her moments, and how she might die ere the drowsy child could be fully awakened. Her pallid lips moved—just moved, and that was all.

"Father in Heaven!" was the slight thin sound, "hallowed be thy name—thy will be done on earth as in heaven—forgive us our trespasses, as ——"

A ghastly rattle shook the repentant sinner's neck.

"Forgive us our trespasses ——"

There was a choking gush, as of wind and water in the throat.

"Forgive us ——"

Her head turned slowly, and fell on its side with a kind of leaden sound; her arm relaxed its hold; and the guilty creature lay there a corpse — her last prayer smothered in its utterance, and her immortal part starting from its now useless tabernacle, to waft itself on the journey for the Strange Land.

<center>~~~~~~~</center>

CHAPTER IX

Her image 'tis — to memory dear —
That clings around my heart,
And makes me fondly linger here
Unwilling to depart.

—THOMAS WELLS

MORE than two years had now passed away since my leaving the country; and I am coming, reader, to tell of things which nothing but a resolution to relate *all* my adventures, could wring from me. There is a sacredness in some of our sorrows, which prevents them from being fit subjects for the rude and common gaze. Wife of my youth! of my early youth! Forgive me if I transcribe your name, and your worth, for the admiration and example of those who may hear my mention of you!

When I left my bar-keeping duties, for the reasons I have alluded to, I found it necessary to change my residence for a cheaper one. Passing along an upper and quiet street of the city, one day, I noticed a plain, clean-looking house, of wood, with the sign, "Boarding," on the door. I inquired there, and finding I could be accommodated, soon took up my quarters in it. My fellow-boarders were in the humbler walks of life; but I soon found an attraction, which made up for every deficiency.

My landlady was a widow, with only one child, her daughter Mary. She was a modest, delicate, sweet girl, and before I had been in the house a week, I loved her. I do not choose to dwell upon the progress of our affection, for it was mutual. The widow knew nothing of my former intemperance — in fact, I had desisted during my residence with her, from any of my dissolute practices.

Six months passed away. I had obtained employment soon after taking up my abode there, in a factory not far from the house; where, though I was forced to labor, and my remuneration was moderate, because I did not understand the business well at first, I was in a fair train for doing better, and getting

higher wages. The widow grew sick. She was of the same delicate temperament which her daughter inherited from her, and in less than a fortnight from
the commencement of her illness, she left the world for ever.

Poor Mary! I have seldom seen such violent and inconsolable grief as followed the death of her mother. She leaned on me for support, and no doubt,
the deprivation of any other comforter forced her to look to one, who, with
all his faults, had a pure passion for her—as the only resource from utter
friendliness.

As soon as it could with propriety be done, after her mother's death, Mary
and I were married. And a more happy union never took place; for, possessed
of a treasure which no temptation would have induced me to jeopardize, I had
quite reformed, and no longer visited my former haunts; while Mary was the
most industrious, prudent, and affectionate of young wives. My sweet Mary!
ah, even as I write, a tear is almost falling upon the words—for, wicked as I
have been, my heart is not callous enough to be unaffected by remembrance
of that hapless one. My wife was a *good woman*, if ever God made one. She
was not learned or accomplished in the branches that constitute what is called
a fashionable education; but she possessed something a million times better
than all the abstractions of philosophy, or the ornaments acquired at a genteel
boarding-school. She had a gentle, kindly heart; she had good temper; she
had an inherent love of truth, which no temptation could seduce aside, and
which she never failed to put in practice; she had charity, a disposition to look
with an eye of excuse on the faults of her fellow-creatures, and aid them as far
she could in their poverty, and console them in their griefs.

The weeks passed on. We were doing very well for people in our humble
circumstances. Debt was unknown to us, at least to any great degree. We never
purchased until we saw the means of payment, and never promised, unless
we had made such arrangements that we felt pretty sure we could perform. I
say *we*, for though my wife was a meek woman, I never took any step without
consulting over the matter with her: there was no such thing as *my* and *thy*.

But about a year after our marriage, the serpent came into our little Eden!
Ambition—the poison that rankles in the hearts of men, and scorches all
peace, and blight the bloom of content—ambition entered there. What is
called low life, affords, perhaps, as much scope for this intoxicating passion,
as that sphere which called forth the ardor of Napoleon, or which brings into
play the mighty minds of statesmen. And petty as the objects among the poor

may seem, they are striven for as eagerly, and the chase after them is attended with as many doubts, and as many fluctuations and fevers, as mark the gaining of generalships or cabinet offices.

One of the proprietors at the factory where I was employed, owned some vacant lots, in a rather pleasant part of the city, one of which he proposed I should purchase from him. Straightway visions of independence and a home of my own, and the station of a man of property, floated before my eyes. I accepted the offer, and as the terms were very favorable, I for a time found no inconvenience from my new purchase. Not long afterward, I thought I had a good opportunity of hiring money enough to put up a convenient house upon my lot—and I took advantage of the opportunity. As ill-luck, and partly my own ill-judgment, would have it, when the house was about half finished, my means fell out, and I could not go on with the work. We pondered, my wife and I, and we worried, and turned a great many projects in our minds—but none were able to be put in effect. At this stage my creditors grew alarmed, and demanded what was due them. Had it been to save my life, I could not raise the money. They were inexorable—and at one fell swoop all my towering dreams of happiness and a competency were crushed to the dust, by their seizing on my little property, and putting it to a forced sale. The house, unfinished as it was, did not bring one quarter what I had expended upon it. I was half crazed with mortification and disappointment.

Yet—yet we might have been happy. Yet we might have risen, and baffled our evil genius—yet we might have gained our little place back again, in time—and, wiser by experience, kept our wishes within moderate bounds, and journeyed on pleasantly until our appointed number of years had been fulfilled. But the Great Master, in his unfathomable wisdom, allowed it not to be so. For comfort in my sorrows, I frequented my old places of resort, the drinking-shops, and the bar-rooms: I bent beneath the storm, and went back to habits which, until then, my poor Mary had never even suspected as belonging to me.

How well do I remember the first night I returned home, and showed my wife that she had bound her fortunes to a *drunkard!* She had been sitting up for me, for many weary hours, until midnight passed away, and exhausted nature could stand it no longer. She sank her head on the table by her side, and slept. The noise of my shutting the street door awakened her, and she sprang to receive me, and inquire the cause of my absence. Alas! the light she carried in her hand showed her too plainly the bitter reason of that absence—the terrible truth that I was intoxicated! Steeped as my senses were in liquor, I was alarmed at her sudden paleness, and the sickly look which spread over her features. She almost fell to the ground—so agonized were her feelings.

The fatal habit once taken up again, seemed to revive with even more than its former strength and violence. I disregarded my business; and, before long, grew so heedless of my wife's comforts, that I neglected to provide even those matters which are indispensable to subsistence. Where was my former love? Where the old tenderness, and the vow I had made to love and protect? Ah, reader! intemperance destroys even the remembrance of love—and this is one of the most horrible of its consequences. To think that the affection of the early years—the kind and innocent tenderness, which was reciprocated from heart to heart, and which was as a fountain of fond joy—to think all this is given up, merely for a beastly and gross appetite, is painful and fearful indeed!

I sicken as I narrate this part of my story. The recollection comes of the sufferings of my poor wife, and of my unkindness to her. I paid no attention to her comforts, and took no thought for her subsistence. I *think* I never proceeded to any act of violence—but God only knows what words I spoke in my paroxysms of drunken irritation, to that humble, uncomplaining creature. Yes; I remember well, with what agony she has often leaned over my prostrate form, and the hot tears that fell upon my bloated face. I remember the gathering degradation that fixed itself round our name. I remember how my wretched Mary's face grew paler and paler every day—the silent uncomplaining method of her long, long time of dying—for my conduct killed her at last. I remember the scorn and jeers of unfeeling neighbors—the avoidance of me by my old friends—the sinking, grade by grade, until it was at length as though there were no lower depths in which to sink—all are burnt into my mind, Oh, how ineffaceably!

Then came the closing scene of that act of the tragedy. My wife, stricken to the heart, and unable to bear up longer against the accumulating weight of shame and misery, sank into the grave—the innocent victim of another's drunkenness. Oh, that solemn—that terribly solemn hour of her death! Thank God! I was sober at the time—and received her forgiveness. I did not weep as she died, for my throat and the fountains of my eyes, were alike parched and dry. I rushed madly from the house—I knew not and cared not whither. Hell seemed raging in my breast. All my cruelty—all my former love—all my guilt—all my disregard of the sacred ties—seemed concentrated in a thought, and that thought pressing like a mountain of fire all round my heart.

It was night. I walked madly and swiftly through the streets, and though the people stared, I recked not of their notice, but kept my way. What would I have given for power to call back but one little year? One moment only, did I think of drowning my horrible agony in drink; but I cursed the very reflection, as it was formed in my soul. Now, I thought upon Mary's tenderness to me—upon her constant care, and regard, and love; and now, the idea of the repayment I had made her, filled my bosom.

As I wended thus heedlessly on with long strides, I came off against the entrance of a tavern which, in times past, I had frequently visited. In the door, talking with a party of companions, stood a form which, in the imperfect light, I thought I recognized. Another moment, he turned, and his face was shone upon by the gas-lamp; I was right in my conjecture—It was Colby. With a sudden revulsion of feeling, I remembered that it was he who had tempted me, and through whose means all my follies and crimes had been committed. I sprang madly toward the place where he stood.

"Devil!" cried I furiously, seizing him by the throat, "you have brought death to one for whom I would willingly have suffered torments for ever! It is fitting that you pay the penalty with your own base life. Die! villain, even on the spot where you started me upon *my* ruin!'"

I clutched him with a grasp of desperation. Those who stood near, were motionless with amazement and fright—and in two minutes more, I had added *murder* to my other crimes. Happily for both, myself and the one I would have made my victim—as he had made me his—the bystanders recovered their self-possession sufficiently soon to interfere, and prevent the accomplishment of my sanguinary purpose. They dragged me from his neck, and relieved him from the imminent danger of his situation; for as sure as there is a heaven above, I would have killed that man, had I been left to myself three minutes longer.

~~~~~~

CHAPTER X

Dehortations from the use of strong liquors have been the favorite topic of declaimers in all ages, and have been received with abundance of applause by water-drinking critics. But with the patient himself, the man that is to be cured, unfortunately their sound has seldom prevailed. Yet

the evil is acknowledged—the remedy simple. Abstain. No force can
oblige a man to raise the glass to his head against his will. 'Tis as easy
as not to steal—not to tell lies.

—CHARLES LAMB

DURING the days that followed, one thought alone—apart from my engrossing grief and remorse—possessed my mind. It was a desire to leave the city,
where I had come merely to go astray from the path of honor and happiness,
and find relief for my sorrow in a new place, and amid the faces of strangers. It
may easily be supposed, that after what I had described in the last chapter, I felt
no desire to continue in my course of dissipation. Whether my good resolves
held out for any length of time, will be seen in the sequel. I had my household
effects sold, and gathering in several debts that were due me, I found I had
quite a respectable sum of cash. Careless where I should cast my fortune, so
that I got away from New York, I took passage in a steamboat, and journeyed
to a small town some thirty miles distant. Here I staid for a few weeks; but
getting tired at length of its monotony, I started and went inland, continuing
my travel for a day and a night, and stopping then to rest. I was pleased when
I awoke in the morning, with the aspect of the place, and determined to fix
my abode there.

I informed the landlord of the hotel of my intentions, and asked him if
there was any kind of business upon which I could enter—telling him of the
small sum of cash which I had at my disposal. With an appearance of great
friendliness, he told me, that he was himself just entering upon some speculations, which were very safe and profitable, and which required the assistance
of a partner. He told me if I would join with him, I could more than double
my money, and that my labors would be very light. The man spoke fair, and
his projects seemed plausible. So in the evening, over a bottle of wine, in his
own parlor, we sealed our agreement. I found, in truth, that I had but little call
upon my services. My leisure I employed in roaming about the surrounding
country, and in various country sports.

Though I did not drink to anything like my former excess, I was by no
means abstemious. During the afternoon, and frequently when at evening the
place was filled with visitors, I indulged myself with wine, and with those
drinks, originally derived from our thirsty south—drinks that are very pleasant to the taste, but which have led thousands down the path to the lower

stages of intemperance, and at last to ruin. As I did not pay for them, when they were used, (the landlord and myself having accounts together) I felt no thought of the expense.

Among my amusements, I have said, were walks about the place. In one of these an incident occurred, where I was the instrument of performing an action that served as some small offset to the much evil I have ever brought, through my weakness of mind, to those about me. Through the village of my residence passed a railroad, and the cars generally stopped there some ten or fifteen minutes. Not far from the depot was a mill supplied with water from a large pond, along the dam of which, as is usual, were several short sluices, covered with bridges. It was a pleasant place, and the miller, an intelligent countryman, was frequently favored with my visits at his place of labor.

One day, on the arrival of the cars, several of the passengers, being informed that they were to stop a little longer than ordinary, determined to get out, and stroll a few steps for recreation. Among the number was a lady, elegantly dressed, and leading by the hand a little girl, a child of six or seven years. The lady appeared to be very much pleased with the scenery of the pond, and creek; she strolled along the dam, and occasionally stopped to admire some fine prospect, or cull the beautiful pond-flowers which grew upon the banks in great profusion. While she was resting upon one of the narrow bridges I have mentioned, the child scrambled down the banks to pluck a gaudy blossom that had caught her eyes. I was at that moment standing, leaning on the door of the mill, and gazing listlessly at the bustle around the stopping-place of the cars. All of a sudden, there came a loud shriek! The lady was standing upon the dam, the very picture of distraction, and uttering loud and shrill cries for help.

"She will be drowned! For the love of God, come and rescue her!" she cried to me, as, alarmed by her cries, I ran hastily toward the place.

I saw at once what was the matter; the little girl, reaching over after the flower, had lost her balance and fallen into the pond. With promptness, I divested myself of my shoes and coat, and plunged into the pond. Fortunately I was an excellent swimmer. The current was running in from the other side very strongly, and I knew the child must have been carried some distance. I dashed rapidly out, and catching a glimpse of the end of a ribbon, made toward it, and seized the girl, just as she was sinking, probably for the last time. I brought her safely to the shore, and restored her to the arms of her half delirious protector.

Ding-dong! ding-dong! went the bell of the cars, calling the passengers together, and sounding the signal for starting. The lady, carrying the child, hurried toward the depôt, uttering incoherent blessings on my head; and beseeching, if ever I came to New-York, the place of her residence, to call at her house. As she seated herself in the vehicle, she threw me, from the window, a card, with her name, and the street and number of her dwelling, which I placed in my pocket-book. In the very midst of her flood of gratitude, the train rattled away. As I walked slowly toward the public house where I lived, it may be supposed that my reflections were of a quite complacent nature, for the deed of kindness which I had been performing.

In the course of the ensuing weeks, my want of active employment led me to the glass, as my resource from low spirits. Two or three times I was more than half drunk; and it came to be so, at length, that I could not spend the day as I thought comfortably, without drinking five or six times before dinner, and as many more between that and bedtime. What will the reader think of my resolution of mind? I had made a compact with myself, after my poor Mary's death, that I would drink nothing but wine; and though I stuck to that for a while, I soon caught myself indulging in the stronger kinds of liquor. Perhaps, if I had filled up my time with active employment, I might have kept to my resolution, and even in the end totally reformed. But of what mischief is idleness a parent! That time which hung heavy on my hands, I drowned in the forgetfulness of the oblivion-causing cup.

Reader! perhaps you despise me. Perhaps, if I were by you at this moment, I should behold the curled lip of scorn, and the look of deep contempt. Oh, pause stern reverencer of duty, and have pity for a fellow-creature's weakness! I would ask, with the gentle Elia, that thou shouldst mingle compassion and human allowance with thy disapprobation. With him, too, I say, trample not on the ruins of a man. Thou sayest, perhaps — Begin a reformation, and custom will make it easy. But what if the beginning be dreadful? The first steps, not like climbing a mountain, but going through fire? What if the whole system must undergo a change, violent as that which we conceive of the mutation of form in some insects? What if a process comparable to flaying alive, have to be endured? Is the weakness which sinks under such struggles, to be compared with the pertinacity which clings to vice, for itself and its gross appetites?

I have known one (relates the same pleasant moralist I quote above) in that state, when he has tried to abstain but for one evening, though the poisonous potion had long ceased to bring back its first enchantments; though he was sure it would rather deepen his gloom than brighten it, in the violence of the struggle, and the necessity he has felt of getting rid of the present sensation at any rate—I have known him to scream out, to cry aloud, for the anguish and pain of the strife within him. Many, perhaps, on whom liquor never produced powerful results, will here laugh at a weak brother, who, trying his strength and coming off foiled in the contest, would fain persuade them that such agonistic exercises are dangerous. On them my remarks are wasted. It is to a very different description of persons I speak. It is to the weak—the nervous; to those who feel the want of some artificial aid to raise their spirits in society to what is no more than the ordinary pitch of those around them. Such must fly the convivial class in the first instance, if they do not wish to sell themselves, for their term of life, to misery.

A man once, whom I knew well, and whose name was honored over all New-York for his many virtues, was seen by me to take a glass in an obscure drinking-shop. I afterward found that he *had* to drink, or engage in the fearful contest described above. He was of irritable and weak temperament, and though he knew his habits were secretly hurrying him to the grave, he quailed before the agony of the trial. He had commenced it more than once, but was never able to complete his own conquest. Now, though I have an abiding faith in the ability to reform, through the GLORIOUS TEMPERANCE PLEDGE, and the strength which Providence gives to those who honestly set about a good work—yet I know the awful horrors which such men as the one I speak of, must go through. Reader, if you are not one of that sort yourself, you can conceive not of those trials. Not only has habit made liquor necessary to their enjoyment, but to the very action of the vital powers; and at the very time it quickens and brightens their faculties into a dim kind of action, it warns them how it is wafting them onward to the verge of decay with a horrible rapidity!

The pure and virtuous cast scorn upon such as I have been, and as thousands now are. But oh, could they look into the innermost recesses of our hearts, and see what spasms of pain—what impotent attempts to make issue with what appears to be our destiny—what fearful dreams—what ghastly phantoms of worse than hellish imagination—what of all this resides, time and again, in our miserable bosoms—then, I know, that scorn would be changed to pity. It is not well to condemn men for their frailties. Let us rather own our common bond of weakness, and endeavor to fortify each other in good conduct and in true righteousness, which is charity for the errors of our kind. The drunkard, low as he is, is a *man*. The fine capacities, the noble marks which belong to our race, those glorious qualities which the Great Builder stamped upon his masterpiece of works, are with him still. They are not destroyed, but hidden in darkness, as precious gems cast down in the mire. And the object of the truly wise and good will be, to raise him up again; to reform and brighten those capacities, and to set in operation a train of causes, which will afford him a chance of attaining once more a respectable station in society. Once *thoroughly regenerated*, the remembrance of his old defamation will stand before his eyes like a pillar of fire, and warn him back from any further indulgence in his vicious courses.

I am the more particular in my remarks upon this matter, because I have seen so many cases of hopeless and confirmed intemperance, made thus by the injudicious severity of the neighbors and relatives of the unhappy victim. Little aware of the strength of the chains which bind him, and the horrors which surround a man in those moments when he is without that stimulus which custom has rendered necessary to him, they cast every slight upon the drunkard, and are unguarded in their expressions of anger and contempt. A little moderation perhaps, a little friendliness and sympathy, bestowed at the proper moment, would work a complete revolution in his character. But it is not bestowed, and the wretched one goes on from bad to worse, until there is no hope left. I remember a case in point.

While living with my uncle in the country, one of our most esteemed neighbors was a young farmer, lately married, and come with his wife to settle in the town. He had bought a fine little farm, and occasionally when work was pressing, he employed me to assist him, my uncle consenting. During the time I spent in that way, I became acquainted with the circumstances I am going to relate. The name of our neighbor was Fanning.

As was customary in those parts, in the hot days when we were getting in the harvest of hay, and the early grain, a couple of jugs of ardent spirits were brought into the field for the use of the work-people. It has since been a wonder to me that all of the villagers were so tacitly agreed as to the benefit of this custom. Now, medical men, and not only medical men, but all men of common sense know that intoxicating drinks are highly detrimental to the strength, and improper for use during laborious employment. They sap the very essence of energy, and prostrate the arm of the strong man. A feverish impulse may be given for a moment; but it reacts in a tenfold deficiency of power for twenty times as long a time. Be that as true as it undoubtedly is, however, among Fanning and his fellow-townsmen it was the common custom.

Fanning had a brother, a middle-aged, gentlemanly man, who possessed a small estate, invested in stocks, from whence he drew a moderate stipend. A portion of the year he was employed in a village near by as school teacher.

I knew the man, and loved him well. He was a quiet, good natured person, and wherever he went, he made friends. I recollect his looks, too, and some little peculiarities he had. He was small in figure, with bright black eyes and very long fine glossy hair, which used to fall quite down upon his shoulders. Notwithstanding the modest disposition of 'the little teacher,' as the people used to call him, his laugh and his voice was loud among the loudest, at the merry-makings in the neighborhood, which he invariably attended. He wore a round jacket always, which was one of his peculiarities. His size and his juvenile method of apparel, made him look like anything but a pedagogue.

The teacher, when he was not employed in his profession, would frequently aid his brother, in the work of the farm. He used to come into the field, in hay time, and give his assistance there. We always welcomed him, for his pleasant mirth cast a charm on all around.

"Mr. Fanning," said one of the men, one day, "if you work with us, you should do as we do. The jug has passed round, and every person drinks but yourself."

"Is it needful, then," said the teacher, laughing, "that I partake of the liquor, in order to be on even-footing with the rest?"

"Of course," was the general rejoinder; "of course."

"Well, then," said Fanning, "here goes."

And he took down a moderate draught.

The whole conversation was intended as a mere joke, of course — such light talk as work-people amuse themselves with during the intermission between their morning and afternoon labors. But it proved in the end, a fatal joke to the poor teacher.

The next day, the same bantering was passed, and Fanning drank again. It is hardly necessary that I should narrate the particulars, of the method by which he became a lover of the liquid that at first he regarded with such apathy. It was all, however, plainly to be traced to the accidental invitation given him in the harvest-field. Before the end of the summer, he could drink his two or three glasses with great satisfaction, and even became an habitual visitor at the bar-room.

I have noted down thus minutely the incident which led to the teacher's intemperance, because I think it by no means an isolated case. There are many, no doubt, who will get this book, who may be the witnesses, and even practisers, of a habit of having liquor in the fields during the hot farm-work of the summer. For this lamentable habit, contrary as it is to the dictates of prudence and common sense, is not an altogether exploded one.

The teacher, as I have said, grew to the desire for drink. He conducted his school that winter, as usual, though before the end of the session, he had more than one fit of intoxication.

Summer came again. The pernicious jugs were brought into the field, and the elder Fanning was their best customer. Hardly a week passed without his being completely steeped two or three times in drunkenness. I have myself seen him lying beside the hay-cocks, divested of sense and rationality, more like a brute than a human being. He had always been attached to me, and would frequently obey my persuasions to go home, or to desist from any further indulgence in liquor, when, to any one else, he was abusive and obstinate.

"Frank!" said he to me one day, when he was just sobered from a spree, "I am a very wicked and foolish man—if things go on in this way, what is to become of me?"

I made no answer, though I was highly pleased at hearing him talk thus.

"Yes," he continued, "it certainly will not do. I cannot—I *will not* allow myself to become a common drunkard. The thought is horrible!"

A good resolution, once formed, may be broken, it is true; but the very process of reflection which leads to the forming of the resolution, is favorable to improvement. If brought back often to such reflections, it is twenty to one but the improvement will be effectual at last.

We had been sitting together, the teacher and I, in his apartment, as he made the remarks I have quoted above. We rose and went down to the common sitting-room, where Mrs. Fanning was engaged in some domestic employments.

"Is my brother home?" asked the teacher.

The woman made no reply, and Fanning repeated the question.

"If he is," was the answer, with a sneer, "it's not likely he cares about seeing a drunken sot!"

The teacher said nothing, but sat down upon a chair near the window. Soon after the farmer came in, but took no notice of the now sobered inebriate. He brushed through the room with a haughty glance, as much as to say, I feel no wish to be familiar with such as thou.

I was standing in the door, just about to depart, and my feelings could not help sympathizing with my poor friend, thus scorned by those who were nearest and dearest to him. True, he had acted wrongly, but they need not have thus wounded him in so unprovoked a manner. He rose from his chair, and we walked forth together. I could see that he felt very much agitated. As I diverged from the road to go my own way, I prayed Heaven to continue in his soul the sentiments he had a few moments before expressed to me.

Without doubt, had he not been treated thus scornfully by his brother and sister-in-law, the reflections of the teacher would have led to his becoming a temperate man. But in his lonesomeness and weariness of heart, he retreated to the bar-room. He drank deeply, and that night saw him in a more severe intoxication than ever before. Provoked very much at his conduct, the farmer and his young wife would hardly use him with ordinary decency. It was only the odium of having him taken up as a common vagrant, that prevented their turning him entirely out of doors.

"Oh!" he has many a time said to me, "if there were only some little fastening of good-will among my family, where I could cast anchor, I feel assured I might be saved yet. But I am maddened by the coldness and contempt of my brother and his wife, when I am in a fit state to feel it. It is more poignant than even the pangs which are a result of my drinking!"

Twenty times, in his lucid intervals, did he express this opinion to me. I have no doubt it came from his very heart.

And now, all his friends dropped off from him. He was considered by them, I suppose, as a disgrace to their name. They would cross the street to avoid meeting him; they would forbid his entrance to their houses; and every contumely was heaped upon him. Of course, he could obtain his old employment of teacher no more; and the children, who formerly loved and respected him, now looked upon him with disgust. This, he told me, was one of the bitterest of his punishments.

I solemnly believe that even yet, degraded as he was, he might have been reformed, by his friends seizing a lucky moment, and by their treating him as a fellow-creature, instead of a beast. But they did not so. His frailties were visited by their virulence; and they forgot entirely that common bond of fellowship, which, as we all sin more or less, should have caused them to be lenient. Which of those friends or relatives can say — I have, on my conscience, none of the responsibility of that man's intemperance and death?

The teacher was of naturally delicate constitution, and he could not long hold up under the results of his conduct. Each successive indulgence left him a weaker and a weaker man.

Three years had not passed away, after his taking that draught from the jug in the harvest-field, before he was upon his dying bed — the dying bed of a drunkard. With his last breath he proclaimed that his wretched fate might have been prevented, had not the thoughts of reformation, whenever they arose in his mind, been stifled by the proud and contemptuous treatment he received from his relatives and friends.

<hr />

CHAPTER XI

Whene'er thou meet'st a human form
Less favor'd than thine own,
Remember, 'tis thy neighbor worm,
Thy brother, or thy son.

—ANONYMOUS

WHEN I had been some five months in this village, I thought one morning that it would not be amiss for me to have a settlement with the landlord. Since the time I had confided my funds to him, I had heard very little of our joint speculations; and I supposed I might have quite a handsome amount of cash due me by this time.

Upon my mentioning the subject, he assented at once — stating that he had for a day or two intended suggesting the same thing to me. We therefore went into his little private parlor, and he drew out his books, and commenced reckoning. What was my amazement when he informed me, that the amount due *from me to him* was not quite one hundred dollars! I supposed at first he was in a vein of pleasantry, and laughed at him. But he gravely pushed his accounts over to me, and told me to look for myself. Considerably alarmed, I did so, I saw that one single item, that of *liquor* alone, was summed up to more than the sum I had originally put in his hands, for purposes of profit. I indignantly asked him, if he thought I was going to submit to such flagrant injustice. With an impudent coolness, he retorted, that if I chose to attempt redress, I might begin as soon as I thought fit. Had he not been liberal, he said, his demand against me would have stood much higher.

The man was a rascal—that was evident. But whether I had any chance of recovering back my money was not quite so clear. Upon consulting with a man of law, in the course of the day, I found that my prospect was gloomy indeed. I have since thought, that the landlord himself gave the lawyer his cue. Quite mad with resentment and agitation, when I returned to the house, I told the landlord plainly my opinion of his conduct. He retorted. My temper rose, and I struck him to the earth. I rushed from the house, swearing that I would not stay in so vile a place another night.

I had a small sum of money, and I immediately engaged passage to New York. In an hour I was on my way thither. The reflections that filled my mind, were anything but agreeable. To be swindled—to be the dupe of a villain, and one too whom I had looked on as a friend—was bad enough. Besides which, I could not but be conscious how much I was to blame for my own carelessness, and my want of sobriety, which, after all, was the foundation of the ill-luck.

The latter part of my journey was by steamboat. As the light of day dawned in the east, our craft swung alongside the wharf; and I went on shore in the city, where, four years previous, I had come an innocent and honest country youth. My unsophisticated habits had worn away, but at the expense of how much of the pure gold, which was bartered for dross!

Of course, I had no plan marked out as to any method of life, or any means to get a living. As I walked along the street, but a few rods from the landing-place, my eyes were caught by the sight of tempting bottles of liquor, arranged on a bar. What busy devil was it that tempted me then to go in and drink? Yielding to the fatal impulse, I entered and called for liquor. The ice was broken now, and I felt no more repugnance. There were some jovial-looking fellows there, and I entered into conversation with them. A little while, and we all drank again.

From that moment, I have an indistinct recollection of going through scenes which it makes my stomach now turn, to think upon—drunkenness, and the very lowest and filthiest kind of debauchery. Probably, for I never knew for certain, I spent five days upon that spree. Not at any single time was I sober, or near sober.

At last I awoke. It was a little before sunrise. I lay upon the ground, on a pier jutting out into the river. By one side of me was a high pile of wood—on the other side I heard the dashing of water against the wharf. The air, though chill, was fresh and fragrant; but the torments of the damned seemed raging in my head. Oh, that agony of pain; that thirstiness; that searing, burning dryness; that indescribable feeling of horror; that detestable nausea—never shall I forget!

I raised myself on my hands and knees, and my first thought was to throw myself over into the river, and thus put an end to my miserable existence. But, wicked as I was, I dared not rush thus blindly into the presence of an offended God. I lifted myself, and sat on the heavy piece of timber that formed the edge of the wharf.

What a miserable object! The thing I wore upon my head was crushed out of all shape of a hat; my trowsers were torn and soiled; I had no coat, and but one shoe. My face, I felt, was all dirty and brown, and my eyes bleared and swollen. What use, had I for life? While, at the moment, I feared to die. And as it seemed that even now I felt the icy finger at my heart—I prayed to God that he would not crush the wounded worm.

I arose, and walked forth.

The hours rolled on. The streets filled with clatter and with busy faces; and wherever I passed along, the crowd shrunk from me as from the pestilence.

I remember that about noon, I came out into Chatham Square. On one side were little hills of furniture of every description and quality. Many people were scanning them, apparently with the intent to become purchasers. There were also auctioneers, mounted upon tables, or barrels, and crying the goods and the prices that were bid for them. Toward the middle of the Square stood a row of coaches, and several carts, for hire. On the walks, and through the streets, hundreds of men, women, and children were constantly passing, crowd upon crowd. I stood awhile, and looked upon the scene, though vacantly.

Then I sauntered on again. All around was the deafening noise of people engaged in their thousand employments. I gazed curiously at the shops, which exhibited their merchandise in large handsome windows, many of them having a few of their best articles hung out in front, so that the passer by could not but see them. After awhile, I turned and went up a cross street. So on I wended, and across, and up and down, like a rudderless boat.

Dragging thus about, four or five hours passed away, and I began to grow foot-sore and very hungry.

Signs now appeared of the coming on of night. Lamplighters hurried past me with their ladders; the windows, one after another, began to touch up their gas; and those of the mechanics whose business was earliest through, were to be seen in groups, walking along homeward. As I came out from a narrow street, through which I had been wandering some time, I found myself in the same open place, where at noon I had seen such busy traffic. What could I do? I cast my eyes hopelessly about, and saw no sign of sunshine. I felt quite faint from want of food.

There seemed to be no better plan than to walk down the wide handsome street, leading to the east from where I stood, and knock at every house, stating my destitute situation, and asking for the remnants of a meal, and shelter or the means of shelter, until I should obtain relief. Beggary! It was a bitter pill, but I saw no medium between it and starvation; and at the best, the chances were ten to one that I should not gain what I sought.

I walked along the street. It was lined on each side with lofty brick houses. There was no flash of shop windows, and much less noise, and fewer passengers than in the thoroughfares I had hitherto seen.

As I wearily trod the flag-stones, my eyes would now and then be caught by the front rooms of the basements, some of them with family groups circling round the cheerful fire, some with the table spread for supper, and with many luxuries and comforts to tempt the appetite. Oh, how my mouth watered! Here and there I beheld through the curtains little children, all fresh and neat, and curled, frolicking about in play.

It was a long time before I could screw my courage to make application at the doors. At last I went up the stoop of one of the houses, and knocked softly with my fist. I waited several minutes, and then knocked again; no one came to open for me, and I was about retreating in despair.

"Pull the bell, my man," said a person passing, who noticed my conduct, "they'll never hear your knock."

So I applied my hand to the knob, and drew it just enough to make a slight tinkle. In a few minutes, a black man came, and swinging the door on its hinges, beheld me standing there, abashed and trembling.

"Well, what is it?" said he, after waiting a moment, and hearing me say nothing.

I began my request, but had not spoken more than four or five words, before the menial slammed the door in my face with an execration. Starting like a guilty creature, I hastily rushed down upon the walk again.

I passed several blocks before making another attempt. This time I applied at the lower entrance. A woman appeared to answer the summons.

"Come in," she answered compassionately, "wait a bit, and I'll speak to the mistress."

She went in through a side door, and I could hear talking in the apartment. After a short time the door partly opened.

"No," said some one within, "imposters are so common, and you only encourage them in idleness. Tell him to go; and be careful of the bolt, when he passes out."

The woman came from the room, and her face told the cheerless answer, she was commissioned to bear, without the necessity for words. The next minute I was in the dark street once more.

A third and fourth trial were as fruitless as the first.

At the next, the servant told me to wait awhile, as the family were at their devotions. I stood, and gazed at the circle in the inner apartment; for the door was open, and I could see all. An elderly gentleman was reading a portion of Scripture, and the rest were listening with sedate attention to all that came from his lips.

"*Inasmuch*," I heard him say, in a slow emphatic voice, his eyes fixed reverently on the book before him; "*Inasmuch as ye have refused it to the least of these my brethren, ye have refused it to me*."

More he read of the same purport—and then closed the book and knelt, the rest following his example.

For fifteen minutes, nothing was heard there but the accents of fervent prayer. Then all arose, and after a decorous pause, the servant introduced my case. He was sufficiently bred to his station, to refrain from urging my claims in any other way than a statement of my destitute condition; yet I could not have had a more favorable advocate. When he finished,

"Richard," said the elderly gentleman, "give the poor fellow this."

The servant took the gift, and put it in my hand. It was *one cent*.

And Richard hurried me out of the light; for he felt his face suffused with a blush. And as I was leaving the door, he unclasped my finger and placed there a silver coin, just twenty-five times the value of what his master had bestowed upon me.

For my life I could not have subjected myself to any more rebuffs. I remembered a low groggery, where cheap lodgings were to let, and turned my wretched steps toward the place.

<center>~~~~~~</center>

CHAPTER XII

What brings vice and guilt below?
Strong drink brings!
—TEMPERANCE SONG

MONTHS swept onward in their silent course. I know not how I lived; I have never been able, to this day, to account for the method of my subsistence—but yet I did live. Sometimes, finding a chance shelter in a half finished building, left open by the work men—sometimes, sleeping in the purlieus of the markets, or on the docks—sometimes, going for two days with hardly a morsel of food, for I was a drunkard still; and though necessity at times made me sober for awhile, I always managed to get liquor by one means or another, at last. Can it be believed that, at the very moment the eyes of the reader are scanning these pages, there are hundreds—ay thousands—roaming about the by-places of this mighty city, in the same condition, and with the same appetite, which I have described as mine during those fearful months? It seems now, as I look back to it, like a dream—a hideous phantom of a diseased mind. But there came a sudden shock after a time, and I was aroused from that mockery of a dream. Thus it came.

It was the midnight of a Sabbath in winter. Darkness spread over the great city, and the slumbering dwellers therein. The streets, the mighty veins along which currents had coursed all day, were now still and deserted. Every hour the booming of the public clocks pealed out, each stroke falling distinctly and solemnly through the frosty night air. Over head, the stars did not shine. It had been snowing, and the wind occasionally blew the drifts so as to make a perfect tempest of fine ice, dashing into the face of the late traveller. The drowsy watchman sought some sheltered nook, and drew himself close together, shivering with the rigor of the night.

Starting at one of the eastern wharves, is a street running up from the river—a narrow, dirty street, with many wooden houses, occupied as taverns for seamen and abiding places for degraded women. At one of these taverns, myself, and a party of ill-favored, gallows-looking fellows, were arranging our persons, preparatory to sallying forth in the streets. What object could we have in view, at that late hour of the night, but wickedness?

There were four of us. The leader of our gang, who was addressed by the name of Picaroon, had several weapons about his person that were evidently capable of doing dangerous work.

"Come lads," said he, "the business we are on, will be none the worse for a few glasses. Let us drink."

At the word, we helped ourselves, and tossed the liquor down our throats.

We made our egress from the place, and sticking our hands in the capacious pockets of our coats, we walked rapidly after the Picaroon, who strode ahead, as if he knew at once the road to be taken.

The wind whistled, and the fitful blasts, laden with the drift-snow, assailed our progress, and dashed in our faces as we walked along. But our leader turned neither to the right or left, and hardly deigned to bend his head to the heaviest demonstration of the tempest.

After awhile we reached a section of the city, mostly occupied by merchants for their warehouses and stores. The Picaroon now proceeded more cautiously, and turning up Wall-street, led us to a place, not far distant from the Exchange, where we stopped—partly to take breath, and partly to reconnoitre. The night was so dark, that a man at a rod's distance could not have been seen. So we listened awhile, to hear if any of the guardians of the hour were stirring.

"I believe," said the Picaroon, in a low tone, "that we are on the right track. This, I think, is the place we seek."

And he pointed to a basement immediately in front of us, which from its appearance, and the sign over the door, looked like a broker's office.

"Now boys," continued our conductor, in the same cautious voice, "let us begin. Banks, where is the key I gave you in charge?"

The person he addressed handed it to him in silence.

"Curses!" exclaimed the Picaroon, vainly trying to put it to successful use, "the thing has failed, after all. I more than suspected it would. The next time, I'll take the duplicate myself."

"Then we'll burst open the door," said one of our party.

"Of course," the Picaroon rejoined, "we have nothing else to do. Here Evans, hold this lantern!"

And coming up at his orders, I took the light, which was shaded on all sides but one, and held it as he directed.

They proceeded to their work of crime. *They?* Why should I not say *we?* For though a passive agent in the affair, I stood by with apathetic consent, and aided in it. Sunk, sunk at last, to be the companion and abettor of thieves!

"D—n the door! how firm it is!" said Banks, as his cautious blows with a sort of crow-bar, produced no effect. The Picaroon had previously used two or three saws, and was now at work with a chisel.

Our other companion was assisting actively, also, and I stood, and threw the rays from the lantern as they desired.

Crash! crash! went the instruments of our burglary, with a deadened sound, for we knew there were private watchmen in this part of the city—and though we feared little from their vigilance such a night as that, we thought our blows, if too loud, might reach their ears, and bring on a discovery.

Yielding, at last, to saw-teeth, chisel-edge, and crow-bar, the fastenings gave way. One stout thump with the latter instrument, and our entrance was clear. But it was louder than any of the preceding ones.

"Hell!" uttered the Picaroon, furiously, "I would rather have worked two hours longer than heard that blow! But it is too late now; so, Banks, come in with me, and you two keep watch here!"

He had hardly stepped out of sight, when a watchman's rattle rang on the curb-stone, not a hundred feet from where we stood. The Picaroon and his companions heard it too, and dashing from the door, threw the lantern on the ground, and fled along the street.

"Quick! quick! for your lives!" cried the Picaroon to us as he passed. "Both of you, run for your lives!"

My companion took advantages of the timely warning; but the watch were now upon our steps. I heard them close behind me, and stumbling in the darkness, fell upon the ground. They seized me, and carried me away a prisoner. The whole occurrence passed over like a whirlwind. Neither of my three companions were taken.

Was I not sunk low indeed? The very stupor, the deadened nature of my faculties—even when not under the influence of liquor which my course of

life had superinduced—was not sufficient to hide from me the horrible feature of my situation. A criminal, one who had violated the laws, and was justly
obnoxious to their severest punishments—where could I look for a friend, or
whence hope for favor?

It were a stale homily, were I to stay here, and remark upon the easy road
from intemperance to crime. Those who have investigated those matters, tell
us, however, that five out of every six of the cases which our criminal courts
have brought before them for adjudication, are to be traced directly or indi-
rectly to that fearful habit. I have sometimes thought, that the laws ought not to
punish those actions of evil which are committed when the senses are steeped
in intoxication. But if such a principle were allowed to influence judicial deci-
sions, how terrible an opening there would be! How great a temptation, even,
to the letting loose of the worst passions! An idiot is not responsible for his
actions, to be sure; but the drunkard deliberately brings his idiocy upon himself, and must not take shelter under it from the consequences thereof. And
yet, that mercy and charity which should ever be present in our minds, must
lead us to throw the mantle of excuse, as far as possible, over the bad done
by the intemperate. None know—none can know, but they who have felt it—
the burning, withering thirst for drink, which habit forms in the appetite of
the wretched victim of intoxication.

〜〜〜〜〜

CHAPTER XIII

Be free! not chiefly from the iron chain,
But from the one which passion forges, be
The master of thyself!

—MRS. EMBURY

WHEN I was turning over in my mind, the second day of my confinement
in prison, the method I had best pursue, under all my present difficulties,
the darkest and fearfullest despondency fell upon me. It seemed like a cloud
stretching all around and over me, and hiding every glimpse of the cheerful
light. The thought of my boyhood in the country—of a hundred different
scenes in the happy life I had spent there—came to my remembrance. Then
my journey to New York, and my companions of the market-waggon. The antiquary, Lee, my benefactor, to whom I had made so poor a return, and Colby,

the instrument of my disgrace. I pondered upon all, and even the minutest incidents of that journey. Lee! Should I not apply to him in my tribulation? But no; I had injured him deeply, and my pride revolted at the idea of his knowing my present situation. And as for Colby, since the death of my poor wife, and our rencontre at the tavern, I would as soon have taken a serpent in my hand as received a favor from him.

The despondency I have mentioned, clung to me for days. I, a young man, on whom fortune had more than once smiled, whose very start of life in the city was signalized by a stroke of good luck, that might have led me on to a competence and happiness; and here I was, imprisoned for a heinous crime. More than once the fiendish resolve entered my mind, of foul self-murder! But ever the image of my sainted Mary came to me in those prison walls, and looked down, and smiled pleasantly; and I could not renounce all hope of ever seeing her again, by sealing up the sum of my wickedness beyond all power of pardon.

The time approached for my trial. So callous was I, and so resigned to my fate, that I cared little whether it went well or ill for me.

A day or two before I was to be brought up in court, one of the officers of the prison entered, stating that a gentleman without desired to see me; and he had hardly spoken the words, when the person in question was ushered into my cell. He was a middle-aged man, and what he could wish with me I could not conceive.

"Is your name Franklin Evans?" said he.

I answered in the affirmative.

"Do you know that card?"

And he handed me a dirty piece of pasteboard, with a name written upon it. The name was "*Lucy Marchion* — Bleecker-street."

Surprised at the question, and utterly unconscious of what the man's conduct could mean, I made no answer, but stared at him in surprise.

"Listen," continued he. "The lady, whose name you hold in your hand, was many months since at a distant place in the country, with a dear child. Accidentally the child fell into a dangerous stream of water, and would have been drowned, but for the kindness of a brave young stranger, who rescued it, and restored it to the lady. She was hurried away, almost on the instant, leaving in that stranger's hand, her name and residence. By some mark upon the card, the whole circumstance was brought to her mind this very morning, when a police officer called, and handed it to us, making inquiries, which it is unnecessary here to repeat."

The man ceased; and I knew the whole affair intuitively. In a preceding chapter I have mentioned the incident, where I preserved the little girl's life. The card I had placed in my pocket-book, never thinking of it since. Upon the morning after my arrest, my person had been searched, and everything taken from me — the authorities thinking, that perhaps some clue might be gained to my accomplices. The card, they fancied, could possibly afford some such clue. They went to the address upon it. Mr. Marchion, the husband of the lady, and father of the little girl I had preserved, was a lawyer, well known for his talent and respectability; and, at the solicitation of his wife, he immediately started upon a mission of benevolence to the prison where I was.

"Tell me, young man," said he, when all this was fairly understood between us, and he knew that he had indeed found the person for whom his wife had never ceased to pray down blessings — "tell me the whole story of your crime, for which you are now in durance. Keep back nothing; and I will see what can be done for you."

"Is there any prospect," inquired I, anxiously, "for acquittal, think you?"

"That question I can best answer," said he, "after your story is told."

I knew that I could place implicit reliance upon his honor, and I related the whole incidents of my folly and my crime. I told him, that for weeks my faculties had been drowned amid a sea of intemperance. I said that when I started off with the Picaroon and the others, I knew not where they were going, or for what purpose; and that, though I stood by, I had no hand in the active commission of the burglary. My defence, I could not help seeing myself, was a very weak one; but it was the best I had to offer, and the love of liberty was strong within me.

"Perhaps it would be wiser," said Mr. Marchion, when I concluded, "for me to express no opinion now; and yet I would advise you not to give up hope. The judge, whom I know well, is one that will not be apt to look upon your conduct, placed in the light you have given to it by the narrative just closed, with a too rigorous eye; and I feel assured that what you have spoken is the truth."

And as he departed, I felt new cheerfulness spring up in my breast. So pleasant is it, in time of dismay, to have one good heart, on whose friendly aid you can rest your troubles.

Before the trial, Mr. Marchion came to me two or three times again, to get the locality of the tavern whence we had started, on the night of the burglary. He also took from me the names of two or three persons, whom I had known in my better days, for witnesses that I had once borne a fair reputation. I felt some doubt, as I gave him that of Mr. Lee, among others, whether the character my old friend might give me, would prove to my advantage or no.

The crisis came at last. The prosecuting attorney proved by the officers the fact of the crime, beyond the possibility of cavil. The officers swore, also, that according to all appearance, I was one of the robbers. They had arrested me on the spot, in a vain endeavor to fly.

Mr. Marchion himself conducted my defence. He skillfully enlarged on the danger of circumstantial evidence—produced his witnesses to my former good name and honorable conduct—and then expatiated on the unhappy method of my having fallen into habits of intemperance. The keeper of the low tavern proved my evident ignorance, when the Picaroon led me away, of the business on which he was bound: and with all the dexterity for which his profession is celebrated, my fervent advocate dressed up what good points there were in my case, and closed by a pathetic appeal jointly to the jury and the court.

All was of no avail. The jury, after being out an hour or two, came in with a verdict of "*Guilty.*" I could hardly support myself under the sickening sensation which followed the utterance of that word. My head swam, my ears tingled, and I heard not the foreman continue, "and recommended to the mercy of the court." Had I done so, I should hardly have hoped for any leniency—so sure had I been, after Mr. Marchion's eloquent appeal, that I must be acquitted.

The judge consulted with those on each side of him for a few minutes, and then rose to pronounce sentence. I could hardly believe my ears, when they conveyed to me, as he went on, the intelligence that I was *not* to be sent back to prison. Amazed and overjoyed, I noted but little of the details of his discourse: how that in view of the peculiar nature of my case, sentence was to be suspended, and I discharged—or something of that sort. I only heard the word *discharged*, and could hardly remain in the box until he finished his speech. Then, as the officer in attendance came to me, and took me by the hand, and told me I was free, I rushed aside, and caught Mr. Marchion's arm, which I dampened with my tears. *Free! Yes*, after all—after being on the very verge of punishment for felony—to come off thus! Was it not, indeed, a fit cause for rejoicing?

~~~~~~

CHAPTER XIV

Kneel! and the vow thou breathest there
At that lone hour shall float on high;
Spirits of light shall bless thy prayer
The dead, the crowned, shall greet thy sigh.
—MRS. HALE'S MAGAZINE

THE kindness of Marchion and his wife did not pause, merely at saving me from an ignominious fate. I pass over the gratitude of the lady at our first meeting, the very next hour after I was liberated from bondage—simply stating, that it was fully such as a mother might be supposed to offer one who had saved her offspring from sudden and painful death.

"All that we could do," said the lady, "would not pay you, generous man, for the service you have rendered me."

And she called the little girl to her side, and bade her thank the preserver of her life. Marchion stood by, and looked on with a friendly smile.

But stop—thought I to myself, my eyes being caught by the sight of my own soiled and tattered garments—am I a fit person for the company of well-dressed and cleanly people? What excuse should I make? But Marchion already knew a large part of my history, and of my former follies; and some good spirit seemed whispering to me, no excuse but the truth. So in answer to their inquiries, I told them my whole life, without any alteration or concealment.

"Young man," said the lady, when I ended, "had you related all this to us some months ago, we should have shrunk from you, or set you down as a liar. But my observation, of late, has led both my husband and myself to the knowledge of cases, exceeding even yours in wonder and in depth of misery."

She then told me that her husband, who had in his younger days been an intemperate man, was now a member of one of the societies of the city, whose object was to aid the holy cause of Abstinence; and that at the meetings of those societies, which she occasionally attended, she had heard in the "experience," of those who addressed them, tales of wo that might harrow up a soul with sympathy.

As we sat that evening around the cheerful blaze of the parlor fire, our conversation turned upon the same topics that we had discoursed of in the morning. Mr. Marchion expressed his wonder at the strange and almost miraculous manner in which some persons, who appeared in the very deepest depth of the mire, would become reformed. A little trivial incident—an ordinary occurrence which seemed not worth the importance of a thought—would sometimes change the whole current of their wicked conduct, and present them to the world, regenerated, and disenthralled. One instance, he said, had come to his knowledge in former times, which, if I felt disposed to hear it, he would relate.

I expressed my pleasure at the suggestion, and he commenced his narrative:

"Lift up!" was ejaculated as a signal—and click! went the glasses in the hands of a party of tipsy men, drinking one night at the bar of one of the middling order of taverns. And many a wild gibe was uttered, and many a terrible blasphemy, and many an impure phrase sounded out the pollution of the hearts of those half-crazed creatures, as they tossed down their liquor, and made the walls echo with their uproar. The first and foremost in recklessness was a girlish-faced, fair-haired fellow of twenty-two or three years. They called him Mike. He seemed to be looked upon by the others as a sort of prompter, from whom they were to take cue. And if the brazen wickedness evinced by him in a hundred freaks and remarks to his companions, during their stay in that place, were any test of his capacity—there might hardly be one more fit to go forward as a guide on the road to destruction.

From the conversation of the party, it appeared that they had been spending the earlier part of the evening in a gambling house. The incidents spoken of as having occurred, and the conduct of young Mike and his associates there, are not sufficiently tempting to be narrated.

A second, third and fourth time were the glasses filled, and the effect thereof began to be perceived in a still higher degree of noise and loquacity among the revellers. One of the serving-men came in at this moment, and whispered the bar-keeper, who went out, and in a moment returned again.

"A person," he said, "wished to speak with Mr. Michael. He waited on the walk in front."

The individual whose name was mentioned, made his excuses to the

others, telling them he would be back in a moment, and left the room. He had
hardly shut the door behind him, and stepped into the open air, when he saw
one of his brothers—his elder by eight or ten years—pacing to and fro with
rapid and uneven steps. As the man turned in his walk, and the glare of the
street lamp fell upon his face; the youth, half-benumbed as his senses were,
was somewhat startled at its paleness and evident perturbation.

"Come with me!" said the elder brother, hurriedly, "the illness of our little
Jane is worse, and I have been sent for you."

"Poh!" answered the young drunkard, very composedly, "is that all? I shall
be home by-and-by."

And he turned to go back again.

"But brother, she is worse than ever before. Perhaps when you arrive she
may be *dead*."

The tipsy one paused in his retreat, perhaps alarmed at the utterance of
that dread word, which seldom fails to shoot a chill to the hearts of mortals.
But he soon calmed himself, and waving his hand to the other:

"Why, see," said he, "a score of times at least, have I been called away to
the last sickness of our good little sister; and each time, it proves to be nothing
worse than some whim of the nurse or the physician. Three years has the girl
been able to live very heartily under her disease; and I'll be bound she'll stay
on earth three years longer."

And as he concluded this wicked and most brutal reply, the speaker opened
the door and went into the bar-room. But in his intoxication, during the hour
that followed, Mike was far from being at ease. At the end of that hour, the
words "perhaps when you arrive she may be *dead*," were not effaced from his
hearing yet, and he started for home. The elder brother had wended his way
back in sorrow.

Let me go before the younger one, awhile, to a room in that home. A little
girl lay there dying. She was quite rational. She had been ill a long time; so it
was no sudden thing for her parents, and her brethren and sisters, to be called
for the solemn witness of the death agony.

The girl was not what might be called beautiful. And yet, there is a solemn
kind of loveliness that always surrounds a sick child. The sympathy for the
weak and helpless sufferer, perhaps, increase it in our ideas. The ashiness,
and the moisture on the brow, and the film over the eye-balls—what man can
look upon the sight, and not feel his heart awed within him? Children, I have

sometimes fancied too, increase in beauty as their illness deepens. The angels, it may be, are already vesting them with the garments they shall wear in the Pleasant Land.

Beside the nearest relatives of little Jane, standing round her bedside, was the family doctor. He had just laid her wrist down upon the coverlid, and the look he gave the mother, was a look in which there was no hope.

"My child!" she cried, in uncontrollable agony, "my child! you die!"

And the father, and the sons and daughters, were bowed down in grief, and thick tears rippled between the fingers held before their eyes.

Then there was silence awhile. During the hour just by-gone, Jane had, in her childish way, bestowed a little gift upon each of her kindred, as a remembrancer when she should be dead and buried in the grave. And there was one of these simple tokens which had not reached its destination. She held it in her hand now. It was a very small, much-thumbed book—a religious story for infants, given her by her mother when she had first learned to read.

While they were all keeping this solemn stillness—broken only by the suppressed sobs of those who stood and watched for the passing away of the girl's soul—a confusion of some one entering rudely and speaking in a turbulent voice, was heard in the adjoining apartment. Again the voice roughly sounded out; it was the voice of the drunkard Mike, and the father bade one of his sons go and quiet the intruder.

"If nought else will do," said he sternly, "put him forth by strength. We want no tipsy brawlers here, to disturb such a scene as this!"

For what moved the sick girl thus uneasily on her pillow, and raised her neck, and motioned to her mother? She would that Mike should be brought to her side. And it was enjoined on him whom the father had bade to eject the noisy one, that he should tell Mike his sister's request, and beg him to come to her.

He came. The inebriate—his mind sobered by the deep solemnity of the scene—stood there, and leaned over to catch the last accents of one who, in ten minutes more, was to be with the spirits of heaven.

All was the silence of deepest night. The dying child held the young man's hand in one of hers; with the other, she slowly lifted the trifling memorial she had assigned especially for him, aloft in the air. Her arm shook—her eyes, now becoming glassy with the death-damps, were cast toward her brother's face. She smiled pleasantly, and as an indistinct gurgle came from her throat, the uplifted hand fell suddenly into the open palm of her brother's, depositing the tiny volume there. Little Jane was dead.

From that night, the young man stepped no more in his wild courses, but was reformed.

When Mr. Marchion concluded his narrative, we sat some minutes in silence. I thought I noticed even more than usual interest concerning it, as he had drawn to its crisis — and I more than half suspected he was himself the young man whose reform had been brought about by the child's death. I was right. He acknowledged in answer to my questioning, that he had indeed been relating a story, the hero of which was himself.

~~~~~~

CHAPTER XV

"The planter's house was an airy, rustic dwelling, that brought Defoe's description of such places strongly to my recollection. The day was very warm, but the blinds being all closed, a shadowy coolness rustled through the room, which was exquisitely refreshing, after the glare and heat without. Before the windows was an open piazza, where, in what they call hot weather — whatever that may be — they sling hammocks, and drink and doze luxuriously."
—DICKENS'S AMERICAN NOTES

THE benevolence and good will of the Marchion family, as I have before intimated, led them to pause at nothing which might be of substantial benefit to me. It is almost needless to say that one of the first movements for my improvement, through their means, was my signing the Temperance Pledge. This was, what is in these days called the Old Pledge, which forbade only the drinking of the most ardent kind of liquors, and allowed people to get as much fuddled as they chose upon wines, and beer, and so on. At that time, those who went further, were supposed by many to be altogether too ultra in their views. It will be seen in the remaining chapters of my narrative, whether the Old Pledge was sufficient to remove the dangers which may be apprehended from habits of intemperance. For, though I had now reformed from my hitherto evil courses, and had always subsequently kept the integrity of my promise; I think it will be allowed that the fruits of temperance were not fully reaped by me in that portion of my life, which I am now going to transcribe.

The Marchions supplied me with a moderate portion of funds, and aided me with advice and recommendations in every way. Under their assistance I started myself in a respectable, lucrative, and easy business. I prospered, and the world began to look bright once more.

Some months passed away, when I took a jaunt—partly of business and partly of pleasure—to one of the southern counties of Virginia. In effecting the arrangements I had under my charge, I was now and then forced to wait the convenience of those over whom I had no control. Accordingly, on several occasions, I was detained for days at a time, with no employment on hand except to look about and amuse myself in the best way possible. One of these waiting spells, I well recollect, was at a pleasant, old-settled village, on the banks of a fine stream. I amused the monotony of the time by getting acquainted, as far as I could, with the planters in the neighborhood, and by roaming over their settlements; and even by chatting with the slaves, from whose liveliness and cheerful good-humor, I derived no small share of mirth myself. The Virginians are proverbially hospitable, and friendly to strangers; and taking all things into consideration, the time passed quite as comfortably as I could expect.

One day, I strolled off to some distance beyond the more closely settled part of the village; sauntering lazily along, and having no more particular object in view, than a listless enjoyment of the natural scenery. My walk skirted the banks of the river. Some two miles I had gone on in this way, when I came out upon a little knoll, sloping down to the shore. Upon the highest elevation of the ground, there stood a house, which I could not help admiring for its look of comfort, and the evident good taste which had been active in adorning the grounds and walks around it.

As I walked nearer, to admire some rare plants that stood in pots, by the porch, a middle-aged gentleman came out of the entrance, and saluting me courteously, entered into conversation, and invited me to take a seat in the cool shade of the verandah. My long walk had made me somewhat weary, and I complied with his invitation. I rather thought, from his accent and manner, that he was not an American. In the course of our talk, I learned that he was a bachelor, and had inherited the estate on which he now resided from his father; and that, though somewhat lonely, he generally found sufficient amusement in taking care of the affairs of his plantation. He brought out some excellent wine, before we parted, and we finished a couple of bottles together.

It was almost evening when I went away; and then my host, whose name was
Bourne, only allowed me to depart under a strict promise, that I would visit
him again on the morrow.

Upon my return to the village, I spoke of my entertainment by the planter
at whose house I had passed the day, and inquired into his history. I found,
from what I learned in the village and in my after acquaintance with the planter
himself, that Bourne's father had come over from France, during the trouble-
some times there, in the latter part of the last century. He was among a large
number of gentlemen and citizens, who left that country to obtain quiet, even
at the expense of exile. The cause of his departure from his native land, however, was not a disapproval of the schemes of the revolutionizers, just then
on the point of coming into power. On the contrary, he assimilated strongly
to their doctrines, and afterward took every occasion to instill them into the
mind of his son.

Bourne chose America as the place of his retreat, because of the liberty he
might enjoy there. And here, where I found my friend of the day before, he
had bought himself a plantation, and placed upon it the needful requisites of
slaves and material, for the purposes to which he intended applying it.

Perhaps it may hardly be the appropriate place here, to remark upon the
national customs of this country; but I cannot help pausing a moment to say
that Bourne, as he saw with his own eyes, and judged with his own judgment, became convinced of the fallacy of many of those assertions which are
brought against slavery in the south. He beheld, it is true, a large number of
men and women in bondage; but he could not shut his eyes to the fact, that
they would be far more unhappy, if possessed of freedom. He saw them well
taken care of—with shelter and food, and every necessary means of comfort:
and he wondered in his own mind, as he remembered what misery he had
seen in his travels through various countries of Europe, that the philanthropists of the Old World should wish to interfere with the systems of the New—
when the merely nominal oppression of the latter is overbalanced, so many
hundred times, by the stern reality of starvation and despotism in the former.

The next day, and for many days after, I was constant in my visits to my new
acquaintance. I found him an intelligent and very affable companion; and, as I
had yet to stay some weeks in the place, it may easily be supposed I was not at
all displeased that such means of amusement were at my command. And the
planter, too, seemed highly delighted with our companionship. He had been,

as it were, buried from the world, and saw few visitors, except what chance threw in his way.

So intimate did we at length become, and so necessary to one another's comfort, that I took up my residence in his house; and forwarded to New York information, that I should probably not be home during the season. My business there was under the charge of a faithful and competent person, and I had no fear but what all would go right. The letters I had from him, from time to time, presented the most favorable accounts.

Bourne and I, during the day, were much of the time together, and night always found us over a bottle of wine. I fear that, notwithstanding my strict adherence to the pledge I had given, under the advice of the Marchions, the occasions were not a few wherein I was forced to have assistance, in order to reach my chamber.

My residence and walks about the plantation, made me familiar with all its affairs; and I even took upon myself, at times, the direction of things, as though I were upon my own property. I cannot look back upon this period of my life without some satisfaction; though, take it altogether, it was sadly to my detriment that I ever went to Virginia, as will be seen in the sequel. My evil genius was in the ascendant, and worked me harm in a method as singular, as it has ever since been disagreeable to my reflections.

CHAPTER XVI

> They say 'tis pleasant on the lip,
>   And merry on the brain—
> They say it stirs the sluggish blood
>   And dulls the tooth of pain.
> Ay—but within its glowing deeps,
> A stinging serpent, unseen, sleeps.
>
> Its rosy lights will turn to fire,
>   Its coolness change to thirst;
> And by its mirth, within the brain
>   A sleepless worm is nursed,
> There's not a bubble at the brim
> That does not carry food for him.
>   —WILLIS

AMONG the slaves on Bourne's estate lived a young woman, named Margaret, a creole. She had once been owned by a lady, at whose decease she had been purchased, with others, by the planter, for his farm. The lady had made something of a favorite of the girl, and given her a good education for one of her class. She was of that luscious and fascinating appearance often seen in the south, where a slight tinge of the deep color, large, soft voluptuous eyes, and beau-fully [*sic*] cut lips, set off a form of faultless proportions—and all is combined with a complexion just sufficiently removed from clear white, to make the spectator doubtful whether he is gazing on a brunette, or one who has indeed some hue of African blood in her veins. Margaret belonged to the latter class: and she only wanted an opportunity to show, that the fire of her race burnt with all its brightness in her bosom, though smothered by the necessity of circumstances.

The overseer of the business of the plantation, was a man named Phillips. I never liked him—though, as he always treated me well, I could have no occasion to be rude toward him. He was from the north, too—my own section of the country—and with much prudence and industry, he had some of the smaller vices of the human character. His dwelling was a mile, or thereabout, from Bourne's own residence.

Phillips, it seems, had frequently noticed the beauty of the young slave Margaret, and with a licentious eye. The advances which his situation gave him the means of making, however, had been repulsed, and not always without some appearance of scorn.

It happened, about a week after I took up my abode at the planter's, that Margaret being employed in the field, Phillips came, and, as formerly, offered proposals which the indignant creature rejected with terms of anger. Irritated at her severity, the overseer proceeded to such lengths, that the passionate slave lifted the instrument of labor she had been using, and felled him to the earth with a heavy blow. He lay there senseless, and blood flowed from his wound.

A moment's reflection convinced Margaret of the dangerous nature of the act she had committed. With promptitude, she immediately made up her mind what courses to pursue. She came at once to the homested, and asked for her master. We were sitting together at the time upon the verandah, our usual afternoon retreat. Margaret was ushered there, and told her story. As she went on, I could not help being struck with her beauty, and the influence of the liquor from the bottle by my side, by no means contributed to lessen my admiration.

"If it were to do over again," said the angry girl, her black eye lighted, and her cheek mantling with the rich blood, "I would act the same. He knows well enough what I have said before, when he has spoken his wicked words to me, and the consequence of his deeds he can only lay to himself."

My countenance, perhaps, expressed the feelings of admiration I have spoken of; for she looked at me, as if appealing to my influence with Bourne in her behalf. The glance I gave her, in return, conveyed that whatever might be the result of her hasty conduct, she would at least have one defender and advocate — perhaps one whose word would be effectual.

In the course of an hour, Phillips made his appearance at the house, with his head bandaged, and his face quite pallid. He had lost some blood, and that, joined with the hate which now appeared in his face toward the offending slave, gave him an appearance anything but inviting. I did not wonder, as I looked at the man, that Margaret had been so obstinate in her conduct toward him.

The room being turned into a kind of judgment-hall, and each party's side having had its say, Mr. Bourne was perplexed in no small degree as to the decision he should give. Margaret had evidently had more of his good will, as she had of the justice of the dispute, but the planter feared the danger of making a precedent by letting her off triumphantly. He could not bring his conscience to chastise her, and yet something was necessary in the way of punishment. So, leaning partly to justice and partly to expediency, he put on a severe face, lectured the girl upon the enormity of her offence, added a few words and threats — which the grumbling overseer thought smacked far too much of being done merely for effect — and then signified his desire to hear no more upon the subject, by dismissing each one to his or her avocations.

In a day or two the occurrence seemed forgotten. *Seemed* forgotten — but in fact, the pride of Phillips had been wounded too deeply for forgiveness. His breast rankled with feelings of hate toward her who had defied him, and made him a theme of ridicule. There was one other, too, in whose mind the beautiful creole had roused strong thoughts, though of a nature very different from those which dwelt in the soul of the overseer.

I don't know whether I have intimated, in the preceding course of my narrative, that my nature was not wanting in susceptibility to female charms. The truth was so, however. And moreover, I had imbibed not a few of the pernicious notions which prevail among young men in our great America city, upon conjugal matters. My safety, hitherto, had been from the swiftness with

which my passion passed over. Often had I been struck with a pretty face—
remembered it for four or five days—and then recovered from my delusion
to smile at my own folly.

The loveliness and grace of Margaret had fascinated me; but she was one,
not of my own race, and her very liberty was owned by another. What had
I to do with such as she? Every feeling of prudence and self-respect, spoke
loudly in opposition to my allowing any sentiment akin to love for the girl
in my bosom, or to express it by my conduct. And yet, strangely enough, I
thought nothing of all this; but in my wine-drinking interviews with Bourne,
frequently alluded to the subject, and spoke of the regard I had for *his slave*.

There seems to be a kind of strange infatuation, permanently settled over
the faculties of those who indulge much in strong drink. It is as frequently
seen in persons who use wine, as in them that take stronger draughts. The
mind becomes, to use an expressive word, *obfusticated*, and loses the power of
judging quickly and with correctness. It seems, too, that the unhappy victim
of intemperance cannot tell when he commits even the most egregious vio-
lations of right; so muddied are his perceptions, and so darkened are all his
powers of penetration. And the worst of it is, that even in his sober moments,
the same dark influence hangs around him to a great degree, and leads him
into a thousand follies and miseries.

Something of this kind, I presume, was the cause of my conduct, as I am
going to relate it. Certainly, a man with his senses about him would never have
acted in so absurd a manner. But, *does* an habitual wine-bibber have his senses
about him? Not one day out of the weekly seven, but saw Bourne and myself
for long hours at the bottle!

In one of these revels, I told my host that my affection for the creole had
induced me to come to the determination of marrying her. Instead of placing
so singular a proposal in its true colors before me, Bourne expressed his opinion, that if I liked the girl, it would all be perfectly proper; and he declared, as
an evidence of his friendship for me, that he would give her her freedom that
very day. Moreover, a young lad, a brother of Margaret, named Louis, whom
the planter also owned, was to be given over to me, as I would probably not
like to have it said that a *connection* of mine was a bondsman. For some time
we discussed the matter, and arranged it highly to our satisfaction. In truth,
before we rose from the table, we were neither of us in a state to know whether
we were acting the part of fools or wise men.

Will it be believed? That very afternoon, Bourne, who was a justice of the peace, united myself and the creole in matrimony. The certificate of manumission also, was drawn out and signed, and given into Margaret's own hand. A couple of apartments in the homested were assigned to her use — and I signalized this crowning act of all my drunken vagaries, that night, by quaffing bottle after bottle with the planter.

~~~~~~~

CHAPTER XVII

Haply, for I am black;
And have not those soft parts of conversation
That chamberers have.

—SHAKESPERE

IT needs not that I should particularize the transactions of the next few days. As may reasonably be expected, not a long time elapsed before I awoke from my lethargy. And *when* I awoke! What disgust with myself filled my mind at view of the conduct I had been pursuing! Though since my first chance interview with Bourne, but four or five short weeks had passed away; it seemed, as I looked back over time, more like an age.

Then I reviewed the uninviting circumstances of my marriage, and my distaste arose toward the creole, *my wife*, who, I felt sure, had done her best to entrap me into all this. The more I thought upon the subject, the more did my dislike to Margaret gain strength. She whom but a little while before, I had looked on with the deepest admiration, was now almost an object of hate to me.

Whatever aversion I felt toward the woman, however, I could not but be conscious of her evident affection to me, as it was exhibited from day to day. She saw and was pained with my conduct. She tried a thousand fond arts to gain back the love I had once shown for her. She conducted herself in the most decorous and humble manner. But all to no avail.

Was my former love for the creole, then, become totally extinct? Ah, human love, to be lasting, must be pure and worthily bestowed.

The course of my narrative needs now that another character should be introduced upon the stage. My evil destiny would have it, that an old city acquaintance of mine, Mrs. Conway, a widow lady, visited the neighborhood at this time, and took up her quarters in the house of the overseer Phillips, to whom she was distantly related. I had met the lady often at the house of persons whom I knew in New-York; and of course, nothing was more natural than for me to call upon her.

Mrs. Conway was about twenty-five, and very handsome; not with unformed and unripened loveliness, but in the rich swell, the very maturity of personal perfection. Her light hair, blue eyes, and the delicacy of her skin, formed a picture rarely met with in that region; and perhaps on this very account, the more prized. She was a woman of the world, however. Gifted with such singular charms, and her mind ornamented with the most needful and complete culture; she had but one aim, the conquest of hearts. And seldom did she determine to make any individual addition to her adorers, but what her efforts were crowned with triumph. Luckless were the stars that led her southward!

The very next day after this woman came among us, she made up her mind to bring me to her feet. Probably it was partly from natural inclination, and partly to find herself some agreeable method of dissipating monotony, that caused the lady to form this determination. She (I afterward found out all this) mentioned the project to her relative, Phillips, who approved of it, and promised to give it any aid in his power. He had never forgotten the indignity bestowed on him by Margaret, before she became raised to her present situation. Policy afterward led him to disguise his feelings; but they were by no means effaced.

It needs not to explain all the artifices which were used for effecting what the plotters desired to accomplish. Fortunately for them, they had a willing subject to work upon; and in much less time than they could have anticipated, I was indeed in the toils.

I do not think I admired Mrs. Conway; at least, I did not at first. But I felt no small disposition to feign that sentiment, if it were merely to mortify my ill-assorted wife. For my dissatisfaction at the marriage was of much longer continuance than my love for the creole; and though I felt ashamed to show the people of the household how bitterly I repented of my drunken rashness — for the marriage deserved no other name — I felt sick at heart whenever I thought upon it. We lived together, Margaret and I, but there was often little of peace and pleasure between us.

"I fear that northern beauty has bewitched you," said Margaret, with a smile, as I returned one evening from calling at the overseer's; "you did not use to be so partial to Mr. Phillips's pathway."

"Matters of business," answered I, a little confused; "nothing but business."

"But is she really as handsome as I hear? I have been told by our people, that fancy can hardly conceive any creature more perfect."

"You have been told the truth," said I; "she is wonderfully fair, not dark and swarthy, which I detest!" and I turned away, sure of the effect of the sharp arrow I had winged.

"Indeed!" burst from the surprised Margaret; and she would have spoken further, but her pride came to prevent her.

Surely, a few short days could not have made this sudden change in my affections. And then the creole thought of many little things that had before been airy trifles, but were now too sure a groundwork for her suspicions.

The fears of the jealous woman were to be consummated but too soon, leaving her no further ground to doubt. I shortly made no secret of my attachment to Mrs. Conway. Indeed, I believe that, as it often happens in similar cases, the feeling I began by dissembling, I after awhile really felt in truth. Like an actor who plays a part, I became warmed in the delineation, and the very passion I feigned, came to imbue my soul with its genuine characteristics.

Poor Margaret! it was a wild and fearful storm that raged within her bosom, when she came fully to know the truth of her desertion. I have no doubt she had loved me tenderly, ever since the time of my interference in her behalf when she was arraigned for striking Phillips; and with all the fiery disposition of her nation, she now felt torn with strong passions, to think that another had supplanted her. I do not think I have given a faithful transcript of the creole's character in all its strong points. She was, indeed, a very woman, with some of the most beautiful traits, and some of the most devilish that ever marked her sex. Her ambition of rising above the low level of her companions, had been gratified by the act wherein Bourne conferred freedom upon her. Such freedom had been one of the dearest dreams of her life. And to be the wife of one who occupied a respectable station among the masters of the land, was exalted destiny beyond which her hopes could hardly rise.

She felt that her being a free woman, gave her much power by the law; and that I was bound to her by indissoluble ties. But with excellent policy, she never allowed her knowledge of this to appear in her conversation or conduct.

She had a most difficult part to play; and, as I have in late years, cast my mind back, I could not help being struck with wonder at the dexterous manner in which she avoided many a quicksand, and kept from an open rupture with me, where we had so little in common. Hapless girl! I would that her destiny might have been a more fortunate one!

<center>~~~~~~</center>

CHAPTER XVIII

No man is safe, who drinks. Actions which are the height of injustice are often committed under the influence of liquor, to those whom we are bound to cherish.

—TEMPERANCE ADDRESS

WHETHER Mrs. Conway returned my admiration, and whether she would have accepted the offer of my hand, had I been in a fit condition to give it, I cannot say. The probability is, however, that in our intercourse the same current of events took place which I have described in my own case. In the first stages, she no doubt acted the part of a most unqualified coquet. But in our subsequent meetings, she may have been touched by the ardency of my love, which was more intense, as it might have been called more legitimate, than that I had borne the creole.

As I gazed on the widow's bewitching beauty—her soft sunny complexion, and her mild eyes—as I listened to her conversation, charming for itself alone, and doubly so from the musical tones it flowed in—I felt myself steeped indeed in the extacy of passion.

One day, after drinking with Bourne, I had been visiting the widow, and pouring into her ears some of those wild thoughts and protestations which wine and love can generate. The beauty listened complacently, for when was homage distasteful to a woman? All of a sudden, a capricious thought entered her brain.

"Come!" said she to me, "I wonder if you would prove, by something more tangible than words, the reality of all this fine sentiment?"

"If there is anything, lady, you wish done," I replied, "that mortal man can do, I will attempt it."

And I spoke with an energy that showed my mind.

"In a stroll I took two or three days since," continued the widow, "I saw a fine boy of some eight or nine years old. They told me he belonged to you. Now

I fancy I should like just such a little fellow to be my page, after the fashion of the damsels of old."

"What was his name?" asked I.

"They called him Louis. And now I think of it, some one said he was the brother of the woman Margaret, who lives at your dwelling."

I started, and felt the blood rushing up in my face like fire. Could the widow have intended to strike that chord? Louis was indeed the brother of the creole, and was beloved by her, as a woman might cling to her own child.

The widow waited for an answer several moments in vain.

"How soon gallantry cools when its labor or its money is required!" she said at length, with a contemptuous smile.

"Forgive me, lady, it is not that," and I spoke very earnestly, "it is not that. Ask of me something else. There are reasons," added I, in a quick and confused voice, "reasons I may not mention why that request must be denied. But some other surely will do as well. There are many children among the slaves, and you shall have your choice of them all."

The widow knew the reasons I alluded to full well.

"My choice is made," she replied, calmly and coolly; "it was but an idle notion, and I have done wrong to trouble you with it."

"I beg you," rejoined I, "let some other take the boy's place in your wish."

"Speak no more about it, sir;" the lady answered, in a tone as if intended to cut short the subject; "it is not worth your while to think of a silly woman's whims. Though I don't know, indeed which are worse—false words, or foolish fancies. I beg you, speak to more about it."

But I did speak further about it. I entreated her to select some other, any dozen others, instead of Louis. Her answer was still the same.

Those who have read the preceding chapters of this narrative, and who know the great failing which has attended me from my very outset of life— weakness of resolution, and liability to be led by others—can conceive the result of this interview. Before I left the widow, I promised to comply with her request about the boy. He was mine, I argued, and why should I not do with my own property as I liked, and bestow it as I listed?

The creole, I have said, loved her young brother very fondly. Who may describe, then, what took place in her bosom when this matter was broken to her? At first it caused a kind of stunning sensational of surprise, almost of incredulity. Then came the tempest. All the fearful propensities which had slumbered so long in her soul, were aroused. Was this stranger—this fair-

faced interloper from abroad, not only to destroy the love which had been to
her as life; but her very brother to be taken away and made a servant, for *her*
beck and command? What right had she, this delicate child of another climate, to invade the privileges and the happiness that had been so pleasant?
The spirit of her fiery race swelled in the creole's breast, as she thought of
these things: and she cursed her rival with a sharp and bitter tongue.

Louis was sent to his new mistress. Before the time of his departure, his
sister was observed to have several long and close interviews with him. What
the subject of those interviews was, they alone knew.

At length came the capstone of the misfortunes of Margaret. Rumors
floated to her ear of preparations for an intended divorce between myself and
her, and of a marriage in prospect of the widow and me. The latter part of the
story was an addition of the busy tongue of common report.

The creole occupied the same apartments in the homested yet: but their
accommodations were no longer shared by me. I spent a great portion of my
time at the overseer's. Bourne was busy with his plantation, it being a season
when its weal depended on his active supervision. We had our daily drinking-
bouts, however, and our friendship was as firmly knit as it had ever been.

As I sometimes glance back at this period of my life, I think with more regret and dissatisfaction upon it, than upon any other portion of my conduct.
My early follies were the result of inexperience in the ways of the world, and
of the errors of impulse; hardly any of them but have some excuse. They were
either committed or begun when I was under the influence of liquor, and had
lost the control of my faculties; or were forced upon me by circumstance, and
might be attributed to the great failing I have before alluded to—weakness
of resolution. But my acts during the few weeks I resided at Bourne's, were
done more in the method of deliberate and premeditated folly. I had my eyes
open, and still went on, as though I were blindfolded.

The true explanation of the mystery is, I think, to be found in my former,
and present habits of drinking spirituous liquors. Those habits were of the
most insidious, sly, and fatal detriment to me. They relaxed my energy of character, what little I had, and left me like a ship upon the ocean, without her
mainmast. I was tossed about by every breeze of chance or impulse, and was
guilty of a hundred foolish things, which the relation of makes my story appear indeed like a work of imagination, instead of what it honestly is, a record
of real events. So evil are the consequence of dissipation!

I can trace the outset of all these frailties, as well as all the calamities that have befallen me in my life, to that fatal night when Colby drew me into the drinking place; where, amid music and gayety, the first step in my downward road was taken.

~~~~~~~~

CHAPTER XIX

In vain the flattering verse may breathe
Of ease from pain, and rest from strife;
There is a sacred dread of death,
Inwoven with the strings of life.

— BRYANT

WHILE matters were in the situation described in the last few paragraphs, a danger was preparing, that threatened destruction not only to the love of myself and the widow, but to our lives, and the lives of the whole family and neighborhood. One of those epidemical diseases that prevail in the South made its appearance, and began to spread in all directions. Alarm and consternation fell upon the people. Beginning at first with striking down a man here and there, the fearful Plague Spirit, after a time, became as it were insatiate in his demands.

At the first appearance of the scourge, Mrs. Conway would have flown back to her native north. I, however, to whom her presence had become very dear, represented the evil as far less than rumor attempted to make it. I smiled at her terrors, and though my own heart accused me of untruth, I told the widow that there was little danger.

Thus she remained in fancied security, until it was too late. When the real facts could no longer be kept from her knowledge, it was quite as dangerous to leave as to remain. And yet, so deeply seated was this woman's love of admiration, that she really forgave me for deceiving her, in consideration of the motive that led me to be guilty of it.

One of the last places where the sickness came, was the village near Bourne's plantation. It was a place of not much travel, and being in a more than ordinarily healthy location, its inhabitants had flattered themselves with a hope of escaping the pestilence which desolated ther [sic] fellow towns. Vain were their hopes. One day authentic information was brought to the planter, that the disease had made its appearance there; and, unfortunately for him, its first stroke was leveled at a poor family whose house stood near the confines of his estate. He was advised to be very cautious, and furthermore enjoined by his medical attendant, who sent the information just mentioned, that fear and anxiety concerning the matter were precisely the things that would bring about the result most dreaded.

All this was kept from Mrs. Conway's ears. I already began to blame myself for my deceit. I took every earthly means to guard her from the dangers that surrounded the place, and never allowed her to hear aught that might produce in her mind those disturbed thoughts which the physician deprecated. New to the climate, and more liable than a native to its deleterious influences, I knew she would stand but little chance of recovery, if once attacked by the dreaded malady.

But amid the general alarm and precaution, there was one person who paid small heed to either. That person was the deserted Margaret. She cared little about bodily danger, for she pined in a deeper rooted sorrow, and not only pined, but with feelings of one much injured, she fostered in her soul the desire of retribution on her injurer. Me, she could not bring herself to regard with any other passion than fondness; but her rival was hated with as deep a loathing, as ever swelled the soul of a jealous woman.

When she heard of the epidemic, her first thought was a desire that the widow would be one of its victims. When the news was brought that it had broken out in our immediate neighborhood, she arranged in her mind a scheme, subtle and worthy the brain whence it sprung—a scheme of revenge. The whole of the thoughts and conduct of the woman, though at the time unknown to me, were afterward fixed too firmly in my knowledge and my memory.

The next day, Louis, her brother, came to the planter's house on some errand for his mistress. Whether that errand required his sister's personal attention or not, I cannot say; but for a long time the child was closeted with Margaret in her apartment. As he left the place, there flashed in his eye a spice of lurking devil, which spoke him to be not a slack partaker of his sister's soul.

Down one of the winding-lanes of Bourne's plantation, that very afternoon, two figures were slowly walking. One was a lady, passing beautiful; the other was a boy, a fine-looking youth, his cheeks tinged with a slight color, betraying though feebly his taint of African blood. The lady was Mrs. Conway; the boy, her attendant Louis.

"It is pleasant," said the widow, "to get once more a taste of the open air; I have been cooped up so long, that it comes to me like something strange and unwonted."

The boy walked on near her in silence.

"Do you not think, Lewy, we are strangely kept in by Mr. Bourne's and Mr. Evans's whims? It was but the other day the latter told me not to stir out of the house to a distance on any account. You don't have robbers here, I hope?"

"I never knew of one about the place, in all my life," answered the child.

"And this sickness," said the lady, "what a fearful thing if it should appear among us! They say, boy, such as I, coming from another clime, stand a double danger from it."

The child looked up in his companion's face with a strange look; and continued to walk on in silence.

"How sweet the air is!" continued the lady. It was more like talking to herself than a listener; but the foible of her sex is proverbial, and Mrs. Conway was no exception to any of her sex's foibles. "How sweet the air is! Life seems pleasant in the South, if it be only for the mild, warm air. Then, the beautiful flowers bloom all around, and are reared with so little trouble; and you have rich fruit here, such as never grows in the rigor of our stormy north. But as much as anything else, I love to hear the birds—the sweet singing birds of the South!"

"What do you think of a bird that can sing tunes?" asked Louis, suddenly.

"I think he would be well worth owning," said the lady.

"Would you like to see such a bird?" rejoined the boy, looking up into Mrs. Conway's face, and with something like a tremor in his voice.

"Certainly," said she, smiling at what appeared to be his childish earnestness; "I would like any variation, however small, of the sameness of this quiet life. Where shall we find the curiosity of which you speak?"

"Through the path yonder," answered Louis, "a little beyond that wood. Andy Warner lives there, and he has the bird hung up in a cage in his room."

"Come on then," said the widow, laughing: "Andy Warner shall show us this prodigy."

And she motioned to go; but the child stirred not. His eyes stared in a wild manner, and he trembled from head to foot.

"How, boy?" exclaimed the lady. "What is the matter? You are sick, Louis, you are sick, I fear!"

"No, I am quite well," answered he, recovering his former appearance. "Come, let us go on to Andy's."

They walked down the lane, and along the path which Louis pointed out. It led to a kind of bye-place. The house he had mentioned was situated at some distance from the principal wagon-way, and on the present occasion, exhibited no sign of tenancy or life. They knocked at the door, which after a moment or two was opened by a woman, who received them with a look so full of startling surprise, that Mrs. Conway knew not what to make of it. They told the woman the reason of their visit—and then she stood looking at them again, in a second long stare of wonder and wildness,

"There!" said Louis, pointing with his finger, "there is the bird!"

Mrs. Conway glanced up, and beheld one of the southern mocking birds, in a cage attached to the wall. The little songster seemed in a sulky vein, however; he hung his head and was totally without cheerfulness or animation.

"Could you make him sing some gay, lively strain now?" said the visitor, turning to her hostess with a sprightly air.

As she looked more fully in the face of the one to whom she spoke, Mrs. Conway started back in alarm. The woman seemed like a ghost—her face pale, and her whole aspect bearing an indescribable appearance of strangeness and insanity. Mrs. Conway was instantly impressed with the idea that she was deranged, and turned in alarm to leave the room.

"Good God!" exclaimed the pale faced female, "she talks here of singing gay strains!"

Fairly terrified, the widow now made a quick exit, and only recovered her self-possession when she found herself in the open air with Louis by her side. They walked swiftly along the path on their return; for the day was now somewhat advanced, and they had strayed quite a distance from Phillips's house.

That very afternoon I had called at the overseer's, and been told that Mrs. Conway was out on a walk. I started forth to look for her, that I might accompany her back. So it happened, that as she came by the dwelling of Bourne, near which she had to pass, I met her.

She immediately began telling me of her afternoon's adventure. As she mentioned the course of her walk, I started, for a dim fear took possession of my mind, to which I dared not give credit, and yet thought too probable.

"But never mind," exclaimed the widow, in continuation, as she finished her story, "I suppose Andy Warner will be at home himself some day, and then I shall, no doubt, get treated with more politeness."

"Did you," gasped I faintly, as the name struck my ear, and a feeling of deadly sickness crept over my heart—"did you say Andy—?"

I staggered and clutched the air, as a man grasping support to keep from falling.

"Did you say Andy Warner?" came up again from my throat in a hoarse whisper.

"Yes, yes, that was the name, I think;" and the alarmed lady turned with an inquiring looking to Louis.

"Then are you lost, indeed," cried I, in tones of shrieking horror. "In that house was the first case of the horrid fever. Andy *died* this very morning, and if you had looked farther, you would no doubt have found his corpse, for it lies there yet!"

One moment more, and a wild shrill cry sounded out upon the air, waking the echoes, and sailing far off in many a sharp cadence. Another followed— and another—and the widow sank down upon the grass in a senselessness so deep, that I thought the contagion would have no chance of working its effect upon her. I was almost out of my senses with agony and alarm. But time pressed, and lifting that form so dear to me, in my arms, I bore her into the planter's residence, and there had those attentions paid which the urgency of the case demanded. In an hour, the widow was somewhat recovered from her fit. But she was still as languid as a babe, and the physician who had been summoned, spoke strongly against the propriety of carrying her the mile's distance which intervened between the house, and Phillips's residence.

So I had it arranged that she should not be removed. In the south range of apartments, there was one with long low windows, opening to the ground. That room was prepared for her reception and there I had her carried.

~~~~~~

CHAPTER XX

I'll tell you friend, what * * *
Where'er I scan this scene of life
    Inspires my waking schemes,
And, when I sleep, * * *
Dances before my ravished sight,
    In sweet, aerial dreams.

—PROFESSOR FRISBIE

How refreshing it is to pause in the whirl and tempest of life, and cast back our minds over past years! I think there is even a kind of satisfaction in deliberately and calmly reviewing actions that we feel were foolish or evil. It pleases us to know that we have the learning of experience. The very contrast, perhaps, between what we are, and what we were, is gratifying. At all events, it is acknowledged that retrospection becomes one of the delights of people immediately after arriving mature years. When merely on the verge of manhood, we love to think of the scenes of our boyish life. When advanced in age, we fondly turn our memory to the times of the early years, and dwell with a chastened pleasures upon what we recollect thereof, beheld through the medium of the intervening seasons.

From no other view can I understand how it is, that I sometimes catch myself turning back in my reflection, to the very dreariest and most degraded incidents which I have related in the preceding pages, and thinking upon them without any of the bitterness and mortification which they might be supposed to arouse in my bosom. The formal narration of them, to be sure, is far from agreeable to me — but in my own self-communion upon the subject, I find a species of entertainment. I was always fond of day-dreams — an innocent pleasure, perhaps, if not allowed too much latitude.

For some days after Mrs. Conway's death, I shut myself up in my room, and hardly went out at all, except in the evening, or early morning. A kind of morbid peculiarity came over me during this while, which, though it fortunately passed off with a change of scene, was very powerful for the time. It was the result, no doubt, partly of my confinement and the somber reflections I held — and partly of my former intemperate habits. It was a species of imaginative mania, which led to giving full scope to my fancy — and I frequently remained for two hours at a time in a kind of trance, beholding strange things, and abstracted from all which was going on around me. On one of these occasions, the incident occurred which I shall now relate.

I was sitting in an easy chair at twilight one evening, near the open window. Upon my knees lay a newspaper, which I had been reading. It contained some extracts from an eloquent temperance address. The quietness of the scene, and the subdued light, and the peculiar influences that had been surrounding me for a few days past, had their full chance to act at such a time, as may well be imagined.

Methought I was wandering through the cities of a mighty and populous empire. There were sea-ports, filled with rich navies, and with the products of every part of the earth, and with merchants, whose wealth was greater than the wealth of princes. There were huge inland towns, whose wide and magnificent avenues seemed lined with palaces of marble — and showed on every side the signs of prosperity. I saw from the tops of the fortresses, the Star-Flag — emblem of Liberty — floating gloriously abroad in the breeze!

And how countless were the inhabitants of that country! On I went, and still on, and they swarmed thicker than before. It was almost without boundary, it seemed to me — with its far-stretching territories, and its States away up in the regions of the frozen north, and reaching down to the hottest sands of the torrid south — and with the two distant oceans for its side limits.

With the strange faculty of dreams, I knew, that two-score years had elapsed, as I stood amid this mighty nation. I was in one of their greatest cities — and there appeared to be some general holyday. People were hurrying up and down the streets. The children were dressed in gay clothes. Business seemed to be suspended — and each one given up to the spirit of the time.

"Is it not," I heard one of the passers by say to a companion, "is it not a glorious thing?"

"Most glorious!" said the second.

I lost all further hearing of their remarks, for they walked on, smiling in each other's faces.

Before long, following a crowd, I came into a wide open kind of amphitheatre, where a man stood up in the midst addressing the assembly. The address seemed to be preparatory to something which was to take place at its conclusions.

"The Snake-Tempter," said the man who was speaking, "is this day to be deprived of his last vassal! Long, long have we looked for the coming of this day. It has been our hope, our beacon of encouragement through seasons of toil and darkness. Who would have supposed, years ago, that it could so soon have arrived?

"Now man is free! He walks upon the earth, worthy the name of one whose prototype is God! We hear the mighty chorus sounding loud and long, Regenerated! Regenerated!

"Oh, could those who have wrought and sickened for the coming of this hour — could they but be present with us — how would their hearts leap with joy! But do we know that they are *not* present with us? Who can tell that their spirits may not be soaring in the viewless air near by, and looking down pleasantly upon us, and blessing us? Who can say, but that they are rejoining in their hearts, and praising the Almighty that these things have come to pass?

"The last vassal of the Tempter is indeed lost him. This day, our charter receives the name of him who finishes the Great Work! We can say then, that of all who live among us, there is none but has his title upon the bond, and his claim to its prerogative."

For some time, the man went on in this strain. Then the assembly dispersed, apparently for the purpose of engaging in the other ceremonies of the occasion.

I had wandered to and fro for an hour or more, when I came out in a wide street, to the sides of which I saw the people flocking from every quarter. Away in the distance there sounded bands of music, which grew louder and louder, as if they were coming toward us.

At length a long and splendid procession was seen, marching with stately pace. First came a host of men in the prime of life, with healthy faces and stalwart forms, and every appearance of vigor. They had many banners, which bore mottoes, signifying that they had once been under the dominion of the Tempter, but were now redeemed. Then I saw a myriad of youths, with blooming cheeks and bright eyes, who followed in the track of those before, as in time they no doubt would occupy their stations in the world. There were rich equipages, also, containing the officers of the state, and persons of high rank. Long, long it stretched, and still there seemed no end.

Not the least beautiful part of the procession, was composed of bands of women and young girls, dressed with taste, and lending their smiles to enliven the scene. I saw many children also, whose happy and innocent looks were pleasant to behold.

All through the long sweep of the multitude, there were innumerable banners, and mottoes, and devices, expressive of triumph and rejoicing. One of them, I noticed, had the figure of a fair female, robed in pure white. Under her feet were the senseless remains of a hideous monster, in whose grapple thousands and millions had fallen, but who was now powerless and dead. The eyes of the female beamed benevolence and purity of heart; and in her hand she held a goblet of clear water.

Toward the end of the march came a large car, upon which was a single personage, a man of middle age, who, as he passed along, was saluted by the shouts of the crowd. He seemed to be the theme, in fact, of all the ceremonials and the rejoicing.

"Who is he?" said I to a by-stander. "Who is he, for whom the people raises their voices so loudly?"

The man turned to me in amazement.

"Have you not heard," he answered, "of the great triumph of this day? The one upon the car is the Last Vassal of the Snake-Tempter; and he goes now to make a formal renunciation of his old allegiance."

"And is this the cause, then, of all the public joy?" said I.

"It is," answered the man.

How it was, I cannot say, but I understood his meaning, though he spoke with strange phrases.

So, yielding myself to the passage of those about, I wended on, until at last we came into a wide field, in the middle of which was an uncovered scaffold. Upon it was the person whom I had noticed in the procession — the Last Vassal. Far around, on every side, countless multitudes of nothing but human heads were to be seen, in one compact body.

"Rejoice!" cried a man from the crowd. "Our old enemy is deserted, and we triumph!"

Then there arose such mighty shouts from the huge concourse, that it seemed as if the sound might pierce the very heavens.

And now, he who stood on the scaffold spoke:

"It gladdens me," he said, "that I shall this day make one of the Army of the Regenerated. You have wrought long and faithfully, and your reward comes in good time. It is well."

Loud shouts evinced the pleasure of the multitude at hearing him utter such remarks.

"We welcome you!" they cried, as with one voice.

"This day," continued he, "I throw off the chains, and take upon myself the pleasant bondage of good. It may not be a truth to boast of, that I am the *last* of the serfs of Appetite; yet I joy that I occupy my position before you now, as I do!"

A venerable old man came forward upon the scaffold, and presented a document to the speaker. He received it with evident delight; and snatching a pen from a table, he wrote his name under it, and held it up to the view of the people.

It were impossible to describe the thunder-peal of hurrahs that arose in the air, and sounded to the skies, as the Full Work was consummated thus. They cried aloud—

"Victory! victory! The Last Slave of Appetite is free, and the people are regenerated!"

<hr />

CHAPTER XXI

Thou sure and firm-set earth,
Hear not my steps which way they walk for fear;
The very stones prate of my whereabout
And take the present horror from the time,
Which now suits with it.

—SHAKSPERE

COULD it be possible that the widow might escape the fatal effects of her visit to the cottage? Whatever chance there might have been for some other more equable mind, I saw that her agitation and ceaseless fear left none for her.

Before the end of the second day after that hapless walk, the signs of the coming horrors appeared on her cheek. They were the signals for a general desertion on the part of the attendants. So great was the panic struck to the souls of people by the stories they had heard of the pestilence, that I found it difficult to get for Mrs. Conway the attentions absolutely necessary to her existence. Even before the disease had made its complete appearance, the servants refused to go near her. The unhappy woman had, however, one most devoted servant. Night and day was I ready at the entrance of her apartment, holding a sleepless watch over its inmate.

I shall not think it worth while for my story, to give a minute account of the lady's illness. The sick chamber is a scene which few love to look upon, or to have pictured for them. The sight of this beautiful tabernacle with its foundations broken, and its mysterious furniture out of place, and its strength bowed down in weakness—whose eye has such unhealthy craving as to delight in the grievous spectacle? The soul of a man loves its dwelling, and though itself not thereof, looks on when that dwelling is harmed by evil, and feels in its recesses a sympathizing sorrow.

At length the time arrived, which at some period or other arrives for all cases of bodily disease — the time of the crisis. The doctor came, and with a wise look, told the listeners that his patient was at the most dangerous part of her malady. He prepared some mixtures of his nauseous drugs, gave directions about the order of their being administered, and then closed by remarking to me that, in the course of the evening or night, the suffering lady would probably fall into a continued slumber, from which she would awake to a new life, or to death.

And where was Margaret of late? The wretched creole lived in her former situation, as far as locality was concerned; but her heart and her happiness were fled for ever. She seldom left her rooms, staying there almost alone, and brooding over her griefs and her injuries, which fancy made many times greater than they really were.

It seems to have been the case, that with this creature's good traits her heart had still a remnant of the savage. When Mrs. Conway's illness appeared favorable, Margaret's bosom felt heavy and sorrowful; and when the sick woman was hovering on the confines of the grave, the other's soul danced with a joyous feeling of life.

When the creole heard that the doctor announced the critical period to have arrived — and heard also what was said about the probable lethargy — the discarded favorite asked her informant again. Receiving the same account, she sat a full minute, apparently gazing on some vision in the air. At length, it seemed to melt from her sight; she drew a heavy breath, and resumed her ordinary appearance.

The God of Mysteries only can tell what passions worked in the woman's breast then, and during the rest of that fearful night. What deep breathings of hate — what devilish self-incitements — what unrelenting, yet swaying resolves — what sanguinary brain-thoughts — what mad, and still clearly defined marking out of fiendish purposes — what of all these raged and whirled in the chambers of that unhappy creature's soul, will ever stay buried in the darkness of things gone: a darkness which falls alike on the dreadful motives of the murderer, and the purity of hearts filled with abundance of good!

Midnight hung its curtains round about the planter's dwelling. Sleep and Repose were there with their pleasant ministerings, and Silence, the handmaiden of both. In the chamber of the sick one there was a lamp, sending forth its feeble beams, and looking as if it were about to gasp its last gasp — ominous emblem of the life that lay flickering near. From the bed which held the beautiful sufferer, sounded breathings faint but regular. There was no nurse or watcher there, for the physician had said it was of no importance, and all were worn out with their long-continued attending upon the invalid. Even I myself had sunk into a deep sleep at the door of the room, exhausted nature refusing to allow any further demand upon her powers.

One of the long windows was partly open, and only a thin piece of gauze was between the ground to which it led, and the room. At that window appeared, time and again, two bright small orbs, fixed, and yet rolling in fire. Ever and anon they would draw back into the shadow; then again they would peer inward upon the room, their directions ever being to the bed whereon the sick one lay.

It was wrong to say that couch had no watcher! Three long hours did those glitterings things, which were human eyes, continue to keep the vigils of that noiseless spot. Three long hours, while hardly a motion, except the swaying back and forth, before spoken of, disturbed the constancy of their gaze, or a sound broke the solemn stillness.

In the deep hour of that night the widow awoke; and as she awoke, her cool blood, for the first time during five days, coursed through veins that did not throb with loathsome heat. Then she knew that she should live.

All around was motionless and soundless, and the lady felt glad that it was so; for her heart was in that mood of blissful calm to which the least jar produces pain.

"Thank God!" sounded in a low murmur from her tongue; "thank God! I shall not die!"

The sounds came faintly; but faint as they were, they sank into ears besides those of the speaker. They sank and pierced, with a dagger's sharpness, the soul of Margaret, the creole: for she it was, whose eyes had been during those long three hours almost winkless at the room window.

And was her rival, then, to get well once more? And were all her late hopes to vanish? That pale-browed northerner *married* to him she loved? Never should the sun rise upon that marriage!

Horrid purposes lighted up the creole's eyes as she softly put aside the curtains, and stepped into the room. With a stealthy pace she drew near to the sick woman's bed. One moment she paused. The widow lay there, still very beautiful, and calm as a sleeping infant. As Margaret approached, the invalid turned and looked at her a moment, but it was plain she knew her not, and probably thought her to be some hired attendant.

Still nearer and nearer came the wretched female: and now she stands by the very bedside. Unconscious yet, the lady is quiet and composed—fearing nothing and suspecting nothing. An instant more, and her throat is clutched by a pair of tight-working hands. Startled with terror, she would shriek, but cannot. What torture fills her heart! She turns, and struggles, and writhes; but those deadly fingers loosen not their grasp.

The murderess presses upon her. Poor lady! Her soul feels very sick, as in one little minute whole troops of remembrances, and thoughts, and dreads come over her. She grows fainter and fainter. Her struggles become less energetic, and her convulsive writhings cease. Still those terrible hands release not. Their suffocating span is continued yet for several minutes.

And now, no longer is it necessary that Margaret should keep her hold; that last faint gurgle tells the consummation of the fell design. Her deed is done. Her revenge triumphs!

Like some ghost condemned to wander on earth for the actions done there, a figure stalked about the garden and the grounds near by, during the remainder of that night. Bright stars shone down, and the cool breeze swept by; but the Shape heeded them not, walking swiftly on in zigzag directions, apparently without any particular point of destination. Sometimes stretching off down a lane, and stopping by the fence, and leaning thereon, and looking at the cattle that lay doubled on the grass reposing: sometimes bending over a flower, and taking it very carefully and inhaling its fragrance; and sometimes standing like a marble statue, motionless, and gazing vacantly for a long time in the bodiless air: these were the freaks of the strange figure.

It was the murderess who wandered there and thus. And as the first streak of light appeared in the east, she started like the guilty thing she was, and returned to her abiding place.

~~~~~~

CHAPTER XXII

This even-handed justice
Commands the ingredients of our poisoned chalice
To our own lips.

—SHAKSPERE

UPON the distraction which filled my breast, when it was found in the morning that the widow had died—and the burial of the body—and the cunning

smoothness of the Creole during the intervening time—I shall bestow no
more than this passing mention. Whether any suspicions of foul play were as
yet aroused in the breasts of other persons, is more than I can say. As far as I was
concerned, however, I had not the most distant idea of the kind; and taking
all things into reflection, the likelihood is that no one thought Mrs. Conway's
death, under the circumstances, aught more than was to have been expected.

But guilt has a vital power, which gives it life, until it is held up to scorn. It
happened so in this case. Louis, the brother of Margaret, was taken sick with
the same disease of which the widow was supposed to have died. Strangely
enough, when the Creole plotted with the boy to entice his mistress into the
infected cottage (for that occurrence was the result of design,) she did not
think how the danger would be shared by Louis too. Her soul had strained
its gaze with the single purpose of revenge; and she saw not each incidental
effect. Thus it is with evil intentions. I have noticed that the bad are always
short-sighted: in the plots they form, and the manœuvres they engage in, some
little thing or other escapes their view, and proves, after a while, to be a seed
of punishment and remorse.

Again the curtains of darkness hung around the planter's dwellings and
again had the balancing point of the sickness arrived for a sufferer there. That
sufferer was little Louis. He had left the house of the overseer, and now lived
at his old abode. There was the same breathlessness and the same want of
movement, as on the preceding occasion; but instead of the sick room being
almost deserted, as in the former case, many persons waited there. Perhaps
they had become more callous to fear, because it was not a new thing; perhaps
it was, that they thought the influences of a sick child's apartment more gentle
and less dangerous than the former one. Margaret stood in a position so quiet,
and with eyes so stony in their gaze, that she seemed like one entranced. On
the result of the pending sleep of her brother, it seemed as if her reason and
her life were wavering.

At last the slumberer awoke. The Creole shrieked! for it was plain Louis but
aroused himself a moment, to sink shortly in that deep senselessness which
knows no waking here on earth. He shifted himself uneasily on his bed. A film
came over Margaret's eyes—a film of fear and agony; and when it passed off
and left her sight clear, she saw, laying before her, the quiet ghastly corpse of
her brother.

Those who were present felt awed by her terrible grief. She screamed aloud, and threw her arms around the boy, and pressed his forehead to her lips. She called him by all the old endearing epithets, and seemed crazed with her sense of desperate sorrow. The wild exclamations that started from her mouth, the listeners heard with wonder.

"Do not go!" she said, looking on the inanimate form of the boy. "Do not go. The pleasant days are not all past. If you leave me my heart will crack!"

Then in a whisper:

"O, never tell me of her kindness. Lead her into the hut I say. She is a witch, and can steal hearts."

She paused, and looked intently at some phantom before her.

"Why, how long she sleeps! She shall sleep longer, though, and deeper, after to-night. Softly! softly! softly!"

The heart-strings were too much wrought, and the Creole sank heavily down upon the floor, in a fit. Those who stood by looked strangely into each other's faces, but no one spoke.

It was evident that something wrong had been done, and weighed heavily on the wretched woman's mind. Her words, and her strange gestures could not but have a meaning to them. Gossipping [*sic*] tongues, once started upon such matters, are not easily put to rest; and before long the dark rumor came to Mr. Phillips's ears, that his kinswoman had been murdered—murdered by her, too, on whom, of all who lived around, he wished an opportunity of showing his dislike.

The overseer, whatever might have been his deficiencies, was a shrewd clear-headed man, and in ferretting out a mystery, had few equals. In the present instance, his wits were sharpened by a sense of duty toward the dead widow, and a desire for revenge. He worked with sagacity, and allowed no incident to escape him, small or large. As might be expected, he soon discovered enough to make his surmises a positive belief.

Many of what the people would have called trifles, were noted down by this man; and the sum of these trifles presented an array dangerous enough to warrant the suspicions even of the most incredulous. The strange appearance of Mrs. Conway's body was remembered—how the bed was all disordered, as if from a violent struggle—the livid spots upon her neck—the open window—and the tracks of some person's feet from the grounds without, through the room—even the fact that Margaret's couch had the next morning borne no sign of occupancy the preceding night—were hunted out by the indefatigable observer. Many other minor and corroborating incidents were also brought to light—the whole making the case of the suspected women a dark one indeed.

Mrs. Phillips applied to the proper authorities for a warrant, and had Margaret lodged in prison, as one who, at the very least, was involved in deep clouds of suspicion.

In the meantime, I myself was as one petrified. Never in all my life did I receive such a shock, as when authentic information was first brought me of the charge against the creole! I could not join the overseer in efforts to worm out the facts of the case; neither could I do aught to screen the murderess of one whom I had so loved. I shut myself up in my room for several days, waiting the conclusion of all these horrible circumstances.

Let me hasten toward that conclusion. I have already dwelt long enough, and too long, on this part of my history, which, notwithstanding the space I have given it, did not occupy more than five or six weeks from the commencement of my acquaintance with Bourne. And I feel glad that I have arrived at the end of the chapter, for my mind revolts at the ideas the narration of these things has already called up in most disagreeable distinctness.

The overseer continued his investigations, but he might as well have spared himself the trouble. From some train of motives which the great Heart-Viewer alone can fathom, the creole soon after sent for Phillips and myself, and made a full confession. Upon her story as she told it me, and her own acknowledgement, I have given many of the incidents in the preceding two chapters, which, at the time they took place, were totally unknown to me. That very night she committed suicide in her cell. I never saw her again.

~~~~~~

CHAPTER XXIII

What can mar the sweetest peace?
Alcohol!

—TEMPERANCE SONG

THINKING over what had taken place, as I prepared for my journey back to New York, I sometimes fancied I had been in a dream. The events were so strange—and my own conduct, in respect to some of them, so very unreasonable, that I could hardly bring myself to acknowledge their reality.

Bourne was loth to part with me. Our short friendship had been in many ways very pleasant to us both. It was seldom, indeed, that his retirement was enlivened with the voice of a stranger, or his lonesome hours made glad by the company of one he loved. At the last interview but one which we had before my departure, we discussed in soberness the transactions of the past month. I think that both of us, though we did not so express ourselves at the time, arrived at the conclusion that the drinking-bout, where I and he settled the wretched step of marriage between myself and the creole, was the starting point of all the late evils.

I had hardly arrived in the city, and was at my home there, before a messenger came with a request that I would visit Mr. Lee, my old antiquary friend, who lay very ill. I went, and found him quite as sick as was reported. He knew me at once, however, and rose in his bed to give me a cordial shake of the hand.

"The reason I have sent for you," said he, "is to prepare you for an evidence that, notwithstanding what has passed between us in days gone by, I have thought proper to bestow upon you a portion of that wealth, which it has been my honest pride to gain."

I was amazed with wonder.

"Sir," said I, "what reason can you have for such favor toward one who is to you almost a stranger?"

"My own fancy, Evans," he answered, "my own whim, perhaps. But we are not strangers. And I have always taken blame to myself, that I did not watch over you with a more fatherly care, when you were first thrown, as it were by the hand of Providence, under my charge."

"Indeed, sir," said I, agitated and affected almost to tears, by the old man's kindness, "I did not expect this."

"No matter," said he, "I have made inquiries, from time to time about you, though you knew it not, and have kept the track of your course of life. I feel assured that your wild days are over—that experience has taught you wisdom, and that the means I shall place at your command will not be put to improper uses."

The sick merchant, raised himself, and propped against his pillow, enjoined me to listen a few minutes, and he would briefly relate the story of his life—and why it was that in his old age, he was alone in the world, without family or intimates. I shall give his story in my own words.

Stephen Lee, at an early age, received from his father a sufficient capital to enable him to start himself in business, in the mercantile profession. Though he was ambitious, he was prudent, and soon sailed on the forward and brilliant track to success. Fascinated by the charms and accomplishments of a young female cousin, he paid his addresses to her, and they were shortly married.

For several months happiness seemed hovering over them, and all prospects were fair for a life of cloudless content. A year elapsed, and Lee's wife bore him a son. The delighted father now thought that the measure of his joy was full. A few days after her confinement, there began to be a strange lassitude about the young merchant's wife—her health was as good as is ordinary in such cases, but as the time passed, her countenance grew more pallid and sickly and her eyes lost their luster. The physician could give no satisfactory account of all this; and Lee himself for some time was in the dark also. But too soon did the fatal truth come to his knowledge, that *ardent spirits* was the cause of that pallor and that lassitude. His wife was an habitual gin-drinker!

Lee, though shocked at this disgusting fact, imagined at first, that the habit had been formed by using drink as a stimulus to keep up her powers of body in her sickness. But it was not so. During the time that had intervened between their marriage, the miserable woman, for very shame, had desisted from the practice. But a single taste, revived the old appetite in all its strength.

It happened one day, when the infant was some ten weeks old, that the mother, stupefied by excess of liquor, let her babe fall against some projecting article of furniture, and received a blow from which it never recovered. In the course of the week the child died, and though the physician never stated the exact cause of its death, it was well understood that the fall from the arms of its drunken mother had been that cause.

Two or three years passed on. Another infant was born to Lee—but it met with a fate not much better than the first. Its death came from neglect and ill nursing.

And the mother—the lovely and educated wife, with whom the merchant had expected to see so much happiness, she was a drunkard. She lingered not long, however, to bear witness to her own and her husband's shame. She sank into the grave the victim of intemperance.

It was many years before Lee recovered his former tone of character. Naturally cheerful, however, he could not long remain that gloomy being which his misfortunes had for a time made him. He was fond of sporting, and loved the country, which he frequently visited. He loved, too, the old traditions, and reminiscences of the earlier part of our American history, to which he gave up a considerable portion of his leisure. Thus, and in the affairs of his trade, which he still kept on, he had made life pass as evenly and pleasantly as he could.

"You say you are a stranger," he said to me, before I left him, "but you are not half so much so as the rest of the world. My nearest relatives, who were never friendly to me in life, have long since been laid in the grave; and I can make no better disposition of my profits than to give them to one whom I feel confident will not be unwilling to use some part thereof, for suppressing the fearful fiend Intemperance, that has brought such wo upon us both!"

I mused, as I left the place, upon the singular notion of the old man, in remembering me thus. Of course, it was anything but unpleasant to me that I should inherit a respectable competency; and yet I could not help wondering at the method of it.

Not many days elapsed before Lee died, and was laid away to his repose. His will, though the theme of much grumbling to some far-distant connexions, could not be gainsayed, and I came into possession of the property left me.

CHAPTER XXIV

The temperance flag! the temperance flag!
It is the banner of the free!
The temperance flag! the temperance flag
An emblem of our liberty!
—WASHINGTONIAN MINSTREL

So, at an age which was hardly upon the middle verge of life, I found myself possessed of a comfortable property; and, as the term is 'unincumbered' person—which means that I had no wife to love me—no children to please me, and be the recipients of my own affection, and no domestic hearth around which we might gather, as the center of joy and delight. My constitution, notwithstanding the heavy draughts made upon its powers by my habits of intemperance, might yet last me the appointed term of years, and without more than a moderate quantity of the physical ills that man is heir to.

The Marchions were still my firm friends. I visited them often.

"I think, Mr. Evans," said Mrs. Marchion to me one day, "that there is still one thing for you to do, in connection with what has already been your movement upon Temperance. Lately, I find there is more progress made than we are aware of. People now are not content to abstain merely from the stronger kinds of drinks, but they disuse *all*. I have been reflecting in my own mind upon the subject, and I came to the conclusion that *total* abstinence is indeed the only safe course."

I too had been reflecting in my mind upon the same thing, and I had arrived pretty nearly at the same conclusion.

"My dear madam," said I, "there is more truth in your words perhaps, than even you yourself imagine. I have tried the old pledge, and I can conscientiously say that I have adhered to it, ever since the day of my signing it; yet, if I were to tell you all the horrors that have been transacted since that time, in reference to my own life, and which I can trace directly to *wine-drinking*, you would be appalled with fear! Total abstinence is indeed the only safe course, and I will put the principle in effect this very evening."

My deeds were as good as my word. Before the sun rose again I had signed the bond — the holy charter with myself, which has never yet been broken; and which, under the blessing of Providence, shall remain inviolate while I continue among the living.

I do not intend to relate the occurrences of my after life. Indeed, were I so disposed, it would be impossible; for I have brought the chain of events down almost to the very day when the reader will be perusing my story. True, several years have passed since my Virginia visit, which resulted so disastrously to some of those with whom I was brought in contact; but the tenor of action has flowed on so smoothly since then, that I have little to tell which would be interesting.

There is one person, however, who has figured in these pages, on whom I would bestow a paragraph before I close. I allude to my old friend, Colby.

As I was passing one day along a street on the eastern side of the city, my course was impeded by crowd [*sic*], gathered around a tipsy loafer, who was cutting up his antics in the street. The miserable man, it seemed, had been promised by some idle boys enough money to purchase a drink of gin, if he would dance for their amusement. And there he was, going through his disgusting capers.

Pausing a moment, and looking in the man's face, I thought I recollected the features. A second and a third glance convinced me. It was Colby, my early intimate, the tempter who had led me aside from the paths of soberness.

Wretched creature! Had I even wished for some punishment upon his head, in requital of the harm he had done me, a sight of the kind I saw there, would have dissolved all my anger. His apparel looked as though it had been picked up in some mud hole; it was torn in strips and all over soiled. His face was bloated, and his eyes red and swollen. I thought of the morning when I awoke upon the dock, after my long fit of intemperance: the person before me, was even more an object of pity than myself on that occasion. His beard had not seen the razor for weeks, and he was quite without shoes.

The spectators laughed, and the heedless children clapped their hands in glee — little thinking of the desecration such a spectacle brought upon the common nature all shared. I felt sick at heart, and hurried away from the place. How had it happened, that I myself did not meet with the same degraded fortune? Was it not indeed miraculous that I — instead of being a counterpart of the poor sot whom I had just been witnessing with feelings I shall not attempt to describe — was occupying a respectable station in society, and on the fair road to a remainder of my life, passed in honor and comfort? I blessed my Maker as I thought of these things, and besought His favor on that holy Cause of Reformation, where I had myself cast anchor, and where thousands besides were moored, safe from the wild storm, and from the boiling waves that so threatened to ingulf them.

As it is the usage of story-tellers to give some passing notice of all who have figured in their pages, before those pages are brought to a close, I will here follow the custom; though the small number of such persons, apart from the I, who have been the hero of the tale, will render the task an easy one.

My country relations were not forgotten by me in my good fortune. The worthy uncle, who had kindly housed and fed me when I was quite too small to make him any repayment for that service, received in his old age the means to render his life more easy and happy. My cousins too, had no reason to be sorry for the good-will which they had ever shown toward me. I was never the person to forget a friend, or leave unrequited a favor, when I had the payment of it in my power.

The tavern-keeper, to whom the reader was introduced in the first chapter of my story, dragged out a life of intemperance, a discredit to his family and with little comfort to himself. He was found dead, one winter morning, in a room where in a fit of passion the preceding night he had gone, from that which he usually occupied with his wife. An overturned bottle of brandy was at his side. After his death, the tavern was closed.

My friend, the driver of the market wagon, became by chance an attendant at some meetings of the temperance advocates. He was a sensible fellow, and listened with open ears to their arguments. In a visit I lately paid to the island of my birth, I found him a wholehearted and most ardent Washingtonian.

Demaine, I have never been able to light upon more than once or twice, and therefore cannot fully say, what are his fortunes. Probably, however, he is to be numbered among those hundreds of men in our city, whose god is fashion and dress; and who, when they are out of sight of their 'genteel' acquaintances, have to practice the most miserable economy to 'keep up appearances,' in the ball-room or the public promenade. Such fellows are as far removed from true gentlemen, as the gilded sun, in stage melo-dramas, from the genuine source of light himself.

The Marchions continued to prosper, as their kindness of heart and their honorable benevolence to the needy, deserved. They are among the most respectable and respected families in the city.

I hear now and then from Bourne. Things are going on in the old way. Phillips has left him, and bought a plantation of his own.

Andrews, my old master, died of grief at the failure of some stock-jobbing operations, wherein a cunning fellow-broker overreached him. His immense possessions, after his death, were found to be as fallacious as the basis on which they had been reared.

The landlord, by whom I was so swindled in the country village, after my poor Mary's death, was caught at last in one of his tricks; and not having been as cautious as with me, he now has to repent his wickedness within the walls of the country jail. I hope he will be taught better, by the time he is at large again.

I have never heard any thing further of the Picaroon, or either of his two companions. Undoubtedly, they reached the confines of Sing-Sing before long, after I had the honor of their acquaintance.

Boarding-houses are no more patronized by me. The distaste I formed for them in my memorable search for quarters, when I first came to New York, was never entirely done away with. The comforts of a home are to be had in very few of these places; and I have often thought that the cheerless method of their accommodations drives many a young man to the bar-room, or to some other place of public resort, whence the road to habits of intoxication is but too easy. Indeed, the thought has long been entertained by me, that this matter is not sufficiently appreciated. I would advise every young man to marry as soon as possible, and have a home of his own.

Reader! I have brought my narrative quite to an end. I may be presumptuous to flatter myself that it has been of much amusement to you, though I have had that partly in view. Partly — but not wholly. For I have desired, amid the path we have traveled together, and which is now at an end — that a few seeds of wholesome instruction might be dropped at the same time we gathered the fruits and the flowers.

CHAPTER XXV . . . CONCLUSION

As works of fiction have often been made the vehicle of morality, I have adopted the novel experiment of making one of the sort a messenger of the cause of Temperance. And though I know not what the decision of the reader may be, I am too strongly armed in the honesty of my intentions, to suppose that there can be any doubt as to the propriety of the *moral* intended to be conveyed — or to fear any attack upon the story, as regards its principles.

To expatiate upon the ruins and curses which follow the habitual use of strong drink, were at this time almost a stale homily. A great revolution has come to pass within the last eight or ten years. The dominion of the Liquor Fiend has been assaulted and battered. Good men and strong have come up to the work of attack. Warriors, with large hands, and with girded loins, are waiting with resolution, and their energies are devoted to the battle. They are taking the place of those who are wearied, and in their turn give way to others, who have new and greater strength. Will the old fortress yield? It *must*, sooner or later. It may be compared to some ivy-crowned castle, some strong tower of the olden time, with its flanked battlements, and its guards pacing on the top of its walls and laughing to scorn all the devices of those who came against it. The red banner floated on its topmost height — inscribed with its fearful watchword, "Disgrace and Death!" And a million victim [*sic*] came every year, and yielded themselves to their ruin under its control. But the foes of the Castle of Orgies stepped forth in array, and swore to one another that they would devote their lives to the work of reform. Long did that haughty structure resist every blow — firmly did it defy every besieger. But the might of a good motive is more than the highest strength of wickedness; and at last the bars of the gates began to give way, and the thick walls cracked. An outpost was driven in, and a tower fell. How tremendous the shout then that arose from the men who were fighting the good fight, and the faces of their antagonists paled with fear! So they kept on. And other parts of the foundation were undermined, and the heavy stanchions were burst asunder, and the forces of the Red Fiend have been routed, band after band, until but a little are left; and they will soon have to retreat, and go the way of their brethren.

The good of the present age are smiling upon the cause of Temperance. It is indeed a holy cause. How many widows' tears it has assuaged — and how many poor wretched men it has taken by the hand, and led to reputation and comfort once more. It seems to me, that he who would speak of the efforts of the Temperance Societies with a sneer, is possessed of a very heedless and bigoted, or a very wicked disposition. It is true, that the dictates of a classic and most refined taste, are not always observed by these people; and the fashionable fop, the exquisite, or the pink of what is termed 'quality,' might feel not at home among them. But to persons with clear heads, and with breasts where philanthropy and a desire for the good of their fellows have a resting-place, I am fully content to leave the decision, whether, after all, there be not a good deal of *intellectuality* engaged in the Temperance movement.

The Reformers have one great advantage, too, which makes up for any want of polish, or grace. They are sincere, and speak with the convictions of their own experience. In all ages, a revolution for the better, when started, has found its advocates among the poorer classes of men. From them, it gradually rises, until it pervades all ranks of society. It has happened so in this case. The few men who met together in Baltimore, and formed a compact with themselves to abstain from those practices which had been so injurious to them, little thought how their principles were to spread, and how they would be pointed back to with admiration, from the rich as well as the poor — the learned as well as the ignorant.

They called themselves "WASHINGTONIANS." Long may the name be honored — and long may it continue to number among those who are proud to style themselves by the title — upright and noble spirits, determined never to turn back from the work, or to discredit the name they bear, and the Society to which they belong!

Any one who has attended the meetings of the temperance people, cannot but be amazed and delighted at the enthusiasm which pervades them. It is not confined to one sex, or to any particular age or class. It spreads over all. Men and women join in it. Young people, even boys and girls, are inoculated with the fervor, and are heard about the streets, singing the temperance songs, and conversing upon the principles of the doctrine, by which their fathers or brothers have been regenerated and made happy. The enthusiasm I mention, has not been limited, either, to one City, or one State. It is felt over every part of this Republic, and accounts come to us of the wondrous doings of Temperance in Maine, while the same hour, in the Western mail, we receive the story of how many new converts there are in Illinois. Perhaps on no occasion has there been a spectacle so full of moral splendor. A whole nation forsaking an evil mania, which has hitherto made it the mark of scorn to those who, coming from abroad, have noticed this one foul blot in contradistinction to all the other national good qualities—and turning a goodly portion of its mighty powers to the business of preventing others from forming the same habits; and redeem, as far as practicable, those who have already formed them: I consider it a sight which we may properly call on the whole world to admire!

In the story which has been narrated in the preceding pages, there is given but a faint idea of the dangers which surround our young men in this great city. On all sides, and at every step, some temptation assails them; but all the others joined together, are nothing compared with the seductive enchantments which have been thrown around the practice of intoxication, in some five or six of the more public and noted taverns called "musical saloons," or some other name which is used to hide their hideous nature. These places are multiplying. The persons engaged in the sale of ardent spirits are brought to see that their trade, unless they can join something to it, as a make-weight, will shortly vanish into thin air, and their gains along with it. Thus they have hit upon the expedient of MUSIC, as a lure to induce customers, and in too many cases, with fatally extensive success.

I would warn that youth whose eye may scan over these lines, with a voice which speaks to him, not from idle fear, but the sad knowledge of experience, how bitter are the consequences attending these musical drinking-shops. They are the fit portals of ruin, and inevitably lead thither. I have known more than one young man, whose prospects for the future were good—in whom hope was strong, and energy not wanting—but all poisoned by these pestilent places, where the mind and the body are both rendered effeminate together.

To conclude, I would remark that, if my story meets with that favor which writers are perhaps too fond of relying upon, my readers may hear from me again, in the method similar to that which has already made as acquainted.

THE AUTHOR

THE END

SUPPLEMENTARY TEXTS

THE MADMAN

BY THE AUTHOR OF

'FRANKLIN EVANS.'

"Lo! See his eyeballs Glare!"
—MONK LEWIS

EDITORS' NOTE: *Seemingly the first installment of a serial novel,* The
Madman *was published in the New York* Washingtonian and Organ, *a publication of the Washingtonian temperance societies. Appearing on January 23,
1843, only weeks after the publication of* Franklin Evans, *it did not carry Whitman's name, only the byline identifying it as the work of the author of* Franklin
Evans. *For more details and an account of the discovery of this and another
previously unknown Whitman text in the* Washingtonian and Organ, *see Holloway, "More Temperance Tales by Whitman."*

CHAPTER I

THE little tables of one of the large eating houses in the upper part of Fulton
street, were crowded. It was an hour past noon. At that time, all classes of
our citizens, except they who aspire to rank among the fashionable, or in the
neighborhood of fashionable, either are engaged in the pleasant business of
eating, or taking measures for soon being so. The waiters, in their shirt sleeves,
hurried to and fro, obeying the mandates of the customers. The carvers and
cooks, at a little place partitioned off in a corner in the back part of the room,
were tasked to their utmost. Knives and forks jingled, plates clattered, the
names of the variety of dishes were sung out without a moments [*sic*] cessation.

It might have been noticed, by the curious eye, that nine out of ten who
sought the accommodation there, *gulped* down their food with the most alarming haste, and in a manner which inferred that the crisis of some important
transaction were just on the eve of happening—and its favorable conclusion

depended on the celerity of mastication and swallowing. The large plain clock, at the top of the back wall, received many a hurried glance — as though the eaters timed themselves, and sought to get through the dining operations, within a given movement of the minute hands.

And there were two features which an observer might have noticed with great satisfaction. Each customer, upon finishing his meal, walked up to the counter and paid for it, according to his own computation — his own honesty being the only bar between a little petty cheating and the fair payment for what he had been served with. It is asserted that the instances of deception, from customers, are so rare as hardly to deserve mention. What a pleasant commentary on the attacks of foreign slanderers with respect to our national integrity! The second feature was the absence of any ardent liquors — no temptation existing for any one to nullify the healthy action of the powers of the stomach upon what had been eaten, by drinking the unwholesome draught.

When the business and the confusion were at the highest, the door opened and admitted Richard Arden. Who was Richard Arden?

Any one who has been familiar with life and people in a great city cannot have failed to notice a certain class, mostly composed of young men, who occupy a kind of medium between gentility and poverty. By soul, intelligence, manners, and a vague good taste, they assimilate to the former method. By irresolution of mind, evil acquaintances, a kind of romance which pervades the character, and incapacity for the harder and tougher and more profitable purposes of life, they attach to the latter. Poverty, too, many times, is the source of much meanness. It causes the commission of a thousand things which result at last in the brushing off from the unfortunate poor one, of that fine sensitiveness which forms the most exquisite trait in the character of a *true gentleman* — that character which it ought to be our highest ambition to attain. I don't know, either, whether it may not be wrought out as well by a person surrounded by the disagreeables of want, and ill-breeding — as by one who has all the advantages of society and fashion. Let me make an impression in this passing remark, good reader.

Richard Arden had but fifteen cents in his pocket — and with that he intended to purchase his dinner. He had no certainty that he could get another meal afterward. Yet he was not cast down in spirit. He held his head well aloft. He bore upon his countenance the expression of one whose mind was but little agitated. He was a philosopher.

"Pork and beans, No. 8!" sung out Irish John, the waiter.

The words themselves may seem identified with any thing in the world but refinement and romance. But they involve quite an amount of comfort, nevertheless. The smoking plate was brought—the crispy brown [beans?] upon one side, and the rich fat slice of meat upon the other. Young Arden applied himself with great cheerfulness to the matter of devouring the savory viand.

What a hubbub! What a clatter of knives and forks!

One of the surest tests of good breeding is the manner of performing the little duties of meals and the table. A person whose fork dashes into the food before him, and whose knife divides it with the ferocity of a wild beast, has been unfortunate in his earlier education; and one remnant, at least, of the manners of a clown is still resident with him. Hurry is a vulgar trait, at best. At the table it becomes doubly so—inconsistent with health and prudence, as with decorum and enjoyment.

Our hero—for the reader has doubtless seen that the person to whom he has been introduced is so—our hero was unexceptionable in the matter to which we have just alluded. Though in our establishment, and surrounded by companions, that would have shocked the fastidious delicacy of an Astor House boarder, or one whose dining hour was five or six o'clock, Arden comported himself with the quiet and deliberation which are at the root of good taste. So we think we have established for our principal character a claim to be considered a gentleman—an important point.

At the opposite side of the table sat a man of rather pleasant countenance, whom Arden had seen some few times previous, and with whom, on the present occasion, he happened to enter into some light talk. As they discussed their dinner, they discussed one or two of the ordinary topics of conversation. For some ten or fifteen minutes per . . . tinued.*

How strangely we form acquaintances! How strange, indeed, and how complete a matter of chance, are many of those incidents and occurrences which have a lasting influence on a future destiny—trivial, as they seem at first, but potent for good or evil, in the future.

Arden and the pleasant-faced man, whose name was Barcoure, happened to get through their meal at the same time—to pay at the counter together—

---

*Here the surviving copy of the text is illegible. According to Thomas L. Brasher, Emory Holloway suggested the reading "perhaps this continued."

and to walk forth into the street together. Then they happened to be going a block or two in the same direction.

Why was it that they became acquaintances—and, are [ere?] long, friends?

I cannot tell. At first they saw little or nothing—the one in mind or manners of the other—to attract an admiration or respect in unwonted degree. Yet the next day, when they happened to meet, they bowed. The next day, each gave the other his name. The next week, they were on the footing of intimacy and familiarity.

〜〜〜〜〜

CHAPTER II

BARCOURE was a young man—like my hero. Indeed it may be found, before the end of my story, that the right of main personage may lie between the two. He was of French descent—his father having come to America just after the downfall of the Napoleon dynasty, imbued with that fierce radicalism and contempt for religion which marked the old French revolution, and which still lingers among a by no means small portion of the people of that beautiful and noble country. The son inherited the sentiments, with the blood, of his father. His infidelity and his disregard of all the ties which custom and piety have established, [were?] more tempered with more discretion than his father had possessed—but they were none the less firm.

Perhaps I am not fully justifiable in calling Barcoure an *infidel*. He had ideas of morality and virtue, and, to a degree, practiced them. His system was a beautiful and simple one—in theory—based upon a foundation of stern and strict and rigorous correctness of conduct. He rejected all of what he called the *superstitions* of mankind. He held that each code of religion contained more or less excellence—and more or less fanaticism. A strange and dreamy creature was Pierre Barcoure.

And before I advance any farther, it were well for me to remind the reader that I seek to paint life and men, in my narrative—describing them in such manner, and putting such words into their mouths, as may seem to make the portratures [*sic*] truthful ones. In what they say, I hold no responsibility.

So* these two—Pierre and young Arden—became near and dear to one another.

---

*Brasher notes that this reads "To" in the original but concludes that this is "certainly erroneous." Brasher, 243.

Their friendship was not of that grosser kind which is riveted by intimacy in scenes of dissipation. Many men in this great city of vice are banded together in a kind of companionship of vice, which they dignify by applying to it the word which stands second at the beginning of this paragraph. How vile a profanation of a holy term!

(TO BE CONTINUED.)

THE CHILD

AND

THE PROFLIGATE

EDITORS' NOTE: *Bearing the title "The Child's Champion," a version of this story first appeared in the* New World *on November 20, 1841. In October 1844, a significantly revised text appeared in the* Columbian Magazine *and then again in January 1847 in the* Brooklyn Eagle, *which Whitman was still editing at the time. Its final nineteenth-century publication was in the "Specimen Days and Collect" section of Whitman's 1892* Complete Prose Works, *this time with some of its temperance polemic downplayed.*

We have chosen to reprint the text that appeared in the Columbian Maga-zine *and, nearly identically, in the* Brooklyn Eagle. *This version, titled "The Child and the Profligate" accentuates the temperance message, thereby demon-strating Whitman's ongoing engagement with the movement and his continu-ing tendency toward the didactic. In the few very minor instances where the* Columbian *and* Eagle *texts differ, we have followed the earlier version because it followed more closely upon the publication of* Franklin Evans. *For a detailed annotation of the differences among the versions, see Brasher, 68–79.*

AMONG the victims of the passion for strong drink the greater part become so, I have observed, not from any ignorance of the danger of the path they pursue, but from weakness and irresolution of mind. To the abstemious it is almost impossible to convey an idea of the strength of the desire, formed, after a while, in a habitual drinker. No one can know, except him who has realized it himself. The world points with contempt at the inebriate, and laughs him to scorn that he does not turn from the error of his ways. But oh, if the agony of his struggles could be seen—if the vain and impotent efforts he makes to disentangle himself from the thraldom of his tyrant—if the sharp shame, the secret tears, the throes of mortification and conscious disgrace—were apparent to those who condemn so severely, one little drop of sorrow might certainly be mingled with their anger.

Now and then, though rarely, it does happen that something occurs which turns the tide and converts the drinker with feelings I have mentioned into a reformed man. And it is strange to observe how small and trivial are frequently the causes of this change. A word merely, or an unimportant action, or a casual incident not out of the ordinary routine, forms the starting point whence the hitherto miserable one commences a reformation which ere long presents him to the world with a clearer head and purer soul. Such a word, it my be—such an incident—stirs up the fountains of thought, brings back memories long passed away and awakens the man to beautiful and pathetic recollections of an earlier and more innocent age. Thus fully awakened, and with genial influence of the time in all its sway over him, if the crisis turns for good, it will surely be consummated for good. But should it turn to wickedness again, God have mercy on the fated being!

The incidents of my little narrative are simple and unromantic enough, and yet I hope they will not be found without interest. I tell no tale of fiction either. There are those now in this metropolis who will pursue the tale and acknowledge in their own minds' consciousness of its unadorned truth.

Just after sunset, one evening in summer—that pleasant hour when the air is balmy, the light loses its glare, and all around is imbued with soothing quiet—on the door-step of a house there sat an elderly woman waiting for the arrival of her son. The house was in a straggling village some fifty miles from New York city. She who sat on the door step was a widow; her white cap covered locks of gray, and her dress, though clean, was exceedingly homely. Her house—for the tenement she occupied was her own—was very little and very old. Trees clustered around it so thickly as almost to hid [*sic*] its color— that blackish gray color which belongs to old wooden houses that have never been painted; and to get in it you had to enter a little rickety gate and walk through a short path, bordered by carrot beds and beets and other vegetables. The son whom she was expecting was her only child. About a year before he had been bound apprentice to a rich farmer in the place, and after finishing his daily task he was in the habit of spending half an hour at his mother's. On the present occasion the shadows of night had settled heavily before the youth made his appearance. When he did, his walk was slow and dragging, and all his motions were languid, as if from great weariness. He opened the gate, came through the path, and sat down by his mother in silence.

"You are sullen to-night, Charley" said the widow, after a moment's pause, when she found that he returned no answer to her greeting.

As she spoke she put her hand fondly on his head; it seemed moist as if it had been dipped in the water. His shirt, too, was soaked; and as she passed her fingers down his shoulder she felt a sharp twinge in her heart, for she knew that moisture to be the hard wrung sweat of severe toil, exacted from her young child (he was but thirteen years old) by an unyielding task-master.

"You have worked hard to-day, my son."

"I've been mowing."

The widow's heart felt another pang.

"Not *all day*, Charley?" she said, in a low voice; and there was a slight quiver in it.

"Yes mother, all day," replied the boy; "Mr. Ellis said he couldn't afford to hire men, for wages are so high. I've swung the scythe ever since an hour before sunrise. Feel of my hands."

There were blisters on them like great lumps. Tears started in the widow's eyes. She dared not trust herself with a reply, though her heart was bursting with the thought that she could not better his condition. There was no earthly means of support on which she had dependence enough to encourage her child in the wish she knew he was forming — the wish not uttered for the first time — to be freed from his bondage.

"Mother," at length said the boy, "I can stand it no longer. I cannot and will not stay at Mr. Ellis's. Ever since the day I first went into his house I've been a slave; and if I have to work so much longer I know I shall run off and go to sea or somewhere else. I'd as leave be in my grave as there." And the child burst into a passionate fit of weeping.

His mother was silent, for she was in deep grief herself. After some minutes had flown, however, she gathered sufficient self-possession to speak to her son in a soothing tone, endeavoring to win him from his sorrows and cheer up his heart. She told him that time was swift — that in the course of a few years he would be his own master — that all people have their troubles — with many other ready arguments which, though they had little effect in calming her own distress, she hoped would act as a solace to the disturbed temper of the boy. And as the half hour to which he was limited had now elapsed, she took him by the hand and led him to the gate, to set forth on his return. The youth seemed pacified, though occasionally one of those convulsive sighs that remain after a fit of weeping, would break from his throat. At the gate he threw his arms around his mother's neck; each pressed a long kiss on the lips of the other, and the youngster bent his steps towards his master's house.

As her child passed out of sight the widow returned, shut the gate and entered her lonely room. There was no light in the old cottage that night — the heart of its occupant was dark and cheerless. Love, agony, and grief, and tears and convulsive wrestlings were there. The thought of a beloved son condemned to labor — labor that would break down a man — struggling from day to day under the hard rule of a soulless gold-worshipper; the knowledge that years must pass thus; the sickening idea of her own poverty, and of living mainly on the grudged charity of neighbors — thoughts, too, of former happy days — these racked the widow's heart, and made her bed a sleepless one without repose.

The boy bent his steps to his employer's, as has been said. In his way down the village street he had to pass a public house, the only one the place contained; and when he came off against it he heard the sound of a fiddle — drowned, however, at intervals, by much laughter and talking. The windows were up, and, the house standing close to the road, Charles thought it no harm to take a look and see what was going on within. Half a dozen footsteps brought him to the low casement, on which he leaned his elbow, and where he had full view of the room and its occupants. In one corner was an old man, known in the village as Black Dave — he it was whose musical performances had a moment before drawn Charles's attention to the tavern; and he it was who now exerted himself in a violent manner to give, with divers flourishes and extra twangs, a tune very popular among that thick-lipped race whose fondness for melody is so well known. In the middle of the room were five or six sailors, some of them quite drunk, and others in earlier stages of that process, while on benches around were more sailors, and here and there a person dressed in landsmen's attire, but hardly behind the sea gentlemen in uproar and mirth. The individuals in the middle of the room were dancing; that is, they were going through certain contortions and shufflings, varied occasionally by exceedingly hearty stamps upon the sanded floor. In short the whole party were engaged in a drunken frolic, which was in no respect different from a thousand other drunken frolics, except, perhaps, that there was less than the ordinary amount of anger and quarreling. Indeed everyone seemed in remarkably good humor.

But what excited the boy's attention more than any other object was an individual, seated on one of the benches opposite, who, though evidently enjoying the spree as much as if he were an old hand at such business, seemed in every other particular to be far out of his element. His appearance was youthful. He might have been twenty-one or two years old. His countenance was intelligent, and had the air of city life and society. He was dressed not gaudily, but in every respect fashionably; his coat being of the finest broadcloth, his linen delicate and spotless as snow, and his whole aspect that of one whose counterpart may now and then be seen upon the pave in Broadway of a fine afternoon. He laughed and talked with the rest, and it must be confessed his jokes—like the most of those that passed current there—were by no means distinguished for their refinement or purity. Near the door was a small table, covered with decanters and glasses, some of which had been used, but were used again indiscriminately, and a box of very thick and very long cigars.

One of the sailors—and it was he who made the largest share of the hubbub—had but one eye. His chin and cheeks were covered with huge bushy whiskers, and altogether he had quite a brutal appearance. "Come, boys," said this gentleman, "come, let us take a drink. I know you're all a getting dry;" and he clenched his invitation with an appalling oath. "So, curse me if you sha'n't have a suck at my expense."

This politeness was responded to by a general moving of the company toward the table holding the before-mentioned decanters and glasses. Clustering there around, each one helped himself to a very handsome portion of that particular liquor which suited his fancy; and steadiness and accuracy being at that moment by no means distinguishing traits of the arms and legs of the party, a goodly amount of the fluid was spilled upon the floor. This piece of extravagance excited the ire of the personage who gave the "treat;" and that ire was still further increased when he discovered two or three loiterers who seemed to slight his request to drink. Charles, as we have before mentioned, was looking in at the window.

"Walk up, boys! walk up! Don't let there be any skulker among us, or blast my eyes if he shan't go down on his marrow bones and taste the liquor we have spilt! Hallo!" he exclaimed as he spied Charles; "hallo, you chap in the window, come here and take a sup."

As he spoke he stepped to the open casement, put his brawny hands under the boy's arms, and lifted him into the room bodily.

"There, my lads," said he, turning to his companions, "There's a new recruit for you. Not so coarse a one, either," he added as he took a fair view of the boy, who, though not what is called pretty, was fresh and manly looking, and large for his age.

"Come, youngster, take a glass," he continued. And he poured one nearly full of strong brandy.

Now Charles was not exactly frightened, for he was a lively fellow, and had often been at the country merry-makings, and at the parties of the place; but he was certainly rather abashed at his abrupt introduction to the midst of strangers. So, putting the glass aside, he looked up with a pleasant smile in his acquaintance's face.

"I've no need for anything now," he said, "but I'm just as much obliged to you as if I was."

"Poh! man, drink it down," rejoined the sailor, "drink it down—it won't hurt you."

And, by way of showing its excellence, the one-eyed worthy drained it himself to the last drop. Then filling it again, he renewed his efforts to make the lad go through the same operation.

"I've no occasion. Besides, *my mother has often prayed me not to drink,* and I promised to obey her."

A little irritated by his continued refusal, the sailor, with a loud oath, declared that Charles should swallow the brandy, whether he would or no. Placing one of his tremendous paws on the back of the boy's head, with the other he thrust the edge of the glass to his lips, swearing at the same time, that if he shook it so much as to spill its contents the consequences would be of a nature by no means agreeable to his back and shoulders. Disliking liquor, and angry at the attempt to overbear him, the undaunted child lifted his hand and struck the arm of the sailor with a blow so sudden that the glass fell and was smashed to pieces on the floor; while the brandy was about equally divided between the face of Charles, the clothes of the sailor, and the sand. By this time the whole of the company had their attention drawn to the scene. Some of them laughed when they saw Charles's undistinguished antipathy to the drink; but they laughed still more heartily when he discomfited the sailor. All of them, however, were content to let the matter go as chance would have it— all but the young man of the black coat, who has before been spoken of.

What was there in the words which Charles has spoken that carried the mind of the young man back to former times—to a period when he was more pure and innocent than now? *"My mother has often prayed me not to drink!"* Ah, how the mist of months rolled aside, and presented to his soul's eye the picture of *his* mother, and a prayer of exactly similar purport! Why was it, too, that the young man's heart moved with a feeling of kindness toward the harshly treated child? Was it that his associations had hitherto been among the vile, and the contrast was now so strikingly great? Even in the hurried walks of life and business may we meet with beings who seem to touch the fountains of our love, and draw forth their swelling waters! The wish to love and be loved, which the forms of custom and the engrossing anxiety for gain so generally smother, will sometimes burst forth in spite of all obstacles; and kindled by one who, till the hour, was unknown to us, will burn with a permanent and pure brightness!

Charles stood, his check flushed and his heart throbbing, wiping the trickling drops from his face with a handkerchief. At first the sailor, between his drunkenness and his surprise, was much in the condition of one suddenly awakened out of a deep sleep, who cannot call his consciousness about him. When he saw the state of things, however, and heard the jeering laugh of his companions, his dull eye lighting up with anger, fell upon the boy who had withstood him. He seized Charles with a grip of iron, and with the side of his heavy boot gave him a sharp and solid kick. He was about repeating the performance—for the child hung like a rag in his grasp—but all of a sudden his ears rang, as if pistols were snapped close to them; lights of various hues flickered in his eye, (he had but one, it will be remembered,) and a strong propelling power caused him to move from his position, and keep moving until he was brought up by the wall. A blow, a cuff given in such a scientific manner that the hand from which it proceeded was evidently no stranger to the pugilistic art, had been suddenly planted in the ear of the sailor. It was planted by the young man of the black coat. He had watched with interest the proceeding of the sailor and the boy—two or three times he was on the point of interfering; but when the kick was given, his rage was uncontrollable. He sprang from his seat, and assuming, unconsciously however, the attitude of a boxer, he struck the sailor in a manner to cause those unpleasant sensations which have been described. And he would probably have followed up the attack in a manner by no means consistent with the sailor's personal safety had not Charles, now thoroughly terrified, clung around his legs and prevented his advancing.

The scene was a strange one, and for the time quite a silent one. The company had started from their seats, and for a moment held breathless but strained positions in the middle of the room stood the young man, in his not at all ungraceful attitude — every nerve out, and his eyes flashing brilliantly. He seemed rooted like a rock; and clasping him, with an appearance of confidence in his protection, hung the boy.

"Dare! You scoundrel!" cried the young man, his voice thick with passion, "dare to touch the boy again, and I'll thrash you till no sense is left in your body."

The sailor, now partially recovered, made some gestures of a belligerent nature.

"Come on, drunken brute!" continued the angry youth; "I wish you would! You've not had half what you deserve!"

Upon sobriety and sense more fully taking their power in the brains of the one-eyed mariner, however, that worthy determined in his own mind that it would be most prudent to let the latter drop. Expressing therefore his conviction to that effect, adding certain remarks to the purport that he "meant no harm to the lad," that he was surprised at such a gentleman being angry at "a little piece of fun," and so forth — he proposed that the company should go on with their jollity just as if nothing had happened. In truth, he of the single eye was not a bad fellow at heart, after all; the fiery enemy whose advances he had so often courted that night, had stolen away his good feelings, and set busy devils at work within him, that might have made his hands do some dreadful deed, had not the stranger interposed.

In a few minutes the frolic of the party was upon its former footing. The younger man sat down upon one of the benches, with the boy by his side, and while the rest were loudly laughing and talking, they two conversed together. The stranger learned from Charles all the particulars of his simple story — how his father had died years since — how his mother worked hard for a bare living — and how he himself, for many dreary months, had been the servant of a hard-hearted, avaricious master. More and more interested, drawing the child close to his side, the young man listened to his plainly told history — and thus an hour passed away.

It was now past midnight. The young man told Charles that on the morrow he would take steps to relieve him from his servitude — that for the present night the landlord would probably give him a lodging at the inn — and little persuading did the host need for that.

As he retired to sleep, very pleasant thoughts filled the mind of the younger man — thoughts of a worthy action performed — thoughts, too, newly awakened ones, of walking in a steadier and wiser path than formerly.

That roof, then, sheltered two beings that night — one of them innocent and sinless of all wrong — the other — oh, to that other what evil has not been present, either in action or to his desires!

Who, was the stranger? To those that, from ties of relationship or otherwise, felt an interest in him, the answer to that question was not pleasant to dwell upon. His name was Langton — parentless — a dissipated young man — a brawler — one whose too frequent companions were rowdies, blacklegs, and swindlers. The New York police officers were not altogether strangers to his countenance; and certain reporters, who notice the proceedings there, had more than once received a fee for leaving out his name from the disgraceful notoriety of their columns. He had been bred to the profession of medicine; besides, he had a very respectable income, and his house was in a pleasant street on the west side of the city. Little of his time however, did Mr. John Langton spend at his domestic hearth; and the elderly lady who officiated as his housekeeper was by no means surprised to have him gone for a week or a month at a time, and she knowing nothing of his whereabouts.

Living as he did, the young man was an unhappy being. It was not so much that his associates were below his own capacity — for Langton, though sensible and well bred, was not highly talented or refined — but that he lived without any steady purpose, that he had no one to attract him to his home, that he too easily allowed himself to be tempted — which caused his life to be, of late, one continued scene of dissatisfaction. This dissatisfaction he sought to drive away (ah, foolish youth!) by the brandy bottle, and mixing in all kinds of parties where the object was pleasure. On the present occasion he had left the city a few days before, and was passing his time at a place near the village where Charles and his mother lived. He fell in, during the day, with those who were his companions of the tavern spree; and thus it happened that they were all together. Langton hesitated not to make himself at home with any associate that suited his fancy.

The next morning the poor widow rose from her sleepless cot; and from that lucky trait in our nature which makes one extreme follow another, she set about her toil with a lightened heart. Ellis, the farmer, rose, too, short as the nights were, an hour before day; for his god was gain, and a prime article of his creed was to get as much work as possible from every one around him. He roused up all his people, and finding that Charles had not been home the preceding night, he muttered threats against him, and calling a messenger, to whom he hinted that any minutes which he stayed beyond a most exceeding short period, would be subtracted from his breakfast time, dispatched him to the widow's to find what was her son about.

What was he about? He had a beautiful dream — and thus it was in seeming.

With one of the brightest and the earliest rays of the warm sun a gentle angel entered his apartment, and hovered over him, and looked down with a pleasant smile, and blessed him. And the child thought his benefactor, the young man, was nigh, sleeping also. Noiselessly taking a stand by the bed, the angel bent over the boy's face and whispered strange words into his ear; it seemed to him like soft and delicate music. So the angel, pausing a moment, and smiling another and a doubly sweet smile, and drinking in the scene with his large soft eyes, bent over again to the boy's lips and touched them with a kiss, as the languid wind touches a flower. He seemed to be going now, and yet he lingered.

In the course of the day Ellis was called upon by young Langton, and never perhaps in his life was the farmer puzzled more than at the young man's pro-posal — his desire to provide for the widow's family, a family that could do him no pecuniary good, and his willingness to disburse money for that purpose. In that department of Ellis's structure where the mind was, or ought to have been situated, there never had entered the slightest thought assimilating to those which actuated the young man in his benevolent movements. Yet Ellis was a church member and a county officer. The widow, too, was called upon, not only on that day, but the next and the next.

It needs not that I should particularize the subsequent events of Langton's and the boy's history — how the reformation of the profligate might be dated to begin from that time — how he gradually severed the guilty ties that had

so long galled him—how he enjoyed his own home again—how the friendship of Charles and himself grew not slack with time—and how, when in the
course of seasons he became head of a family of his own, he would shudder
at the remembrance of his early dangers and his escapes. Often, in the bustle
of day and the silence of night, would he bless the utterance of those words,
"My mother prayed me not to drink!"

Loved reader, own you the moral interwoven in this simple story? Let your
children read it. To them draw forth the moral—pause a moment ere your eye
wander to a different page—and dwell upon it.

AN ADDRESS DELIVERED BY

ABRAHAM
LINCOLN

*Before the Springfield Washingtonian Temperance Society,
at the Second Presbyterian Church, Springfield, Illinois,
On the 22d Day of February, 1842*

EDITORS' NOTE: *Then an Illinois lawyer and legislator, Lincoln delivered this address a few months before Whitman published* Franklin Evans, *following it up by leading reformers and newly sober converts in a parade. This is a transcription from an 1889 pamphlet publication of the speech (Springfield, Ill.: O. H. Oldroyd, 1889).*

ALTHOUGH the Temperance cause has been in progress for near twenty years, it is apparent to all, that it is, *just now*, being crowned with a degree of success, hitherto unparalleled.

The list of its friends is daily swelled by the additions of fifties, of hundreds, and of thousands. The cause itself seems suddenly transformed from a cold abstract theory, to a living, breathing, active, and powerful chieftain, going forth "conquering and to conquer." The citadels of his great adversary are daily being stormed and dismantled; his temples and his altars, where the rites of his idolatrous worship have long been performed, and where human sacrifices have long been wont to be made, are daily desecrated and deserted. The trump of the conqueror's fame is sounding from hill to hill, from sea to sea, and from land to land, and calling millions to his standard at a blast.

For this new and splendid success, we heartily rejoice. That that success is so much greater *now* than *heretofore*, is doubtless owing to rational causes; and if we would have it to continue, we shall do well to enquire what those causes are. The warfare heretofore waged against the demon of Intemperance, has, some how or other, been erroneous. Either the champions engaged, or the tactics they adopted, have not been the most proper. These champions for the most part, have been Preachers, Lawyers, and hired agents. Between these and the mass of mankind, there is a want of *approachability*, if the term be admissible, partially at least, fatal to their success. They are supposed to have no sympathy of feeling or interest, with those very persons whom it is their object to convince and persuade.

And again, it is so easy and so common to ascribe motives to men of these classes, other than those they profess to act upon. The *preacher*, it is said, advocates temperance because he is a fanatic, and desires a union of Church and State; the *lawyer*, from his pride and vanity of hearing himself speak; and the *hired agent*, for his salary. But when one, who has long been known as a victim of intemperance, bursts the fetters that have bound him, and appears before his neighbors "clothed, and in his right mind," a redeemed specimen of long lost humanity, and stands up with tears of joy trembling in eyes, to tell of the miseries *once* endured, *now* to be endured no more forever; of his once naked and starving children, now clad and fed comfortably; of a wife long weighed down with woe, weeping, and a broken heart, now restored to health, happiness, and a renewed affection; and how easily it is all done, once it is resolved to be done; however simple his language, there is a logic, and an eloquence in it, that few, with human feelings, can resist. They cannot say that *he* desires a union of church and state, for he is not a church member; they cannot say *he* is vain of hearing himself speak, for his whole demeanor shows, he would gladly avoid speaking at all; they cannot say *he* speaks for pay for he receives none, and asks for none. Nor can his sincerity in any way be doubted; or his sympathy for those he would persuade to imitate his example, be denied.

In my judgment, it is to the battles of this new class of champions that our late success is greatly, perhaps chiefly, owing. But, had the old school champions themselves, been of the most wise selecting, was their *system* of tactics, the most judicious? It seems to me, it was not. Too much denunciation against dram sellers and dram-drinkers was indulged in. This, I think, was both impolitic and unjust. It was *impolitic*, because, it is not much in the nature of man to be driven to any thing; still less to be driven about that which is exclusively his own business; and least of all, where such driving is to be submitted to, at the expense of pecuniary interest, or burning appetite. When the dram-seller and drinker, were incessantly told, not in the accents of entreaty and persuasion, diffidently addressed by erring man to an erring brother; but in the thundering tones of anathema and denunciation, with which the lordly Judge often groups together all the crimes of the felon's life, and thrusts them in his face just ere he passes sentence of death upon him, that *they* were the authors of all the vice and misery and crime in the land; that *they* were the manufac-turers and material of all thieves and robbers and murderers that infested the earth; that *their* houses were the workshops of the devil; and that *their persons* should be shunned by all the good and virtuous, as moral pestilences — I say, when they were all told this, and in this way, it is not wonderful that they were slow, *very slow*, to acknowledge the truth of such denunciations, and to join the ranks of their denouncers, in a hue and cry against themselves.

To have expected them to do otherwise than as they did — to have expected them not to meet denunciation with denunciation, crimination with crimina-tion, and anathema with anathema, was to expect a reversal of human nature, which is God's decree, and never can be reversed. When the conduct of men is designed to be influenced, *persuasion*, kind, unassuming persuasion, should ever be adopted. It is an old and true maxim, that a "drop of honey catches more flies than a gallon of gall." So with men. If you would win a man to your cause, *first* convince him that you are his sincere friend. Therein is a drop of honey that catches his heart, which, say what he will, is the great high road to his reason, and which, when once gained, you will find but little trouble in convincing his judgment of the justice of your cause, if indeed that cause really be a just one. On the contrary, assume to dictate to his judgment, or to command his action, or to mark him as one to be shunned and despised, and he will retreat within himself, close all the avenues to his head and his heart; and tho' your cause be naked truth itself, transformed to the heaviest lance, harder than steel, and sharper than steel can be made, and tho' you throw it with more than Herculean force and precision, you shall no more be able to pierce him, than to penetrate the hard shell of a tortoise with a rye straw.

Such is man, and so *must* he be understood by those who would lead him, even to his own best interest.

On this point, the Washingtonians greatly excel the temperance advocates of former times. Those whom *they* desire to convince and persuade, are their old friends and companions. They know they are not demons, or even the worst of men. *They* know that generally, they are kind, generous and charitable, even beyond the example of their more staid and sober neighbors. *They* are practical philanthropists; and *they* glow with a generous and brotherly zeal, that mere theorizers are incapable of feeling. Benevolence and charity possess *their* hearts entirely; and out of the abundance of their hearts, their tongues give utterance, "Love through all their actions runs, and all their words are mild." In this spirit they speak and act, and in the same, they are heard and regarded. And when such is the temper of the advocate, and such of the audience, no good cause can be unsuccessful.

But I have said that denunciations against dram-sellers and dram-drinkers, are *unjust* as well as impolitic. Let us see.

I have not enquired at what period of time the use of intoxicating drinks commenced; nor is it important to know. It is sufficient that to all of us who now inhabit the world, the practice of drinking them, is just as old as the world itself, — that is, we have seen the one, just as long as we have seen the other. When all such of us, as have now reached the years of maturity, first opened our eyes upon the stage of existence, we found intoxicating liquor, recognized by every body, used by every body, and repudiated by nobody. It commonly entered into the first draught of the infant, and the last draught of the dying man. From the sideboard of the person, down to the ragged packet of the houseless loafer, it was commonly found. Physicians prescribed it in this, that, and the other disease. Government provided it for its soldiers and sailors; and to have a rolling or raising, a husking or hoedown, any where without it, was *positively insufferable.*

So too, it was every where a respectable article of manufacture and of merchandize. The making of it was regarded as an honorable livelihood; and he who could make most, was the most enterprising and respectable. Large and small manufactories of it were every where erected, in which all the earthly goods of their owners were invested. Wagons drew it from town to town — boats bore it from clime to clime, and the winds wafted it from nation to nation; and merchants bought and sold it, by wholesale and by retail, with precisely the same feelings, on the part of the seller, buyer, and bystander, as are felt at the selling and buying of flour, beef, bacon, or any other of the real necessaries of life. Universal public opinion not only tolerated, but recognized and adopted its use.

It is true, that even *then*, it was known and acknowledged, that many were greatly injured by it; but none seemed to think the injury arose from the *use* of a *bad thing*, but from the *abuse* of a *very good thing*. The victims to it were pitied, and compassionated, just as now are, the heirs of consumptions, and other hereditary diseases. Their failing was treated as a *misfortune*, and not as a *crime*, or even as a *disgrace*.

If, then, what I have been saying be true, is it wonderful, that *some* should think and *act now, as all* thought and acted *twenty years ago*? And is it *just* to assail, *contemn*, or despise them, for doing so? The universal *sense* of mankind, on any subject, is an argument, or at least an *influence* not easily overcome. The success of the argument in favor of the existence of an over-ruling Providence, mainly depends upon that sense; and men ought not, in justice, to be denounced for yielding to it, in any case, or for giving it up slowly, *especially*, where they are backed by interest, fixed habits, or burning appetites.

Another error, as it seems to me, into which the old reformers fell, was, the position that all habitual drunkards were utterly incorrigible, and therefore, must be turned adrift, and damned without remedy, in order that the grace of temperance might abound to the temperate *then*, and to all mankind some hundred years *thereafter*. There is in this something so repugnant to humanity, so uncharitable, so cold-blooded and feelingless, that it never did, nor ever can enlist the enthusiasm of a popular cause. We could not love the man who taught it—we could not hear him with patience. The heart could not throw open its portals to it. The generous man could not adopt it. It could not mix with his blood. It looked so fiendishly selfish, so like throwing fathers and brothers overboard, to lighten the boat for our security—that the noble minded shrank from the manifest meanness of the thing.

And besides this, the benefits of a reformation to be effected by such a system, were too remote in point of time, to warmly engage many in its behalf. Few can be induced to labor exclusively for posterity; and none will do it enthusiastically. Posterity has done nothing for us; and theorise on it as we may, practically we shall do very little for it, unless we are made to think, we are, at the same time, doing something for ourselves. What an ignorance of human nature does it exhibit, to ask or expect a whole community to rise up and labor for the *temporal* happiness of *others* after *themselves* shall be consigned to the dust, a majority of which community take no pains whatever to secure their own eternal welfare, at a no greater distant day? Great distance, in either time or space, has wonderful power to lull and render quiescent the human mind. Pleasures to be enjoyed, or pains to be endured, *after* we shall be dead and gone, are but little regarded, even in our *own* cases, and much less in the cases of others.

Still, in addition to this, there is something so ludicrous in *promises* of good, or *threats* of evil, a great way off, as to render the whole subject with which they are connected, easily turned into ridicule. "Better lay down the spade you're stealing, Paddy, — if you don't you'll pay for it at the day of judgment." "By the powers, if ye'll credit me so long, I'll take another jist."

By the Washingtonians, this systems of consigning the habitual drunkard to hopeless ruin, is repudiated. *They* adopt a more enlarged philanthropy. *They* go for present as well as future good. *They* labor for all *now* living, as well as all *hereafter* to live. *They* teach *hope* to all — *despair* to none. As applying to *their* cause, *they* deny the doctrine of unpardonable sin. As in Christianity is taught, so in this *they* teach, that

> "While the lamp holds out to burn,
> The vilest sinner may return."

And, what is matter of the most profound gratulation, they, by experiment upon experiment, and example upon example, prove the maxim to be no less true in the one case than in the other. On every hand we behold those, who but yesterday, were the chief of sinners, now the chief apostles of the cause. Drunken devils are cast out by ones, by sevens, and by legions; and their unfortunate victims, like the poor possessed, who was redeemed from his long and lovely wanderings in the tombs, are publishing to the ends of the earth, how great things have been done for them.

To these *new champions*, and this *new* system of tactics, our late success is mainly owing; and to *them* we must chiefly look for the final consummation. The ball is now rolling gloriously on, and none are so able as *they* to increase its speed, and its bulk — to add to its momentum, and its magnitude. Even though unlearned in letters, for this task, none others are so well educated. To fit them for this work, they have been taught in the true school. *They* have been in *that* gulf, from which they would teach others the means of escape. *They* have passed that prison wall, which others have long declared impassable; and who that has not, shall dare to weigh options with *them*, as to the mode of passing.

But if it be true, as I have insisted, that those who have suffered by intemperance *personally*, and have reformed, are the most powerful and efficient instruments to push the reformation to ultimate success, and it does not follow, that those who have not suffered, have no part left them to perform. Whether or not the world would be vastly benefited by a total and final banishment from it of all intoxicating drinks, seems to me not *now* to be an open question. Three-fourths of mankind confess the affirmative with their *tongues*, and, I believe, all the rest acknowledge it in their *hearts*.

Ought *any*, then, to refuse their aid in doing what the good of the *whole* demands? Shall he, who cannot do *much*, be, for that reason, excused if he do *nothing*? "But," says one, "what good can I do by signing the pledge? I never drink even without signing." This question has already been asked and answered more than millions of times. Let it be answered once more. For the man to suddenly, or in any other way, to break off from the use of drams, who has indulged in them for a long course of years, and until his appetite for them has become ten or a hundred fold stronger, and more craving, than any natural appetite can be, requires a most powerful moral effort. In such an undertaking, he needs every moral support and influence, that can possibly be brought to his aid, and thrown around him. And not only so; but every moral prop, should be taken *from* whatever argument might rise in his mind to lure him to his backsliding. When he casts his eyes around him, he should be able to see, all that he respects, all that he admires, and all that he loves, kindly and anxiously pointing him onward; and none beckoning him back, to his former miserable "wallowing in the mire."

But it is said by some, that men will *think* and *act* for themselves; that none will disuse spirits or any thing else, merely because his neighbors do; and that *moral influence* is not that powerful engine contented for. Let us examine this. Let me ask the man who would maintain this position most stiffly, what compensation he will accept to go to church some Sunday and sit during the sermon with his wife's bonnet upon his head? Not a trifle, I'll venture. And why not? There would be nothing irreligious in it: nothing immoral, nothing uncomfortable. Then why not? Is it not because there would be something egregiously unfashionable in it? Then it is the influence of *fashion*; and what is the influence of fashion, but the influence that *other* people's actions have on our own actions, the strong inclination each of us feels to do as we see all our neighbors do? Nor is the influence of fashion confined to any particular thing or class of things. It is just as strong on one subject as another. Let us make it as unfashionable to withhold our names from the temperance pledge as for husbands to wear their wives [*sic*] bonnets to church, and instances will be just as rare in the one case as the other.

"But," say some, "we are no drunkards; and we shall not acknowledge ourselves such by joining a reformed drunkard's society, whatever our influence might be." Surely no Christian will adhere to this objection. If they believe, as they profess, that Omnipotence condescended to take on himself the form of sinful man, and, as such, to die an ignominious death for their sakes, surely they will not refuse submission to the infinitely lesser condescension, for the temporal, and perhaps eternal salvation, of a large, erring, and unfortunate class of their own fellow creatures. Nor is the condescension very great.

In my judgment, such of us as have never fallen victims, have been spared more from the absence of appetite, than from any mental or moral superiority over those who have. Indeed, I believe, if we take habitual drunkards as a class, their heads and their hearts will bear an advantageous comparison with those of any other class. There seems ever to have been a proneness in the brilliant, and the warmblooded, to fall into this vice. The demon of intemperance ever seems to have delighted in sucking the blood of genius and of generosity. What one of us but can call to mind some dear relative, more promising in youth than all his fellows, who has fallen a sacrifice to his rapacity? He seems to have gone forth, like the Egyptian angel of death, commissioned to slay if not the first, the fairest born of every family. Shall he now be arrested in his desolating career? In that arrest, all can give aid that will; and who shall be excused that *can*, and will not? Far around as human breath has ever blown, he keeps our fathers, our brothers, our sons, and our friends, prostrate in the chains of moral death. To all the living every where, we cry, "come sound the moral resurrection trump, that these may rise and stand up, an exceeding great army" — "Come from the four winds, O breath! and breathe upon these slain, that they may live."

If the relative grandeur of revolutions shall be estimated by the great amount of human misery they alleviate, and the small amount they inflict, then, indeed, will this be the grandest the world shall ever have seen. Of our political revolution of '76, we are all justly proud. It has given us a degree of political freedom, far exceeding that of any other of the nations of the earth. In it the world has found a solution of that long mooted problem, as to the capability of man to govern himself. In it was the germ which has vegetated, and still is to grow and expand into the universal liberty of mankind.

But with all these glorious results, past, present, and to come, it had its evils too. It breathed forth famine, swam in blood and rode on fire; and long, long after, the orphan's cry, and the widow's wail, continued to break the sad silence that ensued. These were the price, the inevitable price, paid for the blessings it bought.

Turn now, to the temperance revolution. In *it*, we shall find a stronger bondage broken; a viler slavery, manumitted; a greater tyrant deposed. In *it*, more of want supplied, more disease healed, more sorrow assuaged. By *it* no orphans starving, no widows weeping. By *it*, none wounded in feeling, none injured in interest. Even the dram-maker, and dram seller, will have glided into other occupations *so* gradually, as never to have felt the shock of change; and will stand ready to join all others in the universal song of gladness.

And what a noble ally this, to the cause of political freedom. With such an aid, its march cannot fail to be on and on, till every son of earth shall drink in rich fruition, the sorrow quenching draughts of perfect liberty. Happy day, when, all appetites controled, all passions subdued, all matters subjected, *mind*, all conquering *mind*, shall live and move the monarch of the world. Glorious consummation! Hail fall of Fury! Reign of Reason, all Hail!

And when the victory shall be complete—when there shall be neither a slave nor a drunkard on the earth—how proud the title of that *Land*, which may truly claim to be the birthplace and the cradle of both those revolutionaries, that shall have ended in that victory. How nobly distinguished that People, who shall have planted, and nurtured to maturity, both the political and moral freedom of their species.

This is the one hundred and tenth anniversary of the birthday of Washington. We are to celebrate this day. Washington is the mightiest name of earth—*long since* mightiest in the cause of civil liberty; *still* mightiest in moral reformation. On that name, an eulogy is expected. It cannot be. To add brightness to the sun, or glory to the name of Washington, is alike impossible. Let none attempt it. In solemn awe pronounce the name, and its naked deathless splendor, leave it shining on.

BIBLIOGRAPHY

Allen, Gay Wilson. *The Solitary Singer: A Critical Biography of Walt Whitman*. New York: New York University Press, 1967.

Benjamin, Walter. *Charles Baudelaire: A Lyric Poet in the Era of High Capitalism*. Translated by Harry Zohn. New York: Verso, 1997.

Bertolini, Vincent J. "Fireside Chastity: The Erotics of Sentimental Bachelorhood in the 1850s." In *Sentimental Men: Masculinity and the Politics of Affect in American Culture*, edited by Mary Chapman and Glenn Hendler, 19–42. Berkeley: University of California Press, 1999.

Brasher, Thomas L., ed. *Walt Whitman: The Early Poems and the Fiction*. New York: New York University Press, 1963.

Brooks, Van Wyck. *The Times of Melville and Whitman*. New York: E. P. Dutton, 1947.

Caldwell, Charles. *New Views on Penitentiary Discipline, and Moral Education and Reform*. Philadelphia: William Brown, 1829.

Chapman, Mary, and Glenn Hendler, eds. *Sentimental Men: Masculinity and the Politics of Affect in American Culture*. Berkeley: University of California Press, 1999.

Chauncey, George. *Gay New York: Gender, Urban Culture, and the Making of the Gay Male World, 1890–1940*. New York: Basic Books, 1994.

Chudacoff, Howard P. *The Age of the Bachelor: Creating an American Subculture*. Princeton: Princeton University Press, 1999.

Cowie, Alexander. *The Rise of the American Novel*. New York: American Books, 1948.

Denning, Michael. *Mechanic Accents: Dime Novels and Working-Class Culture in America*. New York: Verso, 1987.

Fiedler, Leslie A. *Love and Death in the American Novel*. New York: Dell, 1960.

Fowler, O. S. *Education and Self-Improvement*. New York: O. S. and L. N. Fowler, 1844.

Gilfoyle, Timothy J. *City of Eros: New York City, Prostitution, and the Commercialization of Sex, 1790–1920*. New York: Norton, 1992.

Griffin, Charles J. G. "The 'Washingtonian Revival': Narrative and the Transformation of Temperance Reform in Antebellum America." *Southern Communication Journal* 66 (Fall 2000): 67–78.

Habermas, Jürgen. *The Structural Transformation of the Public Sphere: An Inquiry into a Category of Bourgeois Society*. Translated by Thomas Burger. Cambridge, Mass.: MIT Press, 1989.

Hart, James. *The Popular Book: A History of America's Literary Taste*. New York: Oxford University Press, 1950.

Hendler, Glenn. "Bloated Bodies and Sober Sentiments: Masculinity in 1840s Temperance Narratives." In *Sentimental Men: Masculinity and the Politics of Affect in American Culture*, edited by Mary Chapman and Glenn Hendler, 125–48. Berkeley: University of California Press, 1999.

Holloway, Emory. *Free and Lonesome Heart: The Secret of Walt Whitman*. New York: Vantage, 1960.

———. "More Temperance Tales by Whitman." *American Literature* 27:4 (January 1956): 577–78.

Kaplan, Justin. *Walt Whitman: A Life*. New York: Simon and Schuster, 1980.

Kingsdale, Jon M. "The 'Poor Man's Club': Social Functions of the Urban Working-Class Saloon." *American Quarterly* 25 (December 1973): 472–89.

McGill, Meredith. *American Literature and the Culture of Reprinting, 1834–1853*. Philadelphia: University of Pennsylvania Press, 2003.

McGowan, Philip. "The Intemperate Irish in American Reform Literature." *Irish Journal of American Studies* 4 (1995): 49–66.

Mintz, Steven. *Moralists and Modernizers: America's Pre–Civil War Reformers*. Baltimore: The Johns Hopkins University Press, 1995.

Moon, Michael. *Disseminating Whitman: Revision and Corporeality in "Leaves of Grass."* Cambridge, Mass.: Harvard University Press, 1991.

Mott, Frank Luther. *A History of American Magazines, 1741–1850*. Cambridge, Mass.: Harvard University Press, 1957.

Murphy, Gretchen. "Enslaved Bodies: Figurative Slavery in Temperance Fiction of Harriet Beecher Stowe and Walt Whitman." *Genre: Forms of Discourse and Culture* 28 (Spring–Summer 1995): 95–118.

Reynolds, David S. *Walt Whitman's America: A Cultural Biography*. New York: Random House, 1996.

Sewall, Jonathan M. *A New Epilogue to [Addison's] Cato, Spoken at a Late Performance of that Tragedy*. Portsmouth, N.H.: printed by Daniel Fowle, 1778.

Snyder, Katherine V. *Bachelors, Manhood, and the Novel, 1850–1925*. Cambridge: Cambridge University Press, 1999.

Stansell, Christine. *City of Women: Sex and Class in New York, 1789–1860*. Urbana: University of Illinois Press, 1987.

Stott, Richard Briggs. *Workers in the Metropolis: Class, Ethnicity, and Youth in Antebellum New York City*. Ithaca, N.Y.: Cornell University Press, 1990.

Traubel, Horace. *With Walt Whitman in Camden, Vol. 3: March 28–July 14, 1888*. New York: D. Appleton, 1908.

———. *With Walt Whitman in Camden, Vol. 4: July 16–October 31, 1888*. New York: D. Appleton, 1908.

Turner, Mark W. *Backward Glances: Cruising the Queer Streets of New York and London*. London: Reaktion Books, 2003.

Warner, Michael. "Whitman Drunk." In *Breaking Bounds: Whitman and American Cultural Studies*, edited by Betsy Erkkila and Jay Grossman, 30–43. New York: Oxford University Press, 1996.

Whitman, Walt. *Complete Writings*. 10 volumes, edited by Richard Maurice Bucke, Thomas B. Harned, and Horace L. Traubel. New York: G.P. Putnam, 1902.

———. *Franklin Evans*. Edited by Emory Holloway. New York: Random House, 1929.

———. *Franklin Evans; or The Inebriate. A TALE OF THE TIMES*. 1842. In *Walt Whitman: The Early Poems and the Fiction*, edited by Thomas L. Brasher. New York: New York University Press, 1963.

———. *Franklin Evans; or The Inebriate, a Tale of the Times*. Edited by Jean Downey. New Haven: College and University Press, 1967.

———. *Journalism, Vol. 1*. Edited by Herbert Bergman, Douglas A. Noverr, and Edward J. Recchia. New York: Peter Lang, 1998.

Wilentz, Sean. *Chants Democratic: New York City and the Rise of the American Working Class, 1788–1850*. New York: Oxford University Press, 1984.

Winwar, Frances. *American Giant: Walt Whitman and His Times*. New York: Harper Brothers, 1941.

CHRISTOPHER CASTIGLIA is a professor of English at Pennsylvania State University. He is the author of *Bound and Determined: Captivity, Culture-Crossing and White Womanhood from Mary Rowlandson to Patty Hearst* (1996).

GLENN HENDLER is an associate professor of English at the University of Notre Dame. He is the author of *Public Sentiments: Structures of Feeling in Nineteenth-Century American Literature* (2001) and coeditor, with Mary Chapman, of *Sentimental Men: Masculinity and the Politics of Affect in American Culture* (1999).

Library of Congress Cataloging-in-Publication Data

Whitman, Walt, 1819–1892.
Franklin Evans, or The inebriate: a tale of the times / Walt Whitman ;
edited by Christopher Castiglia and Glenn Hendler.
p. cm.
Includes bibliographical references.
ISBN 978-0-8223-3931-1 (cloth: acid-free paper) —
ISBN 978-0-8223-3942-7 (pbk.: acid-free paper)
1. Temperance — Fiction. I. Castiglia, Christopher. II. Hendler, Glenn, 1962–
III. Title. IV. Title: Franklin Evans. V. Title: Inebriate.
PS3222.F7 2007
813'.3 — dc22   2007003431